Silky!

Also by Leo Rosten

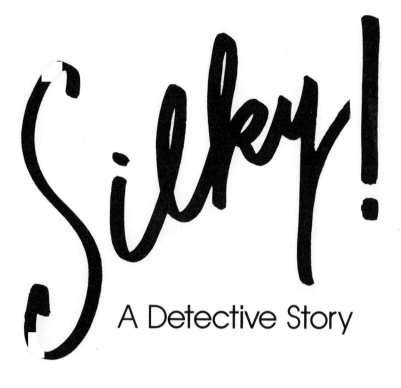

Silky!

A Detective Story

LEO ROSTEN

Harper & Row, Publishers

New York, Hagerstown, San Francisco, London

FIRST EDITION

Designer: C. Linda Dingler

Library of Congress Cataloging in Publication Date

Rosten, Leo Calvin, date
  Silky.
  I. Title.
PZ3.R7386Si   [PS3535.07577]   813'.5'2   78–20215
ISBN 0–06–013671–5

79 80 81 82 83 10 9 8 7 6 5 4 3 2 1

To
the Real Silky

CONTENTS

READER!
YOU HAVE TO READ THIS!!!

Do not blame the Publisher. Certain words in this unusual story are not spelled the way he wants, but the way I want.

That goes for Grammar, too. I have not run across 3 persons in my whole life who didn't understand me when I talk (and 1 of them don't count, being a deaf Iranian), so I do not see why you should not understand me when I write.

A few English teachers will be miffed by my using words like "ain't," and uptight types might raise Hell about words like "cockamamy." That's their problem, not mine.

A word here and there you maybe won't dig right away—on account of your not being Jewish. That is not your fault. I explain those exact words in the back, which the publisher has called a Glossary. That don't bother me, though I have to admit I thought Glossary is the name of a furniture polish.

Remember "Dizzy" Dean, the all-time All-Star baseball pitcher? Diz was a whiz on the mound, but a crazy the way he belted our language around. So a smart-ass sports-writer needled him: "Did you never even hear of the King's English?"

To which Diz uncorked this zinger: "Sure I know the King's English. And so is the Queen!"

There's a guy I really admire.

—Sidney ("Silky") Pincus, P.I.

Silky!

1
WATSON AND HOLMES, INC.

"Silky!" gasped the Gasper.

That's the way to open a story. A story it just busts with thrills, chills, laughs and Sex. A mystery to glue your pants or panties, as the case may be, to the edge of your seat. A whodunit with more cockamamy surprises than hits the *shlemiel* on his wedding night who don't know his doll is a snake-charmer until she lowers her lashes and croons, "Lover, now you can play with my garters!"—and she pulls a pair out of her honeymoon kit, only instead of lace the garters have fangs.

There is no end to human snozzlewobble.

Another reason I open this hair-curler with the line you have just read on top is: All my favorite books, when I was a kid, began that way: like "'*Crack!*' went the bat." Or "'*Bang!*' barked the gun." Or "'*Pow!*' the bully's fist hit our friendly hero's unprotected chin."

The Gasper has slammed my door behind him. "*Silky!*" He is sweating bullets as he zooms to my desk, where he races his motor: "Out there, just blew in a client, Park Avenue type, a real looker—and *built!* Boobies like balloons, believe me, and a pair *legs*—*!*" He kisses his bunched-up fingers, "*Mnyeh!*," then flings out his arm like a horny Italian and opens his fingers so they look like an exploding radish. "This has to be the most gorgeous piece of fluff since God blew the works on Raquel Walsh!"

"Welch," I groan.

"Who cares from nationality?"

"Herschel, get a hold of your goddam marbles. Who is she?"

"A knockout!"

"I mean what's her name?"

"Who knows from *names?*" he blubbers. "She tells me in a voice like hot chocolate it's an emergency!"

"Oh, *boychik.*" I rub my high, fine brow. "If not for you being my nephew—"

"You would piss on my shoes!" he absolutely beams.

"Who told you?"

The phone rings. Herschel dives for it. "Yeah?"

"Dummy!" I explode. "Stop with the 'Yeahs.' Can't we use some class around here?"

He wipes out the boo-boo with a velvet "Hel-*lo*-o. Watson and Holmes, Detective Bureau. Harold J. Tabachnik here. . . . Oh, hi, Mr. Clancy." He lends me the phone. "It's for you."

"Get the lady's name."

He sputters out. When Herschel leaves a room, you feel someone fascinating just came in.

Into the blower I say, "How you making out, Mike?"

My best friend, my buddy, my partner gives a laugh. I have to tell you, that beautiful Irishman, who has a profile like Apollo and the shoulders of a Green Bay linebacker, can charm the birds off any tree with that trillful laugh. "A piece of cake, Silky. I'm in the Burger Queen with the store manager, a joker named Arnie Shotoz, right? So around 2:10 who do you think shuffles up to Speedy Service? You'll *plotz!* Our pigeon from Sheepshead Bay: Soapy Manoosh."

"Soapy the Puker?!" I amaze.

"The same!"

"I'll *plotz.*"

"It's like old times," Mike chuckles. "Soapy orders a Jumbo 'with everything'—takes one bite and throws up. But *everything!* Two customers turn green and an old biddy screams, 'Poison, poison! This customer is already poisoned! Pump out his stomach! Give him an enema!' . . . Shotoz is pale as an oyster, seeing a fat settlement—out of court—staring

him in the puss. I push through the howling loonies, and before
Soapy can spot me, I snatch the half-eaten bar of soap out of
his pocket. The *shmuck* forgot to throw it away before he went
into his act!"

"They never learn," I mourn.

"I survey the up-chuck on the floor and say, 'No dessert
today, Soapy?!' His comeback is very rude. 'Drop dead, you
fink! I have a germ phobia! You know I wash tip to toe before
I touch a piece of food!' . . . But his teeth marks are still in
the Ivory, and sharper than fingerprints. Some *klutz.*"

I have to laugh. In the six years we been in business, Mike
has picked up more Yiddish than half the Jews in New York.
I say, "That's enough evidence for even our Supreme Court."

"So I put the arm on Soapy," says Mike, "and Shotoz dials
a 911, and in 4–5 minutes a patrol car pulls up. Who's in it?
Pirelli and Feinstein. Shotoz hollers them up about the epi-
demic of vomit-dives in the burger chain and I hand the boys
the hot soap like it's uranium. . . . All this time Soapy is doing
his *shtick*, yelling, 'False arrest! Invasion of privacy! I sue! I
sue for tomaine poisoning, hospital expenses, plus 20 grand!'
Pirelli laughs so hard you can scramble eggs on his stomach. No one seen him laugh that way since his wife kicked
off."

Now the Gasper busts in like he's delivering the message
to Garfinkel; and he sticks a card in front of my nose: a Tiffany
special with lettering embossed so high you could read it in
Braille:

KIMBERLEY MARSH

That's all. No address. No phone. We're dealing with Society.

"When you comin' in?" I ask Mike.

"Tomorrow. I want to get back to the apartment. Kathy
ain't been feeling good."

"Kiss her for me." There are few people in this crazy world
I feel about the way I feel about Kathy.

"*Shalom,*" says Michael.

Before I even put the horn back in its cradle, the Gasper grins, *"Now* should I let her in?"

I have to tell you, when Herschel don't grin, he looks like a damp bagel; when he does grin, it is kind of shocking. " 'Let' her in?" I echo. "What is she, a cat? You don't *let* a hi-class client in. You announce her."

While Laughing Boy is playing handsies with the doorknob, I get up and close the window. The rain is really roaring down now, so heavy that the Queensborough Bridge, which you could hit with a meatball from our office on 60th and 1st, looks like it's in London, misty and blurred, like castle towers in a fairy tale. Why don't people realize how romantic that corny bridge is?

"Miss Kimberley Marsh!" Herschel bawls.

I turn.

"—Miss Marsh, *that's* Mr. Pincus."

In she floats . . .

Look, I have played that scene over in my mind a thousand times, and each time I get that same burning ripple up and down my spine. She didn't walk in, you have to understand; she floated in, cool and clean and so beautiful it hurt. . . . Did you ever read *The Great Gatsby?* Then you'll never forget that first time we meet Daisy, drifting in in a cloud of white dress down the long, cool room where the drapes at the high French windows shimmer in a summer breeze. . . . That's pretty good writing—and that's the scene that clobbered my mind that first second my eyes got drunk on the vision of Kimberley Marsh.

I catch a whiff of perfume out of Baghdad. And when I get a load of her architecture, I see that the Gasper didn't go overboard. She is—she is ravishing. The most sensational female I ever saw outside a Broadway musical. Gold and gauzy. Hair the color of honey and smooth with sheen. A skin, peaches and cream. A mouth, a red tulip. Eyes, sort of sleepy, and flecked with emeralds and amber. And stacked?! . . . *"Wham!"* went my heart.

"Thank you for seeing me," she murmurs, breathless, smoky, husky, the way you dream of a woman's voice by candlelight, and especially in the hay. . . .

Do I sound like a pushover? Listen. I have knocked over more than my quota of quiff, some of them fantastic, but never in my 32 years did anyone hit me like this. She has beauty and grace—and class. . . . But she moved in a haze—not just the haze of my feelings—and her expression is worried, or scared. . . . Most of the people who come to Watson and Holmes look worried, but this lady—before she tells me 1 thing about what's bugging her I know she is in trouble up to her ears.

And I had a premonition, you can call it, a dry and choked-up hammering that I was a goner before the game even started and my whole life was shifting into a runaway gear and I was heading for God-only-knows-where-or-what—but it would be for her, and with her, so nothing else could matter. . . .

2
THE GOLDEN NYMPH

Maybe I should of began this story like Herbert Melville, who we had to read in Roosevelt High up on Fordham Road in the Bronx, when he leads off *Moby Dick* with: "Call me Ishmael." Man, there is a grabber! "Call me Ishmael."

When I tell you how Kimberley Marsh knocked me out of the ball park just by floating into my office, with those paralyzing looks and that throaty, smoky voice, with me knowing absolutely nothing about her, you could jump to the conclusion I'm a pushover for a broad, and a bona fida *shlemiel*. Okay, I deserve it. You have a right to holler, "He should lead off on page 1 with 'Call me Shlemiel!' *That* is his opener, and the theme of his whole story!" . . . I give you that. But I will come right back with Al Jolson: "You ain't hear nothin' yet!"

"Miss Marsh," I hear myself soothing. "Perhaps I can help you. . . ." Can you tie that? All of a sudden I am doing a David Niven, oozing with the charm. I am gallant and sophisticated, plus world-weary, and I hold the chair on the other side of my desk for her like it's a throne. That glory melted into it.

She unpeels her gloves. *No* skirt ever came in our office before wearing gloves. A wig, yes. Fake lashes, plenty. Tight pants and no bras, by the dozen. But no la-de-da gloves.

I quick look-see if there's a band of gold where it would be if she's married. No. Thank you, God.

Now she is tapping the end of a cigarette on a tortoise-shell case you don't find in *shlock* stores, and I have my Bic flicking before you could say Jackie Gleason. "Thank you," she murmurs. Real slow. Real—I have to say—peculiar. Dopey.

When she inhales I get the sweet smell. Not perfume. I know that smell. Pungent. Kind of sweet. Pot. . . . *Oy.*

I shoot her a question-mark, but she ain't even looking at me. Oh, no. She has a far-out expression, an absent something that is not here and now . . . I figure that the joint she's puffing isn't her first for the day. But maybe it is, on account of her not being zonked, and her eyes ain't bloodshot. Also her pupils ain't narrow like they would be if she was on acid, or the heavy stuff, horse—that's heroin. . . . Did I rule out "speed"? Well, the amphetamines give a flush and a "high" feeling, and what I'm staring at is the opposite: a low-key Cleopatra.

I tap my pockets like I'm hunting for a smoke. "Darn!" I smile. ("Darn!" That shows you the condition I am in.)

She goes on guard. A cat narrows her eyes that way and glows yellow. Her tongue plays across her teeth for a second before she reaches into her purse. And now out comes *not* the tortoise-shell case, but a pack of Parliaments. It's not open, so she tears the cellophane and holds the pack out, giving me a 3-card Monte smile.

I grin: "I suppose *this* brand is kosher—for squares—like me?"

She fields that one easy. "You are very observant, Mr. Pincus."

"If I wasn't I'd be dead."

Her lashes dipsy-do. "You are also clever . . . but can I trust you? I mean *really?*"

"Ten thousand percent."

The smile she lobs me is varnished with sarcasm. "That's silly. One hundred percent is all there is."

"So I flunked algebra."

"I'm not surprised." She arches a brow. "I *wish* you wouldn't look at me that way."

"What way?"

"As if you can't wait to make a pass at me."

I make it back to my chair without fainting. And I tilt way

back to show how cool I can play it. This is no dumb *shiksa*. . . . I light up the Parliament, and through the blown-out puffs of cancer I size up her assets. You'd be surprised by how much clothes tell you.

She's wearing a simple beige suit, real simple, it couldn't of cost more than 800 clams. I happen to know about things like that because my father, of blessed memory, used to cut cloth for Clarence Nussbaum, and Nussbaum made hi-fashion dresses for some of the fanciest labels in the garment district. Pa always used to say, "I'm in *shmattes.*" But he used to show them to me proudly in the Number 1 windows of Saks and Bergdorf Goodman.

Around the creamy column of her throat is the Status pearl necklace. An antique pin sparkles near her left shoulder. Her cocoa-color blouse is unbuttoned, very casual, down to samples of heaven. Man, oh, man, this girl knows what the boys in the front room want.

Outside, a car backfires. Zip! She is out of her chair and skims past me to the window. It's raining like Noah should start taking reservations again. She rubs some fog off the pane and looks down, frowning heavy.

What else can I say except: "Who you lookin' for?"

"The car that was following me. . . . Perhaps he's waiting for me to come out."

"Are you sure a car was following you?"

"I—" Her lips begin to tremble. "I'm not sure of anything anymore."

Oh, boy. Some fun. This dreamboat is winging it on the Marijuana Sleeper. . . . Maybe she'll see Judge Crater next.

I stand up close to her. I could of found her in a pitch-black basement just by following the Shalimar or whatever foo-foo she has dabbed behind the pink shells of her ears. Through the rain I see plenty of cars parked, and cabs and trucks splashing by, but no wheels are double parked, waiting. I watch and watch, but I do not glom no slow cruisers either. "What kind of car was it, Miss Marsh?"

"A limousine. White."

Right there I see I'm going to have to put in overtime. White is a goddam stupid color for a car playing Follow the Leader. On top of that, using a limousine is plain *meshuggah*. But I'm not ready to bet on that. People ain't logical. . . . Maybe it's an amateur who is shaggin' her. Or a chauffeur whose Arab boss don't even begin to know what his driver is doing for extra green. Or a certified fruitcake. Or a jealous boyfriend, who I wish beets should grow in his belly already. "What car were you driving, Miss Marsh?"

"I wasn't. I was in a taxi. Going to Lincoln Center. I wanted to check on the Gala for the ballet company—a benefit ball. I'm one of the sponsors. Then I saw the limousine behind us, sometimes letting other cars come in front of it, but always sticking to us. I was frightened. I told the cabbie to forget Lincoln Center and hurry here."

I cast soulful lamps on her. I have caught her peddling apple sauce. "What phone booth did you stop at?"

Frown, puzzled. "Why would I do that?"

"To look up this address. How else would you know our location?" I stretch my grin out like a rubber band—to let her see how smart I am, how wrong she is to try to diddle me, and to show her how many fine teeth shine in my macho kisser.

"You *are* foxy," she says. "But I had looked up your address a week ago."

"That's a good answer," I say in what you could call a grave tone. "But it only raises another question: What made you do that?"

She shrugs, "I was frightened. I wanted to call your office when—when this all began. I had been getting strange phone calls. Whenever I answered the ring, whoever it was on the other end hung up. They said nothing. They just hung up."

"No heavy breathing—you know, a creep getting his kicks?"

"Oh, no. No word, no sound, no heavy breathing. . . . Then—I didn't believe it at first—I got the feeling I was being

watched. One night I happened to look out of the window—
I live at the Cloverly, on 5th—and I saw a man across the
street. I am *sure* he was staring up at me. He was a big man,
wearing a hat; his features were in the shadow. He must have
seen me because he walked away fast, then jumped over the
low wall into the park. . . . Around midnight, when I came
into my bedroom, the phone rang. I forced myself to pick
up the receiver. Silence. I said, 'Hello . . . hello.' The caller
hung up." She shivers. "It's awful."

I make heavy with the notes. Hell, I could remember every
single detail, but a customer loves for you to make notes. They
think you're right on the job every minute, that you're taking
them seriously, that you won't fob them off with a half-ass
effort.

She has stopped talking, so I go back to the Q. & A. "Did
you get a look at the driver?"

"No."

"Was there anyone in back?"

"Not that I could see."

I make busy with the pencil. "What make was the limo?"
She noodles for a second. "I'd say a Cadillac."

"You catch any part of the license?"

"No."

"Did you notice was there a *Z* in it?"

"Is that important?"

"Rented vehicles in this state got to have a *Z* in the plate.
. . . Miss Marsh, if you make a blind stab at it, just a guess
I'm not going to hold you to, could you come up with some
names, some *possibilities* for who's been calling you and tailing
you?"

"I've racked my brain . . ." She shakes her head.

"Are you married?"

"No."

I don't say, *"Mazel tov!"* Instead I ask: "Divorced?"

"No."

"Do you have any enemies?"

"Enemies?" Her eyes doubled O'd. "*Why* would I—"

"The choice ain't up to you. The world is full of weirdos. They can get hung up on marshmallows. Some creeps hate women, some hate blondes, some hate rich . . ."

No reaction.

"Let me put it another way, Miss Marsh. Is there anyone who *might* have a reason for hating you? Anyone who's hungry for revenge? . . . A maid you fired? A building employee you complained about?"

The gorgeous head swings left and right to signal negative.

"So we reach the heaving heart depot. . . . You kissed off a boyfriend lately? Tore off a romance? Heave-hoed a randy Romeo?"

She smiles. (Mi*god*, that smile!) "No."

"Are *you* having an affair—like with a married man? . . . Jealous wives can—"

She regards me like I'm oatmeal. "No."

I raise both my palms. "Asking, just asking. We have to tick off every possibility. . . . Are you in *any* kind of trouble?"

"No."

"Run up any big debts?"

"No."

I put the next buzz carefully. "Miss Marsh, can you think of *any* reason someone would be getting ready to—blackmail you?"

Wrinkles. "No, I can't for the life of me imagine who."

"Or why?"

"Or why!" she snaps.

"Then let's turn it around. Have you, by any chance, put the heat on anyone?"

Bells muffle in her throat. "You have a distorted sense of humor, Mr. Pincus."

"Thanks. No charge for laughs. Are you involved in *anything* dicey?"

"Don't be absurd."

"I don't figure that to be absurd. A rich lady like you. . . .

Maybe you're a snow bird, sniffing coke—and you have to get the hard stuff from a pusher. . . . They could put the squeeze on you. Maybe you owe a big, big marker. Maybe they're going to try muscle."

She lays me out with her orbs. "No. Nothing like that. Nothing at *all* like that."

I make a temple out of my long, sensitive fingers and look saintly. "Do you live alone?"

"I *think* you mean—do I have sleep-in help?"

"That's what I mean," I lie.

"A couple. They've been in the family for twenty years. . . . I'd trust them with my life."

"But would you trust them with your money?" (The rich give me a pain in the ass.) "Most people can be counted on not to cut your throat. But how many can you count on to return a scarf, belt or Bible, without you have to goose them?"

Startled pupils. "Are you *always* so cynical?"

"I don't swear a guy's honest just because he never had a chance to steal. . . . Better tell me your live-ins' names." (On Bathgate Avenue, which got its name before they knew who would live there, our only "live-ins" were boarders with kitchen privileges.)

"Johannson. Two *n*'s. Christine and Gunnar."

"Do you own a car?"

"A Rolls"—that figured—"but it's twelve years old."

"What's to apologize?" (The only rolls I ever saw in the Bronx did not move unless some clown threw 1 at you.) "I suppose your rickety old Rolls is in the shop for an overhaul."

"Not at all. What makes you think that?"

"Because you didn't use it today—in such a rain—when cabs are murder to get." I make my smile friendly, but doubtful. "So why did you take—"

She sits up like she sat on a bumblebee-disc from the Magic and Tricks shop in Times Square. "*Mis*ter Pincus! I did not come here to be cross-examined! From the moment I walked in you've acted as if you think I'm—lying!"

Whenever a client goes into a Bette Davis sizzle, I feel obliged to respond like Buddy Ebsen. "Land's sake, ma'am. Don't let's cast aspersions on the asparagus. I'm just plain city folk. All I hanker for is the facts—*all* the facts, if I'm agoin' to be of any doggone use to you."

"Oh, God," she groans. "A comic."

"It stops ulcers. . . . I still would like to know why anyone in their right mind in New York would let a big, clean Rolls stay in the garage and risk yellow fever in one of the beat-up garbage disposals we call taxis."

She tilts her head and I know she is going to burn me. "I did not take the Rolls, Lieutenant Columbo, because Gunnar drives it. *I* couldn't park a tricycle in an empty lot. But Gunnar is on jury duty. *That* is why I took a rather large, quite clean Checker."

You could of buttered your toast with my smile. "You must walk a lot. . . . So let's put the facts together and read the message. What you're dumping in my lap, Miss Marsh, is an open-and-shut case of Peek-a-Boo. You're the target for some shagger. You say it can't be a jealous woman, an enemy, a servant with a grudge, a dope mob, a blackmailer, a blackmailee. Add it all up, and what we have here is mish-mosh. . . . Where else can you look?"

"I wish I knew."

I am willing to give 10–1 she does—know exactly where else to look, but hates like hell to look there. I toss the softball: "Your family."

The pendulum on the big old-fashioned Regulator clock on the wall behind her tick-tocked, nice and soothing. *"Tick-tock, tick-tock."* There's a dandy reason for that big old-fashioned clock being where it is, and when the time is right I'll tell you what it is.

"My family." She sounds sad—and stops.

It says in the Talmud, "When someone stops talking, it's a confession."

(I better tell you it don't say that in the Talmud at all. No place. But whenever I need a quote to nail down my point, I make it up—and say, "In the Talmud, it says . . ." You'd be surprised how many smart people stop thinking whenever they hear the magic word. Like you.)

"Your family," I echo myself.

"Kenneth—my brother—and Howard, Howard Rodenbaker, my stepfather. That's my whole family. . . . Mother died three years ago. Howard loved her, truly. She left him the house they lived in, *so* happily, in Gramercy Park. . . . He couldn't have been nicer to me, or remained a better counselor and friend. . . . He's been wonderful to me, Mr. Pincus. He's good, and honest, and very wise."

I bet you just jumped out of your chair and cried, "Aha! Howard Rodenbaker! Zero in on Howard Rodenbaker!! *There* is your Number 1 suspect!"

If that's what you're thinking, you are full of flak. Kimberley Marsh obviously trusts and even loves her stepfather, and if I start throwing spitballs, she will freeze up. The big thing I do *not* want is for her to shut me out now. Not just because I have a thing for her, which I admit, but because I have a— call it "professional pride" in how I handle a case. Mike and me take a job, we do the job. All the way. As good as we can. . . . We go all out for a customer. We have to do right by the name of Watson and Holmes. (Wouldn't you?)

I say, "What about your brother?"

"Kenneth? Kenneth Ardway Marsh the Third," she sighed, fondly. "Terribly good looking. Very popular. We were more or less raised by Toby—our governess—because Father worked for Exxon, so he and Mother moved around the world a lot, until he died. . . . I suppose there was nothing Kenneth wanted he didn't get. From Toby. From Father. From Mother. . . . In a way, I feel sorry for him. He's been spoiled." I can't say I felt I should drop coins in the orphan fund for poor Kenneth. "We are very close, Mr. Pincus. We always were . . ."

I aimed that one for the bleachers. "Then how come you didn't ask him for help, the minute all this spooky stuff started?"

She looks at me like I have a bad case of the cutes. "Because he lives in Trinidad."

"In the South Pacific?"

"Trinidad," she educates me, "is in the West Indies."

"Near Porto Rico."

"Nowhere near *Puerto* Rico," she knifes. "It's just off the coast of Venezuela."

"Right!" I almost split my face forcing that grin. "I was just testing you."

"Of course. You got straight A's in geography."

"Naw. I once made a collar in Caracas. . . . So why does your brother live in swinging Trinidad?"

"Because Father left him the big house and estate. And the plantation. Sugar. Rum. That sort of thing."

"He must *hate* New York. . . ."

"N-no. He just loves boats and beaches and natives more. I told you Kenneth is spoiled. He's also extravagant. Frightfully. And Father knew that. The only way he could tie Kenneth down to something real—some way to keep him from going through a fortune in no time—was to leave him the place in Trinidad, to live in and operate, instead of money. Speaking of which, I suppose I should give you a—retainer?" She opens her purse. Dainty-like, as if she is handling rare butterfly wings, she lifts out 1, 2, 3, 4, 5 fresh C's—which, in case you are from Kokomo, stands for "centuries," which means 100-dollar bills.

I get her eyes to stop drifting long enough for mine to lock them up. "Money is not the only thing that counts in this shop, Miss Marsh. Not many things come *before* money, but no matter what you think, pesos are not our Numero Uno. For instance, Health. You got health, you got something fish can't buy. So we don't play Russian roulette for a fee. So—2, you couldn't put up enough cash for me or Mike Clancy to commit a crime—like strangle some party you hate. Or steal plans from the Pentagon. Or crawl up one of them cables on the bridge over there to talk down some juice-head who's threatening to jump. Not our bag, lady. Those jobs are for cops, or firemen . . ."

"I'm not asking you to break any laws! I just want you to—"

At this minute, me having forgotten he's been laying in the corner all this time snoozing as quiet as a baby, Mr. Isadore Goldberg decides he is starving for affection. He yawns, gets up on them all 4 lazy legs, and paddles over to Kimberley Marsh, putting his mournful face and head in her lap and making pitiful sounds.

"Your dog!" She breaks into her first real happy of the day. "A Schnauzer?"

"No. A *momzer* . . . Izzy, *kum avek fun ihr!* . . . He don't understand English, Miss Marsh. I know, I know: He don't look Jewish. That's because he's looking at you straight on. But observe his profile and you'll—Izzy! *Voos is mit dir? Kum doo!*"

The mutt sighs me a reproach, and he leaves the beautiful blonde he was sniffing and comes to me, broken friendship written all over his mug. *"Laig zich!"*

Isadore obeys, laying down at my feet, but he sneers at me, I swear, for being a no-goodnik who has double-crossed him.

My ravishing client looks like she thinks I am nuts.

"This pooch was raised by a rabbi," I explain, as plain and frank as a frankfurter.

"Was he circumcised, too?"

I give her "A" for that shot. "The rabbi hired us to find his long-lost sister, a veteran of amnesia. We threw a net from Miami to L.A. and ran her down—in Flatbush. In a grave. . . . Rabbi Goldberg is so broke up he heads for the Holy Land, to die on sacred soil. So who can he leave his darling pup with? Me. . . . Isadore is a sweet pooch, and a comfort to a lonely bachelor—" I pause. In fact, I drag out the pause long enough for her to take the hint and exclaim, "Oh, you poor man. Let me come and cook for you and sew on your buttons!" But she is chasing rainbows. So I finish. "The only catch is,

Isadore won't touch food if it ain't kosher. He's gone ape for chopped liver."

I can't tell if any of this, which happens to be absolutely true, is getting through to my valentine, and I am kind of let down on account of she don't even giggle, which is the whole point of my giving her the full *megillah,* trying to break through something I still can't put my finger on, trying to bust her standoff, her hazy switches in mood, which could not be from grass but from—yep, I'm right. She is *yawning,* for Chrissake! Is she on downers?

"*I* use Valium," I fungo.

"Do tell."

The Friendship Club is closed.

I pick the five fresh C's off the desk. "Okay, we'll try to find the character who's phoning you and tailing you. It's probly the same joker, but it *might* be 2—even 3—different jobbers. . . . By the way, do you think someone's trying to drive you bananas? Mess up your mind?"

She looks me smack in the retina. "I think someone is trying to kill me."

3
M-O-N-E-Y

Oh, peachy. There's a gasser. She don't even say it with a touch of funk, you understand, but flat out, like she's saying, "Alaska gets cold in December."

"Why?" I ask her. "Do you have any—uh—reasonable reason to think someone's trying to knock you off?"

Pause. "I don't know. If I did, I'd have gone to the police."

Bupkes! It all sounds as phony as a kosher oyster.

I scratch my cheek. Whenever I land behind an 8-ball, my damn cheeks begin to itch. Don't ask me why. Whenever I'm stymied, or go up against the unknown, I feel I forgot to wipe the lather off my face that morning and the soap dried up and tightened my delicate skin.

"Miss Marsh, I'll tell you 1 good reason someone could be trying to scare you into a rubber room, or wipe you out for good." She gives me the on-guard expression. "Money," I say. "If you go ga-ga—or die—who's going to make M-O-N-E-Y?"

No answer.

Now, I've had it. I drop the cozies and flip. "Look, lady! Are you on my side or are you playing me for the mark in Button, Button, Who's Got the Button? I feel like I'm pulling teeth, which I do not like, on account of at C.C.N.Y. I did not go for Dentist. I don't even believe in the Tooth Fairy. You want help or you want Patty Cake? I ask for the most obvious facts in this gig and you breeze off to Balmyville, leaving me with egg on my face. How the *hell* am I suppose to help you?!" I suddenly think of what my Uncle Yussel used to say, so I say it: "Out of snow, you can't make cheesecake."

She tosses her head back and ripples out laughs like she's on goof pills, and her honey hair falls over her eyes as she juggles the jollies. "Oh, this is going to be a blast! You are out of sight."

"Not if you take the hair out of your eyes."

She pushes her goldilocks away, still laughing, catching her breath. "I like you, Mr. Pincus. In fact, I'd like to call you anything but Mr. Pincus. . . . What do your friends call you?"

My heart makes flapjacks. "Silky."

"Silky? What a *mar*velous name! Why do they call you Silky? Because you're so smooth?"

"Because when I played for the Knicks I had a high jump-shot it barely touched the strings—dropped in like silk."

You would of thought I told her I was the guy who invented Pampers. "You played for the New York *Knicks?!*"

I give her 1 of my unused snorts. "Nix . . . that's a pun."

She says, "You must have gotten straight A's in lying!"

"Creative Lying. Any mush-head can lie; it takes talent to invent . . . and that's enough with 20 Questions. Let's hit the Repeat key on this tape: How much moola changes hands if you get knocked off?"

She slants her Mona Lisa glance at me. "You're looking at me that way again."

I try to look hurt, a nice pure Y.M.H.A. type on his way to *shul* when a hooker suddenly swings her goodies at him. "Maybe I'm looking at you 'that way' because you've been putting me through a wringer looking at *me* 'that way.' What are you, aside from flaky—a nympho?"

Her eyes flare up; but she cools it. "Tem-per. *Tem*-per."

"You leave your blouse open practicly down to your *pupik*— that means navel, Miss Marsh—and you swish your hips and cross your legs like you're auditioning for the Dietrich part in *Blue Angel.* Is this how you charge your batteries? Giving the boys hot nuts?"

"Don't be vulgar!"

"Vulgar-shmulgar, knock it off. *You're* the sexpot, not me.

I'm not going to be another one of your patsies."

"Oh, my," she slow grins. "Aren't you the jealous one?!"

"Plenty. The gut point is: Do you want protection or do you want to get laid?"

The punch she threw would of split my nose into several portions if I hadn't grabbed her fist in time. She is really boiling. *"Damn* you! Damn your insolence!"

We are bust to bust now, a position I do not mind increasing.

"Let—me—*go!"*

I accede to her request, but not in a hurry. Never make haste with waists.

We are pressed so close together and she is so soft, part of me is practicly behind her. And she is heaving like the T.H.I. is in the 80's. For half a second I am tempted to make great music with her, right then and there—but only for a second. That would screw things up—but good. I wouldn't know if I was coming or going (if you know what I mean), and right now, with 500 green slips and plenty more on call, is the worst time for either.

So I muffle the hots and put my pearly teeth on parade again, easing her back in the chair by her shoulders. "Temper, *tem-*per," I quote her. "We'll do this by my rules, not yours. 1: When I ask, you answer. You don't fake, fudge or clam up; you answer. 2: If you don't know the answer, you say so— nice and clear, and without a guess-which-shell-covers-the-pea ploy. 3: If you want to hit the sack with me, that's groovy— but not here in the office, for Chrissake!" (Talk about being noble! . . . I only wish I meant it.)

She must of read my thoughts, because all of a sudden she is smiling like she won that round hands down, which any fair-minded *maven* would tell you she did not. To rub it in, she is making mock poo-poos. "Yes, sir. I'm *so* sorry, sir. But truly, you have misjudged me."

"Not as much as vice-versa. Let's go back to Square 4: Who gets the insurance *gelt* if you fold."

"Fold?"

"Croak. Fill a casket."

She shudders. "Must you be so graphic?"

"I used to sell coffins. . . . You do have life insurance?"

A nod.

"Mute is out," I remind her.

"Yes, your honor. I certainly do own a life insurance policy."

"For how much?"

Now she smolders. *(You* tell me why.) "That is none of your business."

"Everything about this job is my business. . . . Big insurance is the best bait to bring out big baddies. . . . I assume you're covered for more than 48 dollars?"

She thinks that's funny. "Much more."

"Does the policy run into 7 figures?" As she draws zeroes in her mind I say, "That means millions."

"Oh . . . yes . . . it's over seven figures."

I give her my Chock-Full-of-Goodness soother. "Who's the beneficiary?"

Goody-Two-Shoes puckers her lips, and I can see she's enjoying what she is about to unload. "Nobody knows—except me."

Balls. "That's the dumbest dodge you've thrown me yet. The lawyer who drew up your will knows! The secretary who typed it up knows! Your executor, who has a copy, knows! . . . Play it again, Samantha. Who's your executor?"

"The Bankers Trust."

"So at least 5 more jokers—the estate officers—know. So why can't you tell me? Christ, that's the best—maybe the only— lead I can work on!"

That did it.

"My insurance—like the rest of my estate—will go to the Josiah Harmsworth Marsh Foundation. For psychiatric research." Man, how she chortles over that 1-up.

"You mean you're leaving every single buck to a noble cause?"

"I can do without the sarcasm, Mr. Holmes. Or are you Dr. Watson? . . . The philanthropy idea wasn't mine. It was all in Father's will. Very complicated . . . Howard can explain it." Suddenly she slaps her hand on the desk. "For God's sake, don't you have *enough?* I don't want you to write my biography. I just want you to stop those damn phone calls—and that damn hearse following me. Can you or can't you?"

There's no place to go from there. So I give her a deep sigh, of which I have plenty in reserve. "Sure. Here's what we crank up. 1st, you change your phone number. Make it unlisted. 2nd, you tell the phone company's serviceman not to put the new number on your instruments where any win-dow-washer or delivery boy can read it. Leave the center of the dials blank. 3rd, you keep a careful list of *everyone you give your new number to* . . . so, if the calls that have been bugging you stop, it was probly a stranger—getting kicks from a random number."

Stare. "And if the calls keep coming?"

"Then we know it's no stranger. . . . So we do a snoop in depth on the people on your list. And if that adds up to zilch, we find out which friend did a favor for a friend—of yours, or theirs, or some party you don't know—by slipping them your new and unlisted number."

She must of given every angle an X-ray before she mur-mured, "You *are* clever."

"Frequently. . . . Now about your being tailed. Better not run around alone for a while. Have a friend pick you up, and stay with you—like when you go shopping. . . . Don't make a big thing of it, or your dear friends will spread the word that you've left pot and are into paranoia. . . . Do you like movies?"

"Yes."

"Go alone?"

"Sometimes."

"Don't. A dark theater brings out the worst in our crazies—male or female."

She wrinkles her adorable nose. "Now *how* can I explain that I'm afraid to go shopping alone? Or to a movie?"

"Lie."

"Oh, wow. I suppose you have a list of foolproof lies handy?"
"That's our specialty. For shopping, tell a friend you want her honest opinion before you buy a dress, coat or helicopter. That kills suspicion right in its tracks. It also makes you popular. Nothing flatters people more than being asked for advice. You don't have to take it; just ask for it. . . . For company at the movies, say you don't enjoy a flick unless you can share it with a true lover of *cinéma vérité.*"

She looks like she is getting a hype from Dale Carnegie's successor.

"Remember the best part of this dipsy-doodle," I remind her. "No one has actualy tried to snatch you—or hurt you—all this time. And they had plenty of chances."

"Then what are they up to?"

"It depends on who 'they' are. *If* someone's tailing you . . ." I fade out.

"Do you think I'm *imagining* all this?!"

That's right across the plate, so I ignore it. "Let's test it out, ma'am. Let's give your playmate a nice long leash—so *we* can pick up his—or her—description. . . . Go on with your daily routine. Don't act suspicious. Don't tip our hand."

"Haven't I tipped my hand already?" she jumps me. "I mean, by coming here."

It is a pleasure to have a client who asks a question like that—if you have an answer. Mike and me worked it out before we took space in our first office, which was in a neighborhood where we had hoods for neighbors. "I sure as hell *hope* you tipped your hand."

"Now I'm really confused!"

"So listen. There are 46 offices in this building. Everything from a C.P.A. to a Hi-Fi hutch. How could your shadow guess which 1 of those 46 offices you came to? . . . Tell me. Suppose *you* were doing the tailing. . . ."

"I? I—oh! I would ask the elevator operator."

Anyone who underrates this doll's I.Q. should go back to baking Brownies. "That's exactly why I hope you did tip your hand. The slogan of Watson and Holmes is, 'Brains are better than breaks.' We *shmeer* the help here heavy. So whenever a snooper asks our elevator pilot where a client of ours went, the answer is 'Room 502.' Which this office is not. 502 is Bernard and Frosch, Interiors. But meanwhile, our elevator jockey has gotten a good look at the shadow, and zooms up here."

Her delight is so great she laughs, forgetting she could end up as the *X* newspapers use in diagrams of where the body was found: "Let's hope the driver of the Cadillac *has* asked—"

"He didn't," I regret.

"How can you be so *sure?*" (No one likes a smart-ass.)

"Because if the bloodhound did, by now the elevator man would of told Mr. Tabachnik, who would of bust in here like a shot out of hell, and I would already have an eyewitness 'make'—that means description."

That scored. Her expression suggests she will refer plenty of business to us in the years ahead. If, of course, she lives . . .

I sneak a reach under my middle drawer and press 1 of the buttons. It makes my own phone ring, through no courtesy of Ma Bell. I pick up the receiver. "Hello? . . . From where? Washington?" I analyze my wristwatch. "I'm in conference. Tell Mr. Kineahora to call back in 5 minutes. . . . Thanks."

You think that's cute? I've got enough buttons under there so it looks like a Wurlitzer keyboard.

I stand up. "I've got all we need for now, Miss Marsh. I'll get you a receipt."

As I go past her, Isadore Goldberg comes to life and makes goo-goo eyes at the most desirable female he ever saw. There is no end to this dog's *chutzpah.*

"No," I scowl.

She is smiling. "Would you mind if I taught him French?" She rubs behind his ear. *"Oh, mon petit chou . . ."*

I do not conceal my disgust. Next thing I know she will be making him *Crape-suzannes.*

I close the door snug behind me. I did not want the lady with the candy to pick up any part of what I am going to tell my *nebbish* of a helper.

4

HERSCHEL TABACHNIK, PRIVATE EAR

Herschel is right on the ball as usual, only he don't know what ball it is. He is hunched over his desk, on which is a fat library book: *Criminal Psychology*. His mouth is open and his eyes are slit so close his name could be Fuji Ichimoro. The adenoid-type breathing and Charlie Chan bit are psyche-ups that Herschel uses to help him concentrate, which I personaly doubt he can.

"Enough with Raymond Chandelier," I growl. "Put on a hat."

"We gonna pray?" he amazes.

"You gonna make surveillance. . . . *Red* hair you have to have! The worst color for a shadow."

He leaps to his feet. "I'll dye it!"

"It'll look like a rug. . . . Give me both ears, *bubeleh*. You're zipping down to the lobby. Futz around at the newsstand. When *she* comes down, someone with an umbrella'll meet her. Maybe a servant, maybe a boyfriend, a girlfriend, an old man."

Herschel's eyes are banjos, which he can't play. "She t-told you someone's waiting downstairs for her?"

I spoil the guess with a groan. "You got a brain? Use it! . . . It's raining, man! She's wearing no hat, she's carrying no dome. So how come there's not one drop of wet on her? Not on her head. Not on her jacket. Not on her skirt. . . . Someone *must* of held an umbrella over her coming in. I figure that person is waiting to do the same going out."

If there was air in his popped eyes, Herschel would lift off. "Silky," he gasps, "you are some genius!"

"I wish spare parts ran in the family. And keep your ears peeled. You might hear them—"

"I have very sensitive ears!" he exclaims. "Ask anyone. I can hear a *moth!*"

The rap for mayhem in New York can run to 10 years. "Herscheleh," I reflect, "you are the type who buys a suit with 2 pair pants and burns a hole in the jacket."

"What about they get in a c-cab?" The Gasper can hardly breathe, he's so hopped up. "Should I follow them?"

"If you follow them I will break both your heads. Just lock the looks of whoever meets her into your so-called brain. . . . Get down there—now! After she takes the elevator, I'll hit the stairs. I will barely open the door to the lobby. You signal me when she and the umbrella start for the street and it's all-clear for me to show."

"How should I signal?" Sometimes I think this kid hasn't figured out if 9 comes before or after 10.

"Fiddle with your necktie," I groan. "Or lace up your space shoes."

"Aha! Then *you'll* tail them!" Young Tabachnik, boy detective, waits for the bells and flashing lights to announce he just won the "$20,000 Pyramid."

"No. I will not tail them. I will follow whoever is following *her!*"

Herschel's admiration is so great his mouth is catching flys, for which this is not the best time of year.

I toss him Mike's slouch-hat from the tree. "Move your *tushy.*"

He bangs his hip against his chair only once, I'm glad to see, but drops the hat to even the score. "S-so I'm ex*cit*ed!" he explains and complains, and he bends down to pick up the benny, which causes him to bang his head against the desk, but since he's not bleeding, he completes the complex job of diving through the door I have opened so as to keep him from smashing holes in the glass and ending up in Bellevue for a facial.

I wonder if I'm bongo to let this yo-yo try to do what I

want; but who else can I get? I just can't risk the twosome spotting *me* in the lobby.

I hear the elevator door slam on Herschel.

I make out a receipt for 500 smackers and go back to my office.

The golden girl is standing at the window again, looking out and down. There's nothing fake in her fear.

"What's the score?" I inquire.

"A roofing truck—Ben Fiedler and Son—just parked across the street."

I step next to her. I'll be goddammed if the triangle ad, jutting on top of the truck, don't read "Fiedler on the Roof." Today every *shlepper* has to be a wit.

She turns her back to the world and her front to me.

I paste the wholesome Wheaties ad on my lips. "I'll call you first thing in the morning."

"I could be dead by then!"

"In that case, we return your deposit."

She regards me like I am from New Jersey. "*I* am serious! For God's sake, aren't you worried about what might happen—?"

"Worried, yes. Panicked, no. Someone's played *Gaslight* with you for over a week, so they're in no hurry . . ."

She turns on, her eyes blue saucers, and you can drop me with a canary feather when she says, "I'm sorry about—well, the way I've acted. It's these damn pills. . . . I trust you . . . and I like you." She could be a notary making the deal legal as she kisses me on the cheek. It would of meant more if she didn't peck me like I'm her uncle in an old-age home.

"Why don't you kick the junk?" I pop.

The honeyed eyebrows arch. "For good?"

"For openers."

She shrugs. "One needs an incentive."

"I'll take you to dinner."

She does a slow-motion take. "We-*ell!* Anything to buck up a nervous client?"

"Wrong."

"Mmh," she doubts. "Then why—"

I can hardly believe it's me, except for the goose-bumps, as I hear myself say, "I'm making a play for you, Miss Marsh."

Those long, long lashes flutter, and I'll be a sonofabitch if she don't coy, "Wha, Cap'n Rhaitt Butler! Y' make my po' li'l heart go pitta-pattuh, pit—"

"I can hear it from here. So how's about dinner?"

"Sorry." She drops the coy stuff. "I have a date."

"So do I," I lie. "I'll bust it."

Now she props up her chin with her palm, teasing, sizing me up. "*My* dates aren't easy to break."

I shove the phone across the desk to her. "You'll find a way." I lift the talk-part and hold up my finger. "What number?"

"Oh, no. Uh-*uh,*" she smiles. "I'll dial. It's my favorite exercise." She turns away from me, so I can't see the numbers she is hitting. This is some smart. . . . And the curve of her hips—

The phone rings at the other end, I can tell from the muffled *zzz-zzz.* Her skirt clings to her as she moves her sweet kiester and sits on the desk. And she swings those fantastic gams back and forth, back and forth. She is all soft, waves, juicy, sensual, and ripe as summer fruit. . . . It ain't easy to swallow the golf ball in my throat.

I hear a click and wooly words come on the line. I can't tell if it's man, woman or whatever.

"Darling?" coos Kimberley Marsh. "Kim . . . I can't make it tonight. Sorry." She hangs up.

"That certainly was hard," I remark.

"I never give reasons."

"Just heartburn."

She don't bother topping the peasant.

"What time tonight?" I ask.

"Seven thirty?"

"I'll pick you up at your apartment."

"N-no," she says. "I'll meet you. . . . Where?"

My mind isn't on restaurants. Why don't she stop swinging

that gorgeous stretch of limb? "You like Russian food?"

"I like all food." She runs her tongue across the line of her teeth.

"Let's make it—Kazotski's."

"It sounds like a garage."

"It's a borschtatorium. On 2nd Avenue and 78th Street. A place you won't run into anyone you know."

She slides off the desk and her split skirt slides over her knee and a little up a smooth, smooth thigh. . . . God, I wanted to grab her—send a hand up that long marvel of leg, and over her knee, and up her thigh . . .

She is offering her hand. "Seven thirty."

"Are you going right home, lady?"

Up goes 1 eyebrow. Now she is taunting: The scare has taken a powder. . . . What the hell! I never saw *anyone* run through so many emotions so fast.

"Still worried about me?" she smiles.

"Not much. . . . Just stay alert. I don't want you to fall apart before—"

"Tonight." Again the peck on the cheek.

Something is licking my shoe. I look down. But now Isadore is licking her leg. The *momzer* is smarter than I gave him credit for.

She blows Mr. Goldberg a kiss, then 1 to me for a clincher, and she floats out, all curves and luscious, leaving me with the smell of her and the feel of her lips on my skin and a riot of aches and mixed-up desires.

Isadore starts after her with a gleam in his eyes.

I sigh, "Oh, you lech."

He gives me his man-is-my-worst-friend growl.

I grab my Stetson and topcoat. (You expect a trenchcoat? I'm not Bogart.)

When I hear the outer door close, I head for it. I give a listen. I hear her spike heels clicking in the hall, then stopping, then one of the elevator doors open, and Original Louey, the gimpy operator, sings, "Dropping d-o-o-own." He makes the

words sound like the lead-in to a lyric from an off-beat opera.
. . . Louey is a black man, 40–45, always with the cheerful,
and there ain't a tenant in the building don't like him. He
even helps passengers with bundles. It's hard to believe he's
from Manhattan.

I hear her "Thank you," and Louey carols, "A *plea*sure!"
and crashes the scissors-gate like they are the cymbals in the
1812 Overture.

I swing out and hustle to the door under the red light. Behind
me, Isadore is yowling his equivalent of *"Gevald!"*

I open the EXIT jigger and take the stairs 3 at a time down
the 4 storeys.

I'm breathing hard when I ease open the door to the lobby—
just a crack. It gives me a slanty view of the newsstand. No
Herschel. I widen the opening. I see Mike's hat, and the back
of the Tabachnik neck, which is not famous for eloquence.

Finally, the *shlimazel* turns, and when he spots me, he wig-
gles the knot on his tie like he's choking hisself to death.

I walk out, my back angled away from the street. "Buddy,
how do I get to the I.R.T.?"

To my surprise, he don't tell me. "You sure c-called the shot,
Silky! A classy dude! Waiting for her! With the umbrella. He's
no servant, that's for sure, on account of he put his arm around
her shoulder. A real good-looker. One of them skinny t-tennis-
playing types. Button-down collar. Stylish hair-job. Very dry."

I could kill my own nephew, but it's not his fault her Galahad
got even his short-pants at Brooks Brothers. I hope he's a fag.
"How old is he?" I ask.

"Your age."

I will not give Herschel the satisfaction of knowing what
goes though my head ("May tennis calcify the fag's elbows").
"What the hell are they *doing?*"

Herschel has kept his optics right on our marks. "They're
at the curb. Now he's f-flagging a cab! . . ."

"Did they *talk?*" I grunt.

"Yeah. He ast her, 'How did it go?' She smiled and said, 'Fine, Shelby.' "

" 'Shelby'? You sure?"

"Sure I'm s-sure! . . . Oops! A Yellow's pulling up. . . . He's grabbing the handle. . . . She's in. . . . He's folding the awning. . . . *He's* in! G-good luck!"

I hustle out.

The Yellow is easing past an M.D.'s car in the "No Parking Any Time—Tow-Away Zone."

A Checker pulls up. Two commuter-type broads get out, yakking about yoga exercises. 1 of them starts the usual How-much-is-that? dialogue with the driver—and she ain't even got her satchel open.

Ants invade my pants. There ain't another free cab in sight.

"$2.90," snarls the driver.

"That much? Mi*god*, Mildred, they *rob* you."

"You got 3 singles, Flo?"

I can't wait for these bags to excavate their keys, combs, lipstick, and diaphragms, for all I know, so I con them: "Be my guest, ladies. It's my birthday. I'll pick up your tab!" I hop in and slam the door.

The driver is a punk with a sweatband of Indian beads on his brow. "Are you for real?"

I keep my eyes glued to the slow-moving Yellow as I chat up the honcho, "I am a friend of all Navajos. I love the red man. I—"

"Where *to*, Daddy-O? I can't sit here—"

"Don't wet your pants, Tonto. Your meter's playing our song." I still stall and—bull's-eye! What else?! A white limo passes us, following the Yellow. It is a Cadillac.

"Go!" I whoop. "Go, man—go-go!"

5
BLACK BEAUTY

Charley Brave screeches away from the curb. His heap coughs and rattles like a retired shotgun. It needs a grease job. It also needs springs. Holes in the floor would drain out the puddles. A crank for the window wouldn't hurt. And the brakes must be lined with margarine.

"Don't lose the goddam Cadillac!" I suggest.

A Chevy passes us.

"Let him move in. Easy . . . I don't want the Caddie to spot us."

"Hey," cries my wheel-man, "what are you—*fuzz?*"

"Sergeant Friday of Alcoholics Unanimous. There's a booze bar in that motor vehicle. I'm checking if 1 of our Trustees swigs firewater."

"Some jazz," says Eager Beaver.

The Yellow with Kimberley Marsh and Shelby Whoever-the-hell-he-is turns left, into 63rd, heading west. It's a 1-way street. The Chevy goes straight ahead up lst. The Cadillac slows down. I note with surprise that this buggy is almost as old as I am . . .

A red MG pulls in front of it. The Caddie follows.

"Slow down," I say. "Let that Ford get ahead of us."

The Ford turns and we follow Henry's baby.

"In a minute, pull out of this lane. Cut in front of the limo. Make him hit his brakes. I'll jump out."

The Bead Boy swivels his head and spits—like I'm General Custer. "Cool it, Kojak! I don't go for no rough stuff! And I'm not riskin' a smashed fender—"

"All you're riskin' is a fat tenner!" I slip him a 10-spot. "Give
him room to stop . . . and wait. I have to swap jokes with
the driver." The meter passes the 4-buck notch, which includes
the $2.90 the Wasp broads ran up.

"Make it fifteen and I'll smash his headlight!" cries the Co-
manche.

"I'll knit you a helmet."

The cavalcade, I guess you could call the Yellow, the red
MG, the limo, the Ford and us, moves across 63rd. The MG
turns left on Lex. At Madison I see the Yellow turn right—so
I figure Kim and Sir Galahad are going to her apartment, which,
it being on 5th, which is southbound 1 way, she has to go up
Madison, then over to the park and come down. I don't want
to make my move on Madison, where she might spot me whilst
scanning the boutiques, and I sure don't yearn to pull my stunt
on 5th, which crawls with hep doormen and nosey tourists
who can't wait to *kibitz* any piece of exciting action. The odds
go my way on narrow 63rd Street.

"*Now,* man!"

Tepee Tom swings in so fast he could be turning on a dime,
although he would prefer a nickel, on account of the Vanishing
American's profile.

The Caddie burns asbestos and screams.

I'm out in the drizzle in a flash, waving cars on and away
like I am Undercover Traffic Control. Then I hop to the limo,
whose driver is raging at my Apache, "You rude, incohnsiderate
lout!"

How a*bout* that? This is no New Yorker, because anyone
who's been in Gotham 5 minutes knows that if you cut in
front of a native he will holler "Son of a bitch!" or "You fuckin'
bastard!," and if he's really fractured he will accuse you of
shtupping your mother or making it with a baboon.

I lean closer—and whaddyaknow?! This shagger I have at
last nailed is the color of coffee and cream. A *shvartzer.* Harry
Belafonte with muscle. He ain't wearing no chauffeur's uniform
or cap, neither, but a tailor-made pin-stripe and a pink shirt

and bowtie. He smells of Old Spice and fine tobacco, from the pipe clenched in his choppers.

"That moronic hack hos nearly smashed my mud-guard!"

"Sorry about that, sir." I put a sympathetic elbow on the window-ledge and flash my I.D. from N.Y.P.B.A. That means New York Patrolmen's Benevolent Association, but you'd be surprised how many guppies think it's N.Y.P.D. (I got it after I turned in my shield at Manhattan East.) "May I see your driver's license?"

Mr. Handsome is glaring at Mohican Moe in the Checker. "Why do you not arrest thot *dread*ful drivuh?" he asks me in a baritone, and his accent is *très* elegant. English, Caribbean. "Did you obsuhve the monner in which he changed lanes withoot the slightest effohrt ot signoling?"

"My orders, sir. . . . Can I see your driver's license?"

He looked miffed. "Why?"

"Annual checkup. A Cadillac has run up 41 violations and never shows up in Traffic Court."

"I hov never received a summohns!" He hands me his license, which is welded inside plastic.

I take out my flipover pad and copy the facts:

> NAME: Vernon Matrobe
> ADDRESS: Woodland Drive
>   Yonkers, N.Y.
> DATE OF BIRTH: (He is 31.)
> HEIGHT: 5'10"
> COLOR OF EYES: Brown

No checkmarks after "Corrective Lenses, Hearing Device, Prosthetic Device." On the other side of the license: No entries under "Crime or Infraction."

"Do you own this vehicle, Mr. Matrobe?"

"Yes."

"Is it registered in your name?"

"No."

"*No?*"

The teeth he flashes would make Crest cheer. "I filed the opplication a fortnight ago. Your Motor Bureau is stoffed by illiterates."

"What's a fortnight?"

"Two weeks."

"Right!"

I step to the front now and copy the license number of the chariot. Then I amble back to the window.

"Thank you, Mr. Matrobe." I return his license, plus a rainbow glow of admiration. "Your beautiful accent, sir. Haiti?"

"Trinidod."

"Bam!" goes my ticker. It's bonus time. . . . "No foolin'? *Trin*idad? What a coincidence. I have a friend who owns a very snazzy spread down there . . . Kenneth Marsh . . ."

Does that hit him where he lives, or does he just loathe honkys? He don't answer.

"Do you know Ken?" I display the most unresistible expression from my king-size collection. *"Splen*did chap."

"Severol hondred Americans hov homes on our lovely island."

"But Ken inherited the great big Marsh mansion . . ."

"Om I supposed to be impressed?"

I put 2 fingers together. "We're like that."

"How cozy." He reaches for the ignition.

"Why are you following his sister? . . ."

Man, those eyes burn. Not with affection. With hate? With fear? How can *I* tell: Am I a relative?

The baritone adds steel. "I beg yaw pardon?"

"I asked: Why are you following Kimberley Marsh? . . . If you won't answer, at least flinch."

He don't appreciate humor. He reaches inside his jacket.

I lay a heavy duke on him. "You're not packing a noisemaker, Mr. Matrobe? In this town the rap is heavy for a CCW. That means 'concealed weapon.' "

"I om reaching for a motch."

I'll be a monkey's uncle if he don't pull a matchbook out

of his shirt pocket! He strikes a stick and puffs and puffs on his pipe, then blows out the sulphur, and tosses it at my feet. "I do not know what you are up to, but appahrently it is *not* troffic violations. . . . You are barking up the wrohng tree. *I om* not following anyone. . . . If you hov no further questions, instruct that creton cabbie to move his garbage lorry out of my way."

By now the traffic is backing up behind us and the horns start a concert like it's New Year on the F.D.R. Drive.

"Stop the telephoning," I whisper.

"*Tele*phoning?" He is either puzzled or a pip. "Is it against the law?"

"There's an ordinance against harassment. Even if you don't say a word into the horn, you're invading her privacy, you're hassling her nerves—and you're asking for trouble. From me."

His orbs respond with all the flash of the eyes in a dead herring.

I finger a salute. "And give my regards to Shelby." (What do I have to lose?)

No dice. He looks like he smells rat.

I make feet to the Checker. "Move it. Fast!"

Gitchie-Goomie ignites his heap. "You want I should follow Sambo? I'll do it neat."

This *shmegegge* is turning into a *nudnick* before my eyes. "No."

It's a no-win trap, tagging the Caddie. Matrobe knows I have made him, so he'll give me an exhaust full of raspberry jam with a fakeroo tour of Fun City. "West 84th Street," I grumble. "3–6–0."

That's Mike Clancy's abode. Maybe 12 minutes away.

I have a strong urge to rap with my partner.

6

MICHAEL X. CLANCY

The rain is getting tired now, practicly down to nothing, so the little kids come out all over New York, floating paper boats down the gutters, splashing around in boots, slapping puddles to send wet arrows at each other.

The older boys are throwing footballs around, and the pimple faces are sitting on stoops, making with stale wisecracks whenever a *zaftig* tomato klops along on mile-high cork heels.

The brownstone Mike and Kathleen live in is at the farthest end of the block, and there the street is almost quiet and very deserted.

I ransom the friend of our Little Red Brothers with another 5. By now I have brought so much drama into Sitting Bull's bored-ass career, he wants to kiss my feet.

"Use me on your next caper! We have two-way radios! Call any time of day or night! Tell the dispatcher you want Polansky! Or just say, 'Lockjaw Lennie'! " He is pushing a card into my paw. "It has been a pleasure and a privilege to serve you! You are some fat tipper!"

"Go home, Lockjaw. Wash your socks."

"You should live to a hundred and twenty! If you die sooner, God forbid, call the number on the card!" His spine-buster staggers away like it's ready to join its parents in Ecuador.

As I go up the brown steps of 360, I marvel once more at the certified kooks who serve a suffering public.

The front door is open. I establish myself in the entrance before the 2nd door. The mailboxes are so clean and shiny

they belong elsewhere. I stab the button between "Wimbish"
and "Dostoevsky."

No feedback.

I press again. This time Mike's voice comes through the perforated circle. "Yeah?"

"Mr. Clonsky?" I falsetto.

"Clancy!"

"Can I take 2 minutes of your valuable time?"

"What for?"

"I'm collecting for the Tone-Deaf Daughters of Ukrainian
Chicken-Pluckers."

He laughs that rippling-brook laugh. "I gave at the office,
k'nocker." I hear him call out to Kathy, "It's the kid from Cairo."
To me, "Come up, laddie."

The buzzer gives the love-call of a grasshopper, and I open
the 2nd door—and the back of my head explodes. The whole
world flashes yellow, spinning, crazy, and I choke on a mouthful
of bile, and the whirling stairs turn blue as I hit the tiles, hearing
1,000 nails scratch on a tin blackboard before the whole scene
goes black, bubbling like hot tar, and I fall deaf and blind
down a whirling vortex, I guess you call it, drowning in darkness. Far, far away I hear my moans in an echo chamber, "Oh,
God. Oh, God," and in an awful sick silence all the sweet beat
of life seeps out of me.

Minutes—very long—a week, Halloween, I hear a voice
swearing but can't make out the words, and 2 feet jump over
me, and later still I am picked up and tossed like a sack of
sawdust across a shoulder, and I could be back in Viet Nam,
slung across Mike's shoulder in a fireman's-carry, gushing blood
after the land mine went off, hearing his carbine rattle into
the ambush all the way 'til he got me to the medics . . .

I begin to suck air, bouncing up stairs, and I dimly know I
wouldn't be sucking air now, and Mike might be dead as a
dodo, too, "if the Blessed Virgin hadn't snatched us that day."
When it comes to saving my life, I'll take help from any denomi-
nation.

. . . A soft, soft place to lay on. . . . Beautiful. . . . I try to unglue my lids, but the spinning makes me nauseous.

Kathleen's voice is saying, "No, darlin'. Don't move," and her warm hands are unloosing my choker and unbuttoning my collar.

"Easy, *bubeleh*," whispers Mike. He is bending over me with a worried look, and Kathy's face is next to him, that beautiful colleen with the brogue that ain't put on; and nice, cool wet soothes my burning cheeks and brow. I wonder what sonofabitch is croaking a punk-rock "Sock it to me, baby, the fire's in my tank."

I'm sweating something awful.

Slow, real slow, I sit up. The back of my head falls off.

"What the holy hell happened?" asks Mike.

I wipe my neck with the cold towel. Then Kathy holds a bag of ice-cubes against the pounding goose-egg on my innocent head. "You tell me. I missed the feature. Who wrapped my voice in flannel?"

"I pushed the button for you," says Mike, "and you must of opened the downstairs door—"

"I heard the very click," says Kathy.

"I waited, our door wide open, but you don't show," says Mike. "So I pop in the hall and yodel, 'Silky! Silky!' I get no answer, so I tear down to the landing, and when I hear groaning, I take the stairs like a shot out of hell. There you are, *bubie*, a sack of potatoes. I damn near pull the door to the street off its hinges as I run out—but there's no sign of a stranger, up and down the street. I holler to the kids up the block. The Sullivan boy runs over. And Bo Blake. No, they didn't see a thing. They were chasing a goddam football with their backs to this end of the street. Yazoo Stoner threw the pass, but he don't know from nothin' neither. So I came back and checked your breathing, which was full of pebbles, so I hauled you up here."

Kathy kisses me on the forehead and sits down, looking at me like a misty mother with a beat-up child. "Sure and your color's returnin', love. Michael Clancy, where are your manners? The lad could use a nip."

Kathy looks bad. Her skin has turned sort of waxy since the last time I saw her. "You should be full of shame, Silky, not comin' to pass the time so long."

Like I told you, the lilt and lingo ain't put on. Mike met Kathleen Riordan in County Mayo on the trip to his dying grandmother. Kathy was 24. They were married in the church his mother had been baptized in.

One of the 4 Clancy kids yells from a bedroom, "Mummy, Mummy, Sheila is breaking the doll house!"

Mike comes in with a bottle of 4 Roses and 2 lo-ball glasses. "Want me to take it, sweetheart?"

"I'll go," says Kathy. She bends over and kisses me, and I kiss her just as sweet. And when she goes out, once more I see how full and strong she is built. I couldn't help thinking she is worth 10 of Kimberley Marsh. I hear her cough.

"She looks sick, Mike."

"I know." He looks at the floor, troubled. "She keeps going to doctors. . . ." He pours 2 drinks then lifts his glass. *"L'chayim."*

"L'chayim." To life. That means a hell of a lot more than "Bottoms up" or "Here's mud in your eye." The only toast I ever heard of that even comes close to *"L'chayim"* is the 1 a V.P. used to toss off during Prohibition: "Let's strike a blow for freedom."

Mike settles in his favorite chair and puts his size 12's on the coffee table. "Kathy took off your shoes."

I loosen my belt. I also rub my forehead.

Michael Xavier Clancy. He has curly hair and a good jaw, and those light gray eyes usually dance, but they are not making merry now. He weighs 195, but is light on his feet and practicly a pro with his dukes, that made him light-heavyweight champ of our regiment back when he weighed 178. He sighs. *"Nu,* hero, what in holy hell is going on?"

I take a small, careful sip of fire. When I don't gag but feel

I will gladly hock my right arm for more, I send a bigger portion down the tube. "A black bastard named Vernon Matrobe. He sapped me."

"Did you go up against him?"

"Hell, I never caught a peep of him."

"Then how can you finger him?"

"Because he is the only jamoke in the whole world could possibly of known I was downstairs! He must of tailed *me* after I caught up with him. . . . Some switch. Can you imagine me suckered by a rope trick?"

"Cheerfully."

"I feel like a *shmuck*."

"I'll go along with that."

"Turning my back to a door while I ring a bell!"

"Quote something smart," says Mike. "It makes you feel better."

I close my eyes. "When you go to a restaurant, take a table near a waiter."

"That's a beaut!" Mike beams.

"I am a *putzeroo*," I moan.

He lets me torture myself for a while, then says, "You still are champ for tease-openers. Now, who's Vernon Metro?"

"It's Mat*robe*, not Metro. He was tailing our client—and I 'made' him."

"May I be so rude as to ask who is our client?"

"Kimberley Marsh. She came to the office—when you were phoning from the Burger Queen." The long speech sent extra blood to stir up the other delegates in my goose-egg. "She laid 500 clams on the line, Michael, without me fishing for even 1. . . . And she has like 8 million—don't keel over—in her kitty."

Mike's eyes are fried eggs. "What does she want us to do— blow up the Kremlin?"

"What she wants us to do looked like a lollipop. But now I think it could be the lead in my obituary. And maybe yours."

"Enough with the jokes. Clue me in."

So I lay it on him, the whole *megillah,* which takes a good 20 minutes, just the way it had unrolled. Except I don't tell him how Kimberley Marsh twice caught me ogling her. Or how I responded. I don't want Mike to bust a gut laughing on me. I do tell him how she was way up from grass and down from pills. "I can't figure her, Mike. She is a *gorgeous* piece— and does she know it!. . . . For a dame who thinks someone is trying to drive her up the wall with phone calls and tailing— who tells me her marbles are in a pinball machine on account someone's out to 'off' her, she sure didn't stop sending out sex waves. . . . She could be a fruitcake." I pause, then—what the hell!—I pull out the plug. "Or 1 of them classic Society types: a prick-teaser."

"The bitch," says Mike, but not grinning as he usually does with such a picturesque comment. "You think some character is really trying to wipe her out? Or is she seeing flying saucers?"

"Your guess is as good as mine."

We absorb some alcohol.

"What I keep wondering," he says, "is *why.* Like you told her, if rubbing her out is going to drop a couple of million in someone's greedy lap, that's the kicker. But to a *Foundation,* for Chrissake!"

"That's what she *said,* sweetheart. My vibes tell me we better not buy everything she peddles."

"But why would she try to give *us* phony-baloney? She's hired us to nail the gopher, right? And you show her that motive has to be the key. So what in hell does she gain by trying to fake you out?"

I had been casing that, too, and from every possible angle. "I tell you why. Maybe . . . suppose it never dawned on her— always a rich broad—that money could put thoughts of murder in a beneficiary's mind. Suppose it hits her like a ton of bricks only after I mention it. Suppose *another* beneficiary of the will is her brother, Kenneth. . . . She won't tell me that— about Kenneth—'til she really has proof, or tests out what can only be a suspicion. . . . Like the Talmud says, 'Blood never turns to water.' "

Mike refills our glasses. "Don't get bombed. . . . But what reason could the spade from Trinidad have for tailing her—and clobbering you? . . . Oh-oh. Hold the phone. Is he working for the brother!?"

"Could be. Or her stepfather. Or that Shelby. . . . Whoever's paying the black man, he'd be scared stiff when he learns she's hired a couple of *shamuses*. He can't wait to ask his boss what in hell he should do. He's running scared. So after I grill him in the Caddie, he follows my cab, trying to think, trying to plan some move. When he sees me going up your stairs, he stops his buggy—maybe around the corner—and hustles up the steps after me, tipsy-toe, and while I'm pressing your button and making jokes, he panics (who are *you?*) and saps me."

Mike reaches for 1 of his stogies. "That fits. Nice and tidy. But it could also stink on ice, *bubie*. . . . Let's talk about the clyde who was waiting for her with the umbrella."

"Shelby."

"How does he figure?"

"Figure-shmigure." I feel hot and crummy. "Who knows? Maybe not at all. Maybe he's just a john she's got on her string. Maybe she wanted company. Maybe she felt safer with someone in her cab."

"So why didn't she tell you he was waiting in the lobby for her?" Mike grins sarcasticaly. "And how come he didn't come up with her? He could of waited in the office with Herschel. Not that that's anyone's idea of Disneyland."

My cheek is itching again. "Also, remember that Shelby asked her, 'How did it go?' She laughed, 'Fine, Shelby.' That's a stopper."

Mike lights the stogy. "This job has more cockamamy handles than a scheming octopus. . . . Anyway, we'll make ourselves a cushy fee. Just don't get sapped again, Silkeleh. Or worse. . . . Don't play the *shtarker*."

"Oh, I got the message all right. What I want now is— Matrobe." My mouth practicly waters. "I owe him."

"*If* he's the guy who clobbered you." Mike winks. "Look— it *could* be a coincidence. I'm not saying it is. But it might have been a mugger. We have some nifty swifties in this area."

"A mugger who didn't even snatch my wallet?" I snicker.

"My coming down the stairs could of put his pants on fire."

"Naa. You told me you waited at your door, Mike, then wondered why I hadn't come up, *before* you started down the stairs. In all that time, even a first-time butterfingers could of gotten my dough and wristwatch." I blow out stale air. "It has to be Matrobe."

"I won't knock it. . . . How about I ask Belchy O'Brien to put a trace on the Department's records? Maybe there's a sheet on Black Beauty."

"What's to lose?"

"Why don't you sleep here tonight? You look wiped out."

Suddenly, I remember my date. With her! I never would of thought I'd forget a thing like that. I wonder if I should tell Mike. . . . No. I don't want to. You shouldn't *never* date a client. . . .

I stand up and test my legs. They are not entirely spaghetti. I marvel at my powers of recuperation. Darwin was right about who survives. "I'll go home. And first thing tomorrow—I take Matrobe. In Yonkers."

"You up to that?"

I feel my goose-egg. "The Talmud says, 'The man who wants revenge is never tired.' "

"True?" asks Mike.

"False."

He sighs. "You have the constitution of a horse—and just as much moxie."

"Say good-bye to Kathy."

"Go out the back way. . . . Your welcome wagon could be waiting to flatten you again."

I'm halfway through the shutter before Mike says, "Silky . . ."

"Yeah?"

"It's no skin off my ass, but—are you developing a thing for that Marsh broad?" Before I can fake a denial, he says,

"From what you told me—I get a funny feeling about her. Quail like that—" He flutters one hand, like you do when you mean it's tricky, touch-and-go.

I pull a breezy wink out of cold storage.

"No, chum," he frowns, "I don't buy that. . . . Look, she's just too rich for the likes of us. . . . For the love of Jasus, I don't want her to break your balls."

For a second I was afraid he was going to say, "She'll break your heart."

7

CAVIAR AT KAZOTSKI'S

If you read the food handicappers in the *Times* or *The New Yorker,* you will not read any raves about Maury Lontzman's Chez Kazotski—even though, in my opinion, its "cuisine" runs second only to the Russian Tea Room. I can't say the same for its décor, which Mr. Lontzman shrewdly hides by very dark lighting.

It's that dim lighting and a strolling balalaika, whose strummer is a killer with *Otchi Chórnia,* which makes me give the Kazotski my business whenever I take a but-I'm-not-*sure*-of-you-yet-darling broad out on the town.

But that was not why I chose it for Kimberley Marsh. The Kazotski happens to be a nook none of her family—or friends or enemies—would ever stick their refined noses in.

I got there ahead of time and chose a very cozy booth in the corner. I asked Sergei, the pessimistic Cossack prince who has been reduced to being a waiter, to get a rose from the Glorious Florists next door and put it in a vase and set it between the candles in their wax-choked bottles. You would of thought I asked him to invent a new brand of orchid. His eyes filled with terror: "No, no, *pashálsta!*"

"You are not friendly tonight, Sergei," I observe.

"I have—kachoo!—rose allergy."

"There's no rose within 50 feet."

"The name alone makes my nose run."

This is typical of my life.

So I have to settle for a suffering gladiola, great for a funeral, which Mr. Lontzman himself went next door to buy. "I'll add

this to your bill!" he warns me. "They had to break up a bou-
quet."

"Don't charge me for its abandoned relatives."

All this time, my pulse is somewhat rapid, and I keep sipping
water into my dry throat as I watch the door.

And, at last, She comes in. Even in the dark she spins out
light. She has stepped out of a painting. She glows. Gold flecks
sparkle in her honey hair. . . . Her eyelashes are a lot longer
than they were before, and there's a violet gloss on her eyelid
. . . velvet and emerald . . . the scent of Persian musk. . . .
Her lips are parted and they glisten. . . . "Silky . . ." She is
breathless. She is *always* breathless—unless I confuse her voice
with my breathing. Then that quick, hushed, throaty voice:
"Am I late?"

"Always."

"You darling." She brushes my cheek. "This is Shelby Maitland."

You could of knocked me over with a baby-duck feather. I
am so *vertootst* I did not notice there is a guy with her, right
behind her. He emerges from the Lontzman gloom.

"You told me not to go out alone," she smiles. "And Shelby
needed the walk."

I would like to kick in his shins.

"How do you do?" says Maitland. He has a nice, long face
(from overbreeding), a hi-class nose (which could easily be
cracked), long blond hair (thinning), and a smile so charming
he has to be conceited. He is a personality kid, all right. Very
likable. . . . So is *halvah.*

He has said, "Mr. Pincus . . ." and stuck out his manicure.

I squeeze it without trying to break more than half the fingers. "I don't know my own strenth," I remark.

"I should say that you do. . . ."

All right, so he's fast with the comeback. . . . He is
taller than me, lean, wearing a Brooks Brothers button-down
oxford. Them shirts are made with the buttons set wrong,
to make the collar bulge and crease around the neck. You can

reconize a Brooks collar from Toledo to Tel Aviv, which I do not think stocks them. "Mr. Maitland, will you have—a drink?" I ask it without a drop of enthusiasm, and hit the "drink" to advertise he is not invited to hang around for chow.

"No, thank you," he says. "I really must run."

"You don't look overweight."

She thinks that is funny.

So does he. "I meant, I have a date for dinner."

"So," I grin, "do I."

He glances from me to her and makes a wry, although amused, concession. "Good night, Kim." He leans over and she lets him smooch her cheek, which I prefer to it being vice-versa. "See you Friday?"

"Uh-huh."

Now Maitland clutches my arm, with feeling. "Kim has told me a lot about you—"

"She don't know a lot about me."

"What? Oh." He laughs. "Still, I want you to know I—I'm terribly glad you'll be helping us! Thank you. I mean that. . . . And if I can help—in any way at all . . ."

I do not tell him the best way he can help is to take a cruise to the Land of the Midnight Sun. Instead, I *utz* him: "Glad to have you aboard."

Damned if he don't beam, "Thank you, Mr. Pincus. Thank you." And with that repetition, which phoneys use to pump up Sincerity, Mr. Shelby Maitland, of the Oyster Bay crowd, vanishes into the darkness.

Now Sergei, the suicidal Cossack, has turned very cheerful and is holding Her chair and exclaiming, "Please, nice lady, *pashálsta . . .*" which only goes to show the clout she puts on male chromosomes. Sergei even comes around to hold my chair, which I am already occupying, so's he can get a front shot of her. "To drink, *tovarischi?*" I swear his voice *tsiters* with passion.

"Martini," she says.

"Vodka," say I.

The Cossack buzzes off like to a call from his regiment in Varnishkes.

My dreamboat starts wriggling out of her brocade jacket. The wriggling animates some of her best parts. "Why don't you like Shelby?" she asks. Bingo.

I pretend to think it over. "I have a thing about men who secretly wait in a lobby—with an umbrella."

She stops so fast her right sleeve don't complete its journey. "How on *earth* did you know—"

"It has nothing to do with agriculture."

She inclines her head. "You never cease to surprise me."

"That's good. . . . I notice the man said, 'Thanks for helping us.' . . . I didn't know I was working for him, too."

"Does that bother you?"

"Sure it does. Is he a silent partner? Does he foot part of the bill?"

"Oh, no. You don't understand. Shelby and I have no secrets. . . . We were raised together. He and my brother still are best friends. . . . I guess Shel would do just about *anything* for Kenneth—or me."

"Peachy. . . . Is he in love with you?"

"Oh, God, you're jealous!"

"Plenty."

She laughs. "I am never jealous."

"That's because you are so noble—and emotionally secure." I reach into my jacket, extract my wallet, and remove a snapshot of the most beautiful brunette you ever laid 2 eyes on. "How does she grab you?"

Kimberley has to put the snapshot in the candlelight to study it good. "She *is* beautiful! . . . Very. Who—"

"I'm going to marry her."

She practicly drops the picture, and her mouth opens, and she looks at me—well, dumbfounded.

I am all innocence as I blink on the sweet side, "I thought you weren't jealous . . ."

She *shoves* the picture back across the tablecloth. "You're just too much!"

"For who?"

"For anyone!"

"Not for her," I say as I return the picture to its home near my heart. "She's my kid sister."

It takes like 2 seconds for her to caress her forehead and sigh, "Oh, damn you. *Damn* you! You certainly give a girl a hard time."

"Only those who are hard to get."

She looks at me like I'm either Noel Coward or Mr. *Chutzpah;* considering her background, the odds are strong in favor of the former. "You really are in*cre*dible!"

"Frequently."

At this dandy moment, Sergei brings us our drinks. The rose-hater is so smitten by Kimberley that his little tray is quivering. So is his hand, as he sets down her martini—but steady as he delivers my vodka. The dizzy Cossack drools as he ogles her.

"Tovarish," I moan, "she is my mother!"

"Eh, *Hanh?* Eh?" He gets an attack of the wheezes.

Kim raises her glass. "To my son, the detective."

"Gee, Mom. Thanks *loads.*"

We drink to that.

This bamboozles Sergei, who still hasn't got his first papers, being a wetback who snuck in at Tijuana. He sort of staggers away, puzzled.

Her hair is a stream of gold in the candlelight. I can't help thinking this is a whole different person from the jittery dame who came into the office maybe 5½ hours ago. I don't mean she is less ravishing. To me, she is more—because she is less flaky.

"I hate to interrupt fun and games," I say, "and we have plenty of time for chit-chat—but I should tell you something. . . . I found out who's been shagging you."

She almost drops her glass. Then she catches at the tail end of her breath. *"Already?"*

"I was lucky."

"Who is he?"

I lean back. "How do you know it's a 'he'?"

She's annoyed. "Are you starting that line again?! It's *natural* to assume it's a man. Remember: I saw one staring at my apartment window."

"It's a black man. Very good looking. A Richard Burton voice, with a Caribbean accent. . . . His name is—Vernon Matrobe." I watch her good.

"Matrobe?"

"Uh-huh. . . . Mean anything to you?"

When she knits her brow that way she resembles a college girl doing her Latin. "Matrobe . . . Matrobe . . . no."

"Have you met many blacks in Trinidad?" I ask.

"Some. At large parties. Or at the Casino."

"And you don't remember this character?"

"No. . . . *Why is he following me?*"

"He didn't say. In fact, he denied it."

She goes round-eyed. "You mean you *talked* to him?"

"I almost gave him a ticket for illegal possession of pistachio nuts."

She don't even smile. "But what reason did he give—"

"He said he didn't know what the hell I meant accusing him of the shadow *shtick.* . . ."

"Oh, this is maddening! What can we do?"

"Let me handle that." I don't tell her about the clout I took on the head, on account of that could scare her, and I have other hopes going.

She asks, "Is he the same man who's been telephoning me?"

"He played 100 percent dumb." I pause. "He could of been telling the truth. Or he could be very good with the innocent act."

She bursts out: "Maybe you've scared him off! . . . Maybe the phone calls will stop, too. . . ."

"Maybe . . ."

"You don't sound reassuring."

"You want reassurance, talk to your minister. That's his business. Mine is getting this spool of snakes off your back."

She reaches for the martini. "Did he look dangerous? . . ."

"I don't go by looks," I say. "The most ferocious-looking guy I ever knew was a tulip-nut, and he adopted every stray cat in the Bronx. . . . The sweetest-looking little old lady I ever arrested, when I was in uniform, greatly enjoyed torturing little boys 6 to 8 years old."

"Please . . ." she shudders.

"Mr. Matrobe looked clean, a good dresser, and he uses fancy grammar."

"He could be a psycho!" she exclaims.

"He could."

"Or a blackmailer!"

"Do not cast racial slurs. . . . Is that what you're afraid of? Blackmail?"

She consumes several moments arranging her answer. "No."

"Extortion?"

Pause. "Not exactly."

"How exact does extortion have to be?"

"I mean—there's no dirt in my life . . ."

"But someone is trying to scare the hell out of you."

Pause. "Yes."

"Why?" I push on. "There has to be a reason. I don't think they just pulled your name out of a hat."

"I—uh—well, as you said in your office, I *am* rich. They could want money . . ."

"That's extortion."

She does not answer.

At this point, Mr. Maury Lontzman, our beaming host, appears, brandishing menus. "You will order now, dear friends?"

"No," says Kim. "Two more drinks."

I like a dame who knows the priorities for gracious living.

"And would you mind removing this loathsome gladiola?" she asks. "It belongs near the casket."

Lontzman gives me the visual shaft, picks up the vase and

goes off in 1 of the most eloquent huffs I ever observed.

I look at her and she looks at me and not a word passes for a minute.

I say, "Now we will play Truth or Consequences. Do you think I'm so damn stupid I don't make a connection between the black buzzard and your brother? Trinidad is not the biggest place in the world. Your brother lives there, and you visit there, and Vernon Matrobe comes from there. . . . Who else among those near and dear to you is in the habit of soaking up the sun down Trinidad way?"

Her glance is very steady. "I told you: We all go there. Family reunions. We used to spend every Christmas at Divahli when Father was alive."

"Devalley?"

"Divahli. It's the name of the estate. Father bought it from a Bombay banker. Divahli is a Hindu word. It means 'Festival of Lights.' "

"Does Rodenbaker go down?"

"Oh, yes."

"Maitland?"

"Of course."

I do not like that "of course." . . . "Because he's Kenneth's best friend? . . ."

"Yes. He spends two or three months a year on the island."

"When you're there?"

"*And* when I'm not! Shelby has loads of friends . . ."

My cheek is beginning to itch. "There has to be *some* Trinidad tie-in."

Sergei brings us two more. He is so miffed, he don't say 1 single word. I find that an improvement in the ecology.

I ask, "Do you think Matrobe is working for Kenneth?"

"That's absurd!"

"Why?"

"*Why?*" she exclaims. "Kenneth is my brother! He loves me. He needs me."

"What for?"

She stares into her glass. "I would be the *last* person in the world Kenneth would want to—frighten this way . . ."

"Then how about Maitland?"

She waves that off. "Forget it. Shelby's not involved."

"How do you know?"

"If he was, I would know. There's no sense to that."

"Then how about your stepfather?"

"He's as dear to me—as dear as my father was."

Sergei is back. He has a pad in his hand and a big pencil. "Time is to order," he glares.

"That's an order," I tell her.

We examine the printed goodies.

"How is the Chef's Special?" she asks.

Sergei looks around for spies. "I not recommend it."

"It's Tomaine a la Russe," I say.

"I'll try to resist it."

I ask, "Blini, caviar, herring?"

"Caviar."

Ask a foolish question, you get a foolish answer. . . . "So caviar, Sergei. . . . I usually skip the borscht, ma'am, even though it's good—"

"I am not in love with soup."

"Exile the borscht, Sergei. . . . Now: Shashlik, Chicken Kiev, Blinchiki—which are blintzes—I smother them in sour cream."

"Chicken Kiev."

"1 Kiev, 1 Shashlik," I say.

"And for dessert?!" Sergei demands.

"No dessert," says Kim.

"2 desserts," say I. "The Baklava is too good to miss. . . . Tea or coffee?"

"Coffee," she says.

"You should teach her to love tea!" glares Sergei.

"All right, all right, make it tea!" she surrenders.

"Spasibo!" cries Sergei. "And a bottle of fine wine, of course!"

"A bottle of fine wine," I agree.

"Leaving the choicing on me!" He leaps away like Nureyev, waving the menus.

Kim looks after him. "Is he always that crazy?"

"He's just flipped his *kasha* over you."

She studies me in that strange, sidelong way she has. Then: "Are you annoyed with me?"

If you put a gold frame around her hair and throat and shoulders, it could be at the Louvre. Such beauty, a combo of the elegant and the sensuous—looks like that come up once a generation.

"Silky! I asked you: Are you annoyed?"

I sort out my feelings, which need it. "Sure I am. You hire me to do a job, but you don't want to tell me some essential things. You don't want me poking into something. . . . Whether that makes sense or not, I can't say. . . . I don't know why you're holding back stuff that could make all this a lot easier—and end it sooner. But it's your life, lady, your sleep, your peace of mind—and your money."

"You put it very well," she says.

"But there's a question I still have to ask: Are you protecting someone?"

She takes a very long drag of smoke, so she can decide on her answer. "Let's say that someone I love—is in trouble. I don't know what. I have an idea, but I *won't* jump to conclusions! . . . I've got to wait—until I'm sure. . . . Until I'm sure, I can't tell anyone—not even you. Maybe I will—the moment I do know, the moment all doubts are out of my mind—maybe I'll tell you then."

"And maybe you won't." I am very cool, believe me.

"It—*may* be none of your business . . ." The velvet voice covers iron.

I finish my vodka. "You're the client. You call the shots. Fire me the minute I get out of line."

"I have no intention of firing you."

"And I can quit the minute I'm fed up with playing Mirror,

Mirror on the Wall, who's got the loaded gun?"

That ruffles her. "I hope you won't do that."

Sergei brings us a bottle of Tokay, 1 of my least favorite wines, and opens it. He looks so proud, Kim sips it and says, "Refreshing. A change from the boring Burgundies."

Sergei acts like he has been made a Colonel of the Savage Boyars. He pours the nokay Tokay. Sad as the Sack, he exits.

So now she and me look at each other—in silence. I leave the next move up to her. I think: Maybe she tossed me her whole story as camouflage—to cover up something altogether different, something I don't have the wildest guess about. This is no Simple Simoness. Maybe she is playing me for a setup, in a game involving someone else and something else. . . . Her brother, her stepfather, Shelby. . . . A Mr. X? A Mrs. Z? . . . Suddenly, I get a hot flash: *Is the dear "friend" she's protecting—herself?!* Maybe she is using me—to throw someone else off the track, a track I know nothing about. The possibilities could make a whodunit.

"Silky," she says suddenly, "as you so icily told poor Shelby, I really *don't* know much about you . . ."

I don my Ronald Colman rue. "Miss Marsh, am I 1 of the most fascinating men you ever met in your whole life?"

Time-out for brain-work. "Yes . . . and the most conceited."

"You only say that because it's true."

She leans back and studies me in that tantalizing, sidelong way again. Is she teasing? Is she coming on? . . . "Tell me about being a private eye. I always wanted to know a real private eye."

I shudder, "Don't say 'private eye.' That's out. We are 'private investigators.' More classy."

"Fine. Please tell me."

This is dandy by Sidney Pincus, P.I. One of the payoffs of my line of work is the colorful people I have met, and the fantastic true-life stories I know. If they were only moral, I could make a fortune selling them to *Reader's Digest*. But if Squaresville don't buy them, I tell you who always has: women.

It is absolutely amazing how a hi-class dame goes for a low-down tale. That has been my gateway to a rich, full sex life. "Ask me," I lead off.

So, as we are touching knees under the table down at Maury's, and locking eyes over the romantic candles, Kimberley, whose orbs are like aggies in that soft light, says, "Did he have a gun?"

A wet towel would have worked just as good. "Who?"

"The man from Trinidad."

(Inside, I curse.) "Not that I could see."

She lights a reefer and leans back. "That's reassuring."

"Don't start celebrating. For instance—" I unbutton my jacket and put my elbows out to the side and raise them. "Am *I* heeled?"

"I beg your pardon?"

"Am I carrying a piece? Go ahead, tap me."

She pats my chest and under my arms and down to my pockets. (Listen, at least it's body contact.) "Nothing, Mr. Holmes, nothing at all."

"Wrong. You didn't feel the right place."

"Don't be vulgar."

"Don't be stupid. Try my ankle."

"Your ankle?!"

"The left one . . ."

She bends over and does that and double O's.

"That's a holster," I explain. "With a little convincer tucked in."

"Why at your ankle?"

"Because it's not a place goons expect a piece to be. Also, it's useful if a strongie has you pinned around the neck from behind. Plus, I am on a date. It don't look right for a piece of artillery to bulge out of my suit, or show if I unbutton my jacket. . . ." I stop. She looks freaked out. "Your dress is on fire."

"Mmh," she says, inhaling and very dreamy.

"I just killed the bartender."

"You're charming."

I reach over and take the cigarette out of her hand and sniff it.

Her eyes flare up—so she ain't 100 percent zonked. *"Would you mind returning that?!"*

I give her the fag and stand up. "I hope you enjoy the food. Good night."

"Silky! Please! What are you doing?"

"Going home. I don't like eating with the Queen of the Zombies."

She takes a quick last drag and snuffs out the joint. "I'm sorry. Forgive me . . . please stay."

That's not a hard request to grant.

"I'm just so damn tired of worries," she says. "I've been scared for ten days." She brightens (really, or putting it on, I can't tell). "Tell me: What was your most interesting, exciting, unforgettable case?"

I look thoughtful, for her benefit. "For interesting, the preservation of Pepi Mott's 3 brothers in a meat locker—"

She shudders.

". . . for amusing, the snafola of Mrs. Stoddard—Gwendolyn Tremaine—Blair."

"I'll take Mrs. Blair . . ." She smiles like tutti-frutti. "Did you?"

"Did I what?"

"Take Mrs. Blair?"

I lay silence on her. Silence is an answer, too. In this case, a lie. But I figure she likes to think I ball my double-breasted clients, so I let her think so—with a confidential: "Lady, I never mix sex and money. Sex comes first. . . ."

She laughs. "You *are* something else."

"Mrs. Blair was a client I got through 'Hokey'—Hobart Slocum, one of the most artistic check-hikers in the greater Manhattan area. He milked the personal bank account of Mrs. Blair, who was 46 and loaded. Her hubby is a V.P. at Continental Parachutes, Inc. . . . Well, Hokey was making a very nice liv-

ing on Mrs. Blair, who he only saw once but knew was somewhat dizzy, and he nets hisself like 12 grand, with no overhead
except pen and ink, before Mrs. Blair finds out she is overdrawn
plenty. She gets very mad on her bank when they can't explain
things to her satisfaction, so she decides to hire a P.I.—to find
the unknown forger. She goes to the Yellow Pages—and
chooses Watson and Holmes."

"She probably thought they're still alive," smiles Kim.

"It is a pleasure to tell you a story."

The Cossack prince delivers our caviar—and grated onions
and very thin pumpernickel.

"We take the client on," I continue. "Mike—Mr. Clancy—
passes the word around our snitch circuit, and soon I get a
tip that the penmanship kite has to be the work of one Hokey
Slocum. . . . I turn that over to Headquarters. . . . Inside 14
hours the Forgery Division collars Hokey. . . . He would of
taken a sure 1–5 fall—except for one thing." I pause.

She waits.

I say, "At this point you are suppose to cry impatiently, 'What
was that?' "

She cries, "Sorry! *What was that?*"

"Mrs. Blair had to confront Hokey in the stationhouse, to
tell the cops if she knows him or ever seen him before. Mrs.
Blair is negative. But Hokey puts on such a cornball act, exclaiming he don't know the difference between right and
wrong on account of the brain surgery he had to have—"

"*Brain* surgery?"

"—the brain surgery he had to have for his Korea war wound
in the service of our country, that Mrs. Blair, who did not
know Korea from anemia, gets all choked up. She informs me
that if Hokey will return the boodle and promise never to
do such a naughty thing again, she will drop all charges . . ."

The honey-haired Venus is like a kid listening to "The Night
Before Christmas."

"So I get a neat lawyer, Lester Plosher, and tell him I have
come to love Hokey, as who don't, and can he help that true

artist out in his moment of need? . . . The mouthpiece lays on a deal with an assistant D.A. he knows and despises—a clown named Strable who happens to be very religious, so he is jumping to save a soul, plus gain a contributor to his forthcoming primary campaign for councilman from Staten Island, or some faroff land like that. . . . To Mrs. Blair, Hokey antes up 3 grand—and he signs a promissory note that he will cough up the balance in monthly installments. . . . So justice was done, and a trial avoided to save the taxpayers' money, plus our over-crowded prisons don't have to cram another sardine into the can." I sip the red.

"I *hope* that's not the end," she mourns.

"I would say it was more like the beginning."

But by now the Kazotski is filling up with sour cream addicts, and Sascha Petrovich, the balalaika virtuoso, who is known up and down Yorkville for his fingering (and skill in cadging tips), has launched into the ever-popular "Red Poppy" march.

"Louder, please," says Kim—not to Sascha.

"Well, Hokey makes his monthly payments—the first of each month, on the dot. He borrows the dough from Chomski and Bell, who are actually bondsmen, bailer-outers, but they have a sensitive nose for any type buck, and they charge like 19 percent. . . . The kicker is, that brainy Hokey insists on making his monthly payments to Mrs. Blair in person . . ."

"I don't get it."

"You will. Hokey is a nifty dresser and a talker so smooth you could use his words for eyeglasses. And when, in the 5th month of fulfilling his legal obligation, he cannot go on the cuff for more scratch, from even the firm of Chomski and Bell, Hokey tells Mrs. Blair he is considering hari-kari, even though he never set a foot in Japan. In fact, Hokey cries, 'Madam, I throw myself on your mercy!'—and he throws hisself on her *zaftig* body as well."

Kim begins to choke on her wine. It is a nice way to go.

"1 thing Hokey always could spot a mile away in the smog," I say, "is a middle-age dame who is hungry for love, on account of her hubby is not showing her enough of it."

"Oh, Silky." She is dabbing at her peepers with a napkin. Sergei removes our plates. "You liked?"

We don't answer, so in a sulk he plops the Shashlik and Chicken Kiev before us.

"What *hap*pened?" the Goya across the table asks me.

"Next thing we hear is Mrs. Gwendolyn Blair is filing for divorce. . . . Hokey, who can give lessons in savvy, abets the split by finding the chick in the steno pool at Continental Parachutes from who Mr. Blair has been getting nookey."

"What's 'nookey'? "

"Hormone juice," I say. "Have *you*—"

"Never mind. Don't stop."

"So Mr. Blair don't contest the divorce. Gwendolyn flies to Old Mexico. Inside 2 hours of getting her decree of freedom, she becomes Mrs. Hobart Slocum, III. That 'III' did not refer to Hokey's pedigree, as your Society columnists assumed, but to the number of nuptials he has committed. . . . So in 1 shrewd play, admired by all students of the con, Hokey has wiped out his debt, avoided the slammer, and is now residing in the spacious once-Stoddard Blair spread in Bucks County."

Her laughter, her pleasure, the glow the candles paint in her green-and-amber eyes . . . I was so full of emotion, I refilled her glass.

"It's a lovely, lovely tale," sighs Kimberley. "You really admire Hokey, don't you?"

"I admire talent of any kind, so long it's not cruel."

"Is that the end of the story?"

"There's a P.S. Hokey is now raising Holsteins or some other type animal, and making out good. I never in a million years would of cast him as a dairyman—except for 1 thing. . . . Ask me, 'What's that?' "

"What's that?"

"Hokey always had a thing for oversize boobies. And Gwendolyn had them!"

She laughs very amply.

The Cossack has glided away. Sascha the Moocher now glides over. "Hol-*lo,* Tovarish Pinky! Hol-*lo, krasivi zhénshchina.* That mean *beau*tiful girl."

"It means beautiful woman," I snort.

"The same," shrugs Sascha. "I play for you roh-mon-tic moo-zik."

I slip him a buck. "Later."

"Later is double," he shrewds me.

"Sascha," I say, "did you ever notice that all corpses look pious?"

"What is 'pious'? "

"The plural of 'pie.' *Do svidaniya.*"

He starts picking at the theme song for *Doctor Zhivago* as he sashays off.

Kim is gaping. "Do you know Russian?"

"Enough to play Loew's Kremlin. I had an uncle who spoke it all the time."

She sighs, "Will you tell me something?"

"Sure."

"The truth?"

"Oh-oh."

"Did you make up that story about Hokey and Mrs. Blair?"

I look her straight in the eye as I lie straight through my teeth. "Every word was true."

"Oh, Silky!" she throws her head back and laughs. "I think I adore you."

"Bang!" goes my heart.

She raises her glass to me. "You—are—something."

My heart begins to hammer. This is all impossible . . . crazy. Man, she only knows me like 5 hours. . . . Is she conning me? . . . What for? . . . Who *cares,* who cares? . . . You say love is an illusion? So? What's wrong with illusions? . . . Love is a dream? So don't wake me up . . . I can't hardly breathe, I am throbbing so, beating like one big hot metronome.

In the haze of candlelight and shadows I hear myself saying, "You know, madam, I could blow my mind for you." The words

come out like I have no control over my own goddam tongue.
It is like I hit her. She stares at me. Her eyes are very big
and like in shock. Her hand touches her throat. "Oh, Lord
. . ." She turns away; her eyes are wet. "Don't say that."

"I didn't expect to . . ."

She looks at me and starts to say something and stops and
frowns and looks puzzled; she's hunting for words. "You mustn't
crowd me. I'm a terrible mess just now. . . . I need you, I
really, really need you . . . but I don't want—I can't handle
another affair—"

" 'Another affair'? Thanks a lot."

"Don't be sarcastic."

"How *is* Shelby in the hay?"

She waves her hands at invisible mosquitoes. "Don't be silly."

"Look, sweetheart! Every goddam time I mention Shelby
Maitland, or ask you a question about him and his place in
your life or this gig, you give me the same poopy answer: 'Don't
be silly.' Well, what the hell's so silly about it? Sure, sure, he's
your brother's best friend, and you and him are real close 'cause
you practicly grew up together, and—"

"He's *gay!*" she blurts. "Couldn't you guess that?"

Guess-shmess, I feel a *tanz* in my heart. "How am I suppose
to guess? The toughest sergeant in my outfit in Viet Nam turned
out to be queer—and the neatest, daintiest dancer in a chorus
line I once had to cross-examine turned out to be a stud for
half the divorcees on Park Avenue. . . . I just saw Maitland
for the 1st time—like 3 minutes—in dim light. If I have to
guess, I say he could be A.C.-D.C. . . ."

She looks up so fast I know I struck oil.

"Did you and he—"

"No." She says it so quiet and simple I believe her.

Sergei brings our dessert. We don't eat much of it. I suppose
we are busy analyzing each other's weapon—which is silence.

When Sascha Petrovich comes around with his balalaika—
for his donation—I slip him a fin. He asks me what to play.

I ask her, "What would you like?"

"Anything."

"Sascha . . . play anything."

"Anything is by Tchaikowsky," growls the Kazotski sage. "Who else?"

I have to admit he played like an angel. I think it was a serenade. Sascha even sang it, low and good and full of that Russian feeling that plucks the strings inside you. They have the highest suicide rate east of Budapest.

And in that new smoky cloud of romance, the eyes of Kimberley Marsh tear up again.

I take her hand.

She leans toward me. Her words come out in a murmur: "Shelby is mad about my brother."

Oh, man . . . Mr. Kempovitz, my Hebrew teacher, used to say, "Love can turn 1 person into 2, and 2 into 1." And here, now, at this heart-grabbing moment, Kimberley Marsh has to turn 2 into 4.

Sergei served brandy without my asking, and we "lingered"—like they say—over the brandy.

Sergei sniffed with sentiment over us, like he's watching *Anna Karenina*—and Sascha strummed more *shmaltzy* serenades.

We did not talk, not at all. The candlelight transformed her face so I saw it—beautiful in flickering silver like moonlight . . .

I wondered what was going on in that fascinating, mixed-up head.

"Please take me home," she said.

That's what was going on in that fascinating, mixed-up *keppeleh* . . .

And "home" did not mean, "Come up and have a nightcap," which I had hopes about—a nightcap being a nice way to start making out.

At the entrance to the Cloverly, which is 14 storeys of big, dignified stone slabs, with front doors that belong in a fortress in Florence, Italy, except they sparkle from heavy brass fittings and doorknobs and grillwork, the gray-haired doorman touches 2 fingers to his braided Royal Guard cap. "Evening, Miss Marsh."

She says, "Good evening, Shawn," and turns to me. "I *loved* the story about Hokey Slocum and Mrs. Blair."

"Would you like to hear about Jelly-Bean Snodge and Mitzi the Moocher?"

The smile is sad. "Next time. Thank you, Silky. For dinner, and your patience—and everything." She kisses me on the cheek. "Good night."

I just froze as Shawn opened a door and she went in. Before Shawn closed the armory from the inside, I got a glimpse of an enormous chandelier over a fountain, and marble walls and floors, and runners of Oriental rugs, and 2 golden elevator doors with attendants out of a Sepoy regiment Kipling wrote up.

I had reached for the moon—and grabbed a handful of air.

8
DONNY CHU

Herschel had brought Mr. Goldberg to my apartment, and fed him, and the pooch is so glad to see me, he interrupted his snooze on my best bedspread long enough to open 1 eye to see who that is unlocking the door and coming in, which he does—and goes right back to snoring with a clear conscience.

A lot of men have dogs who jump up and bark happily and show they are half-crazy with joy when they (the men) come home after a tough day's work. But Rabbi Goldberg must of not liked the idea of a pup jumping up and pawing his rabbinical trousers and licking slavishly at his hands—so Isadore was trained to suppress his natural canine traits and act quiet and dignified at all times. Either that or he has dopey metabolism. One thing Isadore ain't: Snoopy.

I find my note pad with the stuff on Vernon Matrobe I copied off his driver's license. Then I dial "0."

The Operator pipes, "May I help you?" in a Puerto Rican lilt.

"What's the area code for Yonkers?"

"914."

"Muchas gracias."

She laughs. *"De nada."*

I dial 914-555-1212.

This operator sings, "Which town, please?" in an accent you could dance to. The N.Y. Phone Company is a paradise for minority groups.

"Yonkers."

"The name of the party?"

"Matrobe. M-a-t-r-o-b-e. Vernon. On Woodland Drive."

It don't take 2 minutes before she has it. "Please *do* make a note of that numbah: 881-6272 . . ."

I scribble that down, then I dial 914 again and the 7 digits.

The phone at the other end rings several times before a woman's voice—hoarse, sleepy, annoyed—answers. " 'Lo."

"I'm sorry to phone at this hour, ma'am, but we have just received an emergency cable for—Mr. Vernon Matrobe. Are you Mrs. Matrobe?"

"No. This M'z Loganberry. The maid."

"Is Mr. Matrobe there?"

"They gone fishin'."

"Do you know when they'll be home?"

"Who you?"

Who *me?* "This," I say in pear-shape syllables, "is Hoo-Ha International Telex. We just received an emergency cable for Mr. Matrobe. From Trinidad. When do you expect him back?"

"Twelve 'clock. Tomorrow."

"Not before?"

"No way."

"Are you sure?"

"He got to be back twelve 'clock, mister, 'cause that's when I leavin' an' *some* body got to be here 'cause the 'frigerator company gonna send a man here to fix the lousy motor."

"Thank *you,* Mrs. Loganberry."

"You betcha."

I took a shower and got into my p.j.'s and commanded Isadore to get off the bedspread. No movement. I raised my voice: *"Arunter fun bet, hinteleh!"* The dog is in a coma. I jab him with a finger, I tug his ear, I pull his tail—what's the use? He purrs happily. . . . I finally have to lift him off like he is a pile of blankets and put him down at the foot of my temple of rest.

It took me a while to fall asleep. It has been probly the most unusual, crowded, confusing day of my whole life—and the most unusual part of it was Kimberley Marsh. Just the thought of her made me moan and toss around. . . . At last I drifted down, down into a dream.

What do I dream of? I'll be damned if I don't dream I am a kid again, visiting my Uncle Fischel and *Tante* Surah. Why? It must of been some type unconscious clairvoyance. You'll see why.

My *Tante* Surah, may that good soul rest in peace, always used to say, "Sidneleh, sooner or later everything depends on *mazel*. So when Luck knocks on your door and asks, 'Is anyone home there?' jump up at once and cry, 'Come in, come in! Here! The most comf'table chair!' "

Whenever my *Tante* Surah said this, my Uncle Fischel, of blessed memory, would holler, "Even the unlucky need luck! *Boychikel*, why is a gold coin *round?* Why? So it can roll— away from you or up to you. . . . Believe me: From good luck to bad luck is an inch; but from bad luck to good luck is a mile. Remember that, thank you, go away, eat fruit, a piece cake, but let me watch 'I Love Lucy,' and good night."

Who could forget lessons like that?

In the middle of that delicious dream, I hear a ring. And a ring. And the steady ringing jolts me out of sleeping. "Thr-r-r-ring . . . pr-r-r-ring . . ."

I unglue 1 eye. 3 minutes past 2, says the clock.

"Thr-r-ring . . . pr-r-ring . . ."

Trouble! God*dam*mit! Trouble.

Then I remember *Tante* Surah's wisdom: Maybe it's not trouble; could be it's Luck. "Come in, come in! Be comf'table."

"Pr-r-r-ring!"

I lift the receiver. "Pincus," I grunt, out of habit from when I was on the Force.

I hear no voice answer—but a mish-mosh of traffic noises: a bus sputtering, a horn, a Honda cracking the air like smashing a mirror. The party at the other end has his mouthpiece turned to the street.

My scalp prickles: That has to be Donny Chu!

The traffic noises cut off, and 2 short whistles stab my ear.

I give 2 quick whistles back.

Then comes his very deep, hoarse voice, that you could imitate by raking gravel. "I—think—it—is—gonna—rain."

"I think it is gonna pour," I answer.

"Hey, pal. Goddam line clean?" comes his gritty basso. "Tell your friend . . . your friend."

I will explain the reason for all this hocus-pocus. Donny Chu turns the mouthpiece to catch the traffic sounds to inform me he is at a pay phone, out in the street and not in his house. This means that his end of the line is clean. His saying "Tell your friend" is a signal not to use his name—first or last—in case my line has a tap.

So I wait. No click. No echo. No buzz.

Now I say, "I think it's clean, friend."

He chuckles. It is like a frog croaking. "How ya feelin', friend?"

Man, I have to hand it to Donald Chang Chu. He never makes or takes a "business" call from his mansion. A servant does that and relays the message, and if it's important and Donny has to reply, he goes out of the house. At once his torpedoes leave their posts in front. One of them gets behind the wheel of the maroon Lincoln Continental and the other sits in back next to Donny.

The Connie drives to a pay phone on some street corner— a different location each time—and the second torpedo steps out first and looks around, and when Donny goes to the street phone, this gun stays close to the booth all the time Donny makes the call.

His personal gorillas are not Chinese, you should know. That way they never understand what Donny is saying if he wants to spiel in the family lingo.

When Donny says on the blower, "I think it's gonna rain," or even, "I like Nifty Nightgown in the third at Hialeah," you have to answer in the same area or he hangs up.

All this don't mean Donny Chu is crocked. He has real good reason to be triple careful—ever since a tap on his phone got his name on a police tape while Donny was arranging pneumonia for a business associate who had double-crossed him. The fink died in Mother Cabrini Hospital that night. But it cost Donny a bundle to buy that tape from "Big Mo" Malloy, a sharpshooter in the Detective Bureau who was on the take. He put the arm on Donny. . . . Donny *had* to burn that tape to beat a very bad rap. Which he did. It cost him. Big. But he did.

"Goddam coppers," he is croaking. "They are suppose to get a court order before they splice a private citizen's line, right?"

"Right."

"Well, how often they obey that law?!"

"I wouldn't know."

"The hell you wouldn't." He snorts. "So—how's your head?"

"Bang!" A gun explodes in my skull. Donny *Chu* in this?! . . . My goose-egg is beating like it is trying to shout at him. . . . I dasn't show surprise—never—with a cat like Chu. So I slap the innocence. "Should anything be wrong with my head?"

"Knock it off!" he grates. "You are talking to your *friend.* . . . I tell you, I went sick to my stomach when I hear you got blackjacked."

I bolt up like my electric blanket short-circuited. "Is the bastard with you?"

"That goddam spade—he had strict orders never to lay no finger on *no* one!"

"Your orders?"

"Sure, my orders! That's why I went sick to my stomach. . . ."

I went dry in my gullet. "So Black Beauty is your boy."

Pause. "N-not exactly, chum. It is complicated. . . . In a million years I didn't figure you working in this gig. . . . You okay in the think tank? It would be a shame something serious happened up there. . . ."

"Something serious did happen up there, Donald. There's

a time bomb in there says I have to pay the jamoke back.
. . . Any objections?"

Throat rattle. "I appreciate your strong feelings. . . . He is
off the job now. . . ."

"You mean tailing a certain female?" I bait him.

"Uh—he got lonesome—for his family. So I'm gonna send
him back—home."

"Trinidad?"

Donny sounds irritated. "Since when I deal open cards over
a goddam wire?! . . . You and me should have a little talk.
So you understand what's goin' on."

My cheek began to itch.

"How's about you and me eat . . . tonight? I mean *tonight*,
tonight."

"Sure . . . where?"

"The Factory." He chuckles, so I know he is already enjoying
what he's going to lay on me. "Six P.M."

"6? That's early for dinner."

"I got reasons."

"You always got reasons, Mr. Friend."

Chuckle, chuckle. "Hey, I hope I didn't bust in on something?"

"Naw . . . I was just sharpening my knifes."

Yuk-yuk. "You still are my most favorite gumshoe. So—six,
pal. Don't be late."

As I put the phone down, my heart is going *"Oomp-boom-
ooomp"* on its drums. Donny Chu is no small-time operator.
He would not call to find a partner for *pisha-payshe*. . . . How
the *hell* does he get into tailing Kimberley Marsh? . . . Why?
. . . How come he uses foreign talent—from her brother's P.O.
yet! Trinidad. . . . Oh, man. It's going to be a doozy.

All this races through my keen, swift brain. I look at the
clock next to my bed. At least 3 years have gone by, but the
clock says only 2:09.

I set the alarm for 7 and take a Valium.

Mr. Goldberg is whining. That pooch has E.S.P. He don't know Donny Chu from Choo-Choo Carmen Cole, the topless queen of the Fandango on Broadway. But Isadore knows I am worried. So he gets on the bed and lays down at my feet, forgetting that the Dog Lib movement don't approve of servility.

In half an hour I am out of sight.

And what do I dream about now? Donny Chu. His shiny bald head and croaky throat and ever-present smile. Genghis Khan with dimples. . . . Then—the cobalt puss of Vernon Matrobe. A sledgehammer hitting my head. I fall. I fly. I get him. And I am laughing like crazy as I tear off his hands. . . .

Even in sleep, revenge tastes like candy.

Besides, like it says in Berakoth: "In our dreams it is not we who sin—but the dream."

You can't beat that. I bet I was smiling like an angel as I dreamed of the slaughter of Vernon Matrobe.

9
THE MOSLER SAFE

The alarm goes off—but soft and mushy, like bells under water. And at once, dear Isadore begins to yowl like an abandoned invalid. So before I do my usual morning triple "S" (shave, s—t and shower), I get the jar of vitamin-enriched chopped liver out of my refrigerator, and some dog biscuits and Izzy's bowl with "Kosher" lovingly painted on it long ago by Rabbi Goldberg, may he rest in peace in the Land of Our Forefathers.

I ladle out the animal's chow with my fingers. The smell of my (or Herschel's) fingers in his food keeps him from eating any other, so he won't get poisoned. Enemies lurk everywhere. . . .

I eat slowly, planning my moves, and I walk to the office, which Isadore loves on account of he exchanges barky greetings with every storekeeper, pedestrian or dog . . .

But that is not why I walk to the office today. I want to think out exactly what I am going to do—when and to who. . . . It will be a helluva day—! Matrobe at high noon. Donny Chu at 6. . . . What's their connection?! What the *hell* is Donny Chu doing in this?

I personaly do not think Donny was responsible for the 9–10 rub-outs that Inspector Borgun claims were pulled off in the Chu-clan style of gangland justice. In my opinion, Donny can't fairly be tagged for more than 5. And the murders were never against law-abiding citizens, you have to remember, but against like a soldier of the Yut Soo Toy tong, or a lieutenant in the Marchesi Syndicate, or (strictly in self-defense, altho in advance of the hired cannon's first move) against the hit man imported from Detroit to snuff Donny on a 30-grand contract that was the envy of professional wasters all around Mulberry Street. . . .

Donny Chu was born in a very tough part of Canton. (I mean Canton, Ohio.) The poop I get is that Donny went to 'Frisco when he was 22, where he wrestled for a living. He weighed only 240 at that point in his colorful and unusual career. Maybe you saw him on TV, in those early phony wrestling bouts that featured monsters, fliers in gorgeous silk bathrobes, marcelled fags, and up-close camera crotch-shots—to build an audience of women, which that sure did. That was when Liberace, in silver sequins and lace ruffs, was dimpling his baby face to make within a few cents of a fabulous fortune.

Donny was a good grunter-and-groaner. His head was shaved like a billiard ball and he wore only a loincloth, and he was billed as "The Canton Chopper." His part was the Baddie, so he had to snarl and spit and lose every match, even against "The Terrible Turk," who had arthuritis, or Frankie Pizarro, "The Killer Kid from Old Madrid," who suffered something terrible from fallen arches.

But that's a long, long time ago. Donny has as much brain as muscle, so he drifted into a tong in N.Y., even tho he was raised as a Methodist. He was handling Laundry and Imported Herbs protection for the Young Brothers, who were known as "Egg Foo" and "Not So." (You'd be surprised how many guys I fractured with that joke when I was a honcho in the Rackets Squad.)

It is 9:20 when I get into the elevator in our lobby, and at once, Cheerful Louey sings his takeoff of the Irving Berlin oldie: " 'Oh, how I love to *go* up in the mor-ning.' . . . You look mahty spiffy. Going to a wedding?"

"To a fight," I say. Just the word makes my blood bubble.

It is 9:25 when I reach for the doorknob of Watson and Holmes. I stop. I can hear Herschel in there. I put my finger to my lips, signaling Mr. Goldberg to remain silent. He nods. That's what he did: nod.

I open the door like the knob is an eggshell.

Herschel Tabachnik is in his Walter Mitty mood, tilted far back in his chair, rocking back and forth, and my ears hear the tune of "Home on the Range"—but the words translated:

> Oy, gib mir a haim,
> Vi di buffalo geyn,
> Vi di deer und di entelope play.
> Vi kaynmul kumt fort,
> Ah discouraging vort,
> Und der himmel
> is rayn gontze taig!

"Freeze!" I growl.

I'll be damned if Billy the Yid don't freeze. Right in the middle of the chorus we all know and love.

"When you sing my song, pardner, lock your thumbs in your belt!"

"I'm wearing sus*pen*ders," he resents.

I wonder if Herschel belongs on "What's My Line?"

"The mail ain't here yet," he says. "You want coffee and a Danish?"

I am in my office. "Sure. Any calls?"

"She didn't," he grins.

I give him a look should of made him an Eskimo. "If you did not work here, what would I do for aggravation?"

He acts like I just gave him the Legion of Honor. "You are all keyed up. You want to be alone. . . . I can take a hint. *Kum mit mir*, Isadore. General Pincus is off to war."

Isadore follows him out, marching.

I go to the Mosler safe, twirl the combo and swing the big door open.

Do you want to know what's in a P.I.'s Mosler Special? (Why shouldn't you? Everyone else does.) Okay:

1. Mike Clancy's .357 Colt Python (that's a revolver) in a holster.
2. Tapes recording how an I.R.S. agent was putting the

heat on Harvey Smedback, our client, for 5 G's—to knock 14 off his tax returns.

3. A 7-page deposition by Mrs. Marion Loshier, revealing how R. O. Brock, her supervisor in the Dan Dee Drugs Bazaar, had taught her how to tap the till—for over a year and $7,800—by pressing a disconnect switch before ringing up Sales, so that said Sales did not make the slightest impression inside the cash register. Mrs. Loshier split the swag with R. O. Brock, who, not satisfied by mere money, persuaded her to spread her legs in rapture for him in his office after business hours—for which she had collected time-and-a-half as well from the Dan Dee Holding Corporation.

4. Xeroxes of deposit slips that Mike bribed a teller at Sturdevant Trust to slip us—on the job for Arnold H. Coleby, who salvaged only 650 grand, *nebbech*, out of the $2.8 million he expected to net from his Brazilian bonds hype, a true masterpiece of paperhanging.

5. Blowups by 1-Eye Fishback, the best sneak photographer in the trade, of shots he got with a 300mm lens from a room across the street from the Hotel Dashley—pictures used for an out-of-court settlement in the famous Aldington divorce case. The candid pix were so candid, they caught Sylvester Aldington, the polo nut, and an ambitious busboy dancing cheek-to-cheek, naked, whilst Mrs. Aldington was in a Swiss hospital having her face optimistically lifted.

I could go on for pages, our Mosler being large and our practice unusual, but I don't want to bore you with sordid details of this ilk.

What I take out of the safe is a looseleaf book that holds confidential names and unlisted phone numbers. I riffle the pages to the *C* index, where I have

> Bobby Cannell
> Joseph Caplawitz
> Lucy Corbin

These names glow for me. Bobby Cannell is a police stoolie, very savvy, who will also penetrate for private—if the price is right. Lucy Corbin is one of the slickest decoys money can buy when you need a fake nurse, B-girl, divorcée, or like that. Joey Caplawitz is a genius with paper. Any type paper: a document, bill, check, letter. Joey can spot a forgery, or a phony 20-dollar bill, or a watermark that cancels out a legal paper, on account of the mark is more recent than the date. I don't have to tell you a talent like that don't grow on trees. The *paper* comes from trees; Joey comes from Yeshiva U. He dropped out to pursue his unusual branch of chemistry.

The item under Caplawitz is "D.C."—for Donny Chu—and is circled in red, and under it I have:

The "Office"—Orccieto's Clam House, 500 W. 11th St.
The "Track"—T. and J. Jewelers, 6th Floor, 86 W. 47th St.
The "School"—Shaughnessy's Pharmacy, 1142 8th Ave.
The "Factory"—Foo Moy's—12 Mott St.

You will notice that Donny's code name always begins with the same first letter as the first letter of the place he is referring to for where you will meet him.

In my opinion, Donny Chu is very smart to adopt all this jazz. . . . He should never advertise the name of the spot he is going to be in, on account of he is a very profitable target for unfriendly persons in rival organizations—like the Flower Five, or Vittorio Boloccioni's, or Bullets Brannigan's. Plus, Donny is often invited Downtown for questioning by the Gambling Squad, or Safe and Lofts, or Missing Persons(!). . . . Donny is a kind of conglomerate.

Herschel returns like the Pony Express. "Two coffee, as usual, one Danish. They didn't have prune so I took cheese."

"Okay."

"I also put in an apple. You should eat more fruit."

I look at my watch. 9:45.

I spend from 9:45 to 10:10 thinking. You can do a lot of thinking in 25 minutes, if you're not bored. If you are bored, you don't think—you futz around and come up with *kreplach.*

At 10:15 (all these exact numbers are not suppose to impress you with how well organized I am; they add tension to a story, because they give the impression something important will explode any minute) I write this note:

Mike:
I am heading for a lively debate—with the slugger from Trinidad. In Yonkers. Woodland Drive.

If I don't call in by 1:30, I am in trouble—so race up there and call Vernon Matrobe from the nearest phone. His number is 881-6272.

You are Captain Flynn, and have an Assault and B. warrant for him. Tell him his place is surrounded, and if he don't put me outside the door, alive, inside 2 minutes, you will tear-gas the joint and book him for attempted homicide.

Wing it from their, Michael, darlin'. I wish you all success in this wholesome enterprise.

—A. E.

The "A. E." is for Albert Einstein, who Mike thinks I take after—in the clinches.

I am sealing the envelope when the phone ding-a-lings in Herschel's sector. He buzzes me.

"Sh-*she*'s *on*, Silky!" he chortles.

I press the outside tab. "Pincus."

"Marsh." That gorgeous girl has dropped her voice 2 octaves to play solemn.

I smile. "Hi, Marsh."

"Hi, Pincus." She laughs like a kid who just pulled a fooler on her old man. "I just called to give you my new, unlisted number."

"You mean the telephone jockeys were there already?" I amaze.

"Certainly. Howard is a friend of the head of Bell Tel."

"Are your instruments clear? I mean the paper circles?"

"Yes."

"Okay. Don't forget to keep the list of pals you let in on this. . . . What's your number?"

"294-7705."

I write it down.

She says, "I'm reporting in. I lunch with Laura Maitland, Shelby's sister. Don't swear. She's picking me up, sir, just as you ordered. 12:15. We're lunching at Côte Basque. . . . What do I do if the Cadillac follows me?"

"He won't."

"Are you sure?"

"Positive. A new car could shadow you. Keep your eyes peeled. But don't worry . . ."

Her astonishment comes across like a bullet. " 'Don't *worry?*' Will you be in it?"

"No . . . listen. Did you ever have anything to do with a Chinese gentleman named Donald Chu?" I ask it like I'm asking her to pass the peanuts. I spell it: "C-h-u. Not 'chew,' like in gum."

"No."

"You sure?"

"Absolutely. The only Chinese I know is Dorothy Wang—a Brearley classmate. Why?"

"I'll let you know sometime. Meanwhile, forget that name. And I do mean: Forget it!"

"Silky . . ."

It made me glow to hear her say my name. "I'm here."

"Why are they after me?"

I hesitate. "I'll know a lot more by 7 or 8 tonight."

"Where can I call you?" she asks quickly. "At 7. Or whenever you—"

"You can't."

"Then will you call me? Please! I've got to know! I'm going to Howard's for dinner. Gramercy Park . . ."

I look at my watch. "I have to get going now."

"Wait. . . . Will you do something for me, Silky? Something very, very special?"

"What?"

"Be careful. . . . Oh, God, *please* be careful."

I feel a peculiar chill . . . I don't know why . . . I have to keep my voice steady as I say, "I'll be careful."

I put the phone down with a kind of worry I can't explain. She is in more than trouble; she is in danger. . . . Sure, I know that somehow she's conning me, that there's something she never told me—something she always holds back, or talks around, or even flat lies about. (Like the Talmud tells us: "The deaf imagine what they cannot hear—the blind, what they cannot see.")

On a hunch, an inside red light, I dial Kimberley's number. Her old number, I mean. It rings once and an operator cuts in: "I am sorry, but the number you are calling has been disconnected."

"This is an emergency," I snap. "I am Dr. Draykopf, chief of University Hospital. Connect me to the new number."

"I'm sorry, sir, but we are not permitted to give out the new number."

"Give me your supervisor!"

"Hold on, sir."

In 4 moments, a more mature matron comes on. "This is the Supervisor." (It could of been a Mother Superior.) "Can I help you?"

"You bet you can. In fact, you *must.* I am Dr. Jeremiah Finster, chief of the city morgue. My office got a call at 9:46 from a Miss Kimberley Marsh, plus an urgent request for me to return the call. I just did—and some idiot operator told me the number has been disconnected."

"What was the number you dialed, Doctor?"

I gave it to her.

Mr. Goldberg comes over for tea and sympathy. I rub behind his ear. He purrs like a cat. *Now* he has an identity hang-up!

The Supervisor's voice returns, as cool as Luke. "That number *has* been disconnected, Doctor, and we are not permitted to reveal the new number, which is unlisted. But since this is a medical emergency, I will call your party and ask her to return your call. Would you please spell your name?"

"My real name," I say, "is John O. Himmelfarb. Inspector

for the phone company. We are running a security check on unlisted numbers. *Congratulations on sticking to orders,* Supervisor! Good work! Keep it up!"

"Oh, *thank* you, Inspector. I just do my best."

"That's all Ma Bell asks, Super. Good-bye."

I hang up with relief, plus a feeling of having raised the morale of a conscientious employee 100 notches.

I look at the clock. It is time for me to get moving. To Matrobe. I lick my lips. I should taste salt, but I don't. I taste the sweet sense of revenge. . . .

I open my desk drawer and take out 2 tight-packed rolls of quarters. I slip 1 roll in my left pocket and 1 roll in my right.

I leave my office and pause to give Herschel the sealed note. "This is for Mr. Clancy. Be sure he gets it the minute he comes in."

"Roger! . . . When you comin' back?"

I give him an educational moan. "When I finish baking bagels."

"What if *she* calls again?" From his look I can't tell if he is leering or seasick.

"If Miss Marsh calls," I say, "tell her to sleep faster—we need the pillows."

10
2 GUYS—FROM YONKERS

I get my Plymouth Fury out of the Garden of Allah Garage, which is the only car-shed in Manhattan run by a man whose first name is Omar. He is a nice old geezer, who despite his bad breath and wrinkled skin hasn't raised my monthly rate in 2 years, which shows you that with him I never mentioned the Middle East.

I open the trunk of the Plymouth, which is a kind of moving office and lab. I have 4 hats of different colors here, and different style caps, gloves, bright scarfs and dull 1's. In a little box is an actor's kit—horn-rim glasses, fake mustaches, a couple of wigs, stickum sideburns, and like that. . . . I choose a pair of cheaters, which they have plain, clear lenses in them. I take a gum-back mustache and long sideburns and select a Scarsdale-type gray hat, and a briefcase that is stacked with interesting business cards and unusual occupations.

I put the gray hat on the front seat. Into the briefcase I put the mustache, sideburns and cheaters. . . .

I drive 86th Street westbound. I am so eager to get my eyes and fists on Vernon Matrobe that when I hit the Henry Hudson Parkway, I have to keep myself from hitting 85. . . .

I get to Yonkers around 11:50, and it takes me a few minutes to get the Mobil jockey to explain how to get to Woodland Drive.

By 12:04 I ease down it. I see a cutesy-pie "rustic" sign (that means the edges look like the teeth in a busted saw) that says:

THE MATROBES LIVE HERE

I sometimes wonder why such yokels don't add the date they moved in. . . .

The house is stucco, a half-ass bungalow, really, with a synthetic "tile" roof. It is 1-storey—in a style I call Early *Khaloshes*. There is a scrubby lawn, the usual dumb bushes and a gruesome screen porch. This abode never won no prize for Gracious Living.

In front of the bungalow is a blue van with luminous red letters to inform the suffering world that "Warren Warren's Wonderful Appliances" is either installing an electric stove or repairing a neurotic washing machine. In the driveway, where I hope to see the white Cadillac, is a Dodge station wagon, but the garage door is shut tight, so I don't close out that option. Since 2 fishing lines are tied to metal hooks near the roof of the station buggy, I figure Mr. Matrobe has returned from his hobby.

I drive past the crummy dwelling, down the winding lane, then turn around at a DEAD END loop (which is the reason to always case the road before you decide where to park), and I come back on the other side and park near the corner, which is marked "Holly Lane." If I have to leave in a hurry I have that extra margin right near the corner for a quick getaway without someone reads my plates. I adjust the rear-view mirror so I can use it from the back seat. Then I skip into the back.

There is a reversible raincoat on the seat, so's I can change its color by turning it inside out. This is a very easy trick to fool some types, especially children—who are the best eyewitnesses of all, in case you didn't know. I cover myself with the raincoat, the dark side showing, and I slouch down in the back seat and push my hat down low. I want to resemble a bunch of clothes on the way to the cleaner.

You would be surprise how many *shmoes* sit behind the wheel at a time like this. That is stupid. It could catch *someone's* eye. . . . I take the back seat where *no* one expects a stake-outer to be—especially under a bundle of old clothes. . . .

Pretty soon, in the mirror I see a clown in overalls with a

big "W.W.W.A." emblem come out of the house and he is calling, "No trouble at all, Mr. Matrobe. Okey-dokey."

The screen door slams behind him. (In all my life in the Bronx, I never heard a screen door slam the way they do in the suburbs.)

The mechanic climbs into his van. He starts the motor and back-ups a little, turning his wheels, then goes up Holly Lane.

I carefully emerge from my covering. A quick gander reveals no person on the street.

I lock all the doors, except for the left front 1. *That* slab I open and let it lean—unlatched—against the jamb, so in case of a quick getaway I don't have to waste a second's time or co-ordination.

The scene is still tranquil.

I open the briefcase and take out the fake mustache and sideburns. I paste these on, looking in the rear-view mirror to make sure they fit right. Then I put on the clear-lens cheaters, and the gray hat. I snap the brim down. I am ready for the action.

I cross the street and walk up the path. There is a bell outside the screen door. I try the door, but it is hooked, so I press the button.

In a minute the front door opens, but the deep shade of the porch don't let me see who's there.

"Good afternoon," I sing out like the district Good Humor manager. "Mr. Matrobe?"

The screen door opens and in the light I behold a big, tough, beefy, sweaty German type in a crew cut, an undershirt, old khaki pants, and moccasins that must of come down the family from a Mohawk on relief. He smells of fish, all right, which must be packed in his barrel of a chest. His head is as square as a box and he has no neck. His eyes are small and washy blue. This charming vision has a beer can in his right hand. The tin pull-out tab is dangling, the slob was in such a hurry to get the beer down. His color is not in the slightest black. It is pale and mottled.

"Mr. Matrobe?" I gloom.

"Which one?"

"What do you mean which 1?"

"Me or my brother?"

Oh, *sheiss!* I am dealing with a Nordic colony. "I am looking for Mr. Vernon Matrobe."

He turns and yells, "Hey, Vern! It's for you!" To me he says, "You from the insurance?"

"Yep," I say. I would be a jerk not to.

"C'mon in."

I get under the porch roof, and in the doorway to the house, the brother appears. Man. I blink, then shake my head to clear my vision. It looks like the first slob has jumped back to the door. Same square head. No neck. Real pale. Washy eyes. Same face, hair, undershirt, pants, beer can. But no moccasins. This 1 wears dirty feet. "Who are you?" he growls.

"Are you Vernon Matrobe?"

"That's me."

I am so damn disappointed and frustrated and angry, I am about to ask, "Are you sure?" but that would not be smart, under the circumstances. They are both pig-eyeing me.

But this ain't my first time in the fighting ring of life, or my first time on the ropes—so I know the ropes. "The department didn't prepare me for *twins,"* I smile.

"You want to settle the claim?" asks Vernon.

"That is my earnest hope and desire."

"Your goddam client practically tore the hood off the Chevy. Go see for yourself. C'mon. It's in the garage."

"That won't be necessary," I say. I stall by opening the leather straps of the briefcase. "I have the complete report here." I dig deep in and drop the roll of quarters on the bottom. The roll in my left hand I ease into my jacket. My collection of printed cards in the sewed-in pocket of the briefcase contains these useful credentials:

> ROBERT BORDAN
> Landscapes
> 28 Christopher St.
> Greenwich, Conn.

> SHERMAN AND ATWATER
> Fidelity Finance Adjusters
> 828 Broadway
> New York, N.Y.

> RALPH P. INKELESS
> Northeast Census, Inc.
> 249 Harkness St.
> Boston, Mass.

Each card has a phone number I don't bother giving you, as they are not able to ring. When I really want a patsy to call me, I give him or her "my direct line," saying it don't go through no snitchy switchboard. This always impresses pigeons. . . .

I hand Matrobe the Fidelity Finance Adjusters pasteboard. "Oh—it's not just the claim I'm here about," I say. *"That's* been approved by the insurance company and is being processed. Our firm is just checking the auto registration and driver's license. . . . May I see your license, please?"

He reaches into his back pocket and pulls out a squashed-up wallet his pet wombat must use to sharpen her claws on. He flips some cards in plastic covers and pulls 1 out.

"Thank you, sir."

The license is for Vernon Matrobe, all right. All of it. The facts match the facts in my notebook. Only 1 thing: The card has stamped across it, in red:

DUPLICATE

"Ah," I chuckle, *"there's* the little devil we were searching for! 'Duplicate.' "

"Sure. Some sonuvabitch snatched the original."

"When did that happen, sir?"

He turns to his brother. "Vince, when did I lose the goddam license?"

Vince, who is no smarter than Vern, screws up 1 eye; that puts pressure on his brain. "I guess three to four weeks ago."

"I had to fill out some goddam new forms and sign a statement I lost it and everything, to get this one," says Vern.

"He had to fill out a lot of goddam new forms and sign a legal statement to get the new license," Vince echoes.

"That's just what we wanted to know," I say. "That will close our books. Thank you, gentlemen."

I turn to open the door, but Vern has preceded me. He has a peculiar expression on his so-called face, and his barrel chest is pretty impressive. "Where did you say you was from?" he murmurs.

"Fidelity Finance. We won't bother you anymore."

"You already bothered us, Four-Eyes," comes from behind me.

I half-turn. I am now between the Berlin Wall and the Yonkers Monster. The former extends his mugg so close to mine I smell the Rheingold like it's coming out of the tap. "What's your racket, mister?" he asks. "Talk fast. Make it good."

It says in the Talmud, "When you have no choice, be brave." So I'm brave, but in this situation bravery can lead to a very brave shellacking from 2 animals who would feel at home in a cage.

Rule #18 in Sidney Pincus's Police Manual, which is not yet written but clear in my mind, says, "When outnumbered, run. If you can't run, confuse. If you can't confuse, threaten."

"What is on *my* mind," I say nastily, pushing my features closer to the Hun's like only a guy with a fistful of aces would dare do, "is *who to pay the $10,000 reward!* My company has offered that sum for whoever gives information leading to the arrest of the rapist who is going around New York using the name Vernon Matrobe!"

Vern has turned green, which does not go well with his acne, and Vince is whimpering in greed, which goes great with his. "Ten *thou*sand?"

"Rape? . . ." Vern seems punch-drunk and moans, "That dirty bastard! . . ."

The brothers are looking at each other in a way that relieves my fears of bodily harm substantialy.

"No one is blaming *you*, Vern," I say, establishing a new bond with the moron. "Or you, Vince. The police know that no one in his right mind would give a driver's license to a guy with a prison record as long as your arm. Not even for 500 bucks, which is this sex-fiend's usual price. . . ."

"Five hundred?!" Vern screams before he knows what he's doing. "He only give me—"

"Shut up!" yells Vince. He steps in front of me, his back to his outraged brother. "You know the name of that guy?"

I draw myself up like insulted. "If we knew his name, would I be here?!"

This unexpected display of reasoning stumps Vince.

"I don't know his name neither," groans Vern.

"Shut *up*, Vern! For Chrissake, don't tell this guy a goddam thing!" Vince swings around to me. "My brother and me got no information at all! He reported his license was stolen. How's he suppose to know who stole it?!"

I feel I have struck out.

"Of course, if we see some real—" Vince has cunning on his puss like a poster. He is rubbing his thumb against his forefinger, so I know it is a new and encouraging ball game.

"You're right, Vince," I solemn. "If I was in your boat I would do exactly the same thing!"

"They can't pin a rape rap on me!" blusters Vern. "They got no evidence!"

"Correct." I am as pleasant as a day in June. "And that's why you need me. . . ."

"Huh?"

"Come again?"

"To squash the *per*jury rap!" I let that hang in the air a second. "Remember, you swore to a statement saying your driver's license was stolen."

"I didn't swear to it! I just signed!"

I look very sad. "That's perjury *quid pro bonoparte* in this county. Not as serious as perjury *makkes*—but still it's a 3-to-10 in the slammer."

"Oh, my *God,*" croaks Vern, without praying.

Vince is too shook-up to appeal to the same authority.

"Don't let's go bananas, fellas," I say. "If you just tell me all you know about that bastard you sold your license to—a description . . ."

A very strange thing is happening. The Bobbsey Twins are staring at me like I am a creature from outer space.

"—I could get you a piece of the reward. Maybe 5–6 grand—"

Vince puts his hand up and reaches for my lip. "Your mustache . . . is peeling. . . ."

And Vern is pulling at my cheek. "So are his sideburns, Vince." He peels 1 off.

Oh, migod! The stickum on my gimmicks has dried out! . . . My heart stops. My skin shrivels, I prepare to drop dead. . . . In my mind, I start reciting my own *Kaddish*.

Vince says, "We have us a smart-ass here, Vern."

Vern grins, "A Hebe, I think. A real smart-ass . . ."

I am glad to this day I did not throw the briefcase at them and dive through the screen, which I thought of, because their phone rang somewhere, very loud.

"Hold him, Vince," says Vern.

"That won't be necessary, Vince," I say, "because I'll make you guys a deal. I put down 500 bucks, right now—no obligations on your part—"

"Shut up." Vince puts a hammerlock on my tender wrist.

I get set to pull the judo *shtick* I learned at the Police Academy—when Vern appears, pulling a long telephone cord. His face is red as a tomato. He is holding the phone out—to me! "Vince, it's for him. . . . Let him go."

"Thank you," I say hastily. "It's Headquarters."

Into the phone I say, "Roger, 9–3, 9–3." Hell, I have to say *something.* My only weapon is mystification. "Over."

"Listen, *shtarker,"* comes Mike Clancy's voice. It is like warm honey pouring into my ears. "I just read your note. I know it's not one thirty, but I have the feeling you are some *shmuck* to go up against that strong-arm alone. So tell me—you in trouble?"

"Well, Captain, I am absolutely satisfied these 2 boys are clean! They innocently sold the license . . ."

Mike groans. "I can't get there for 40 minutes! The traffic is fierce!"

"Yes, sir. I'll ask them. Hold on." I turn to the goofing Matrobes. "Captain Flynn wants to know, do you want to come down to the station or do you prefer to sign a statement I can take right here—to put you in the clear."

You can't blame them for acting like they have been psyched into post-lobotomy exhibits. The sounds they are making belong in a zoo.

Into the phone, I say, "I'll vouch for them personally! Yes, sir, I'll take their statement, Captain."

"Wait a minute!" suddenly blurts Vern. "How the hell we know you're a cop?"

Cee-rist! It was too good to last. I am back on the hot seat. . . . I have to cool this burner fast. Rule #28 pops in my bean: "Admit what you can't deny. Then lie."

"Good question, Vern," I smile. "I am not a cop. On this

case, the police are using a slew of private investigators. You
have to remember: rape . . ." Into the phone, I snap, "Captain
Flynn, subjects 206 and 207 wish confirmation of my identity,
and your authority in this investigation. Over." I hand the
phone to Vince, who is a shade dumber than Vern.

Mike must of done a gorgeous job, because when Vince hangs
up, his hands are trembling. But I see Vern frown. "Is this
guy on the level?"

"I dunno," says Vince. (New sweat replaces my old.) "The
Captain said there are several fake investigators, using phony
names and business cards, trying to horn in on the reward!"
(My heart shucks 12 years. Was Mike making with fun and
games again?) "He told me to make Mr.—wait a minute, what's
your real name?"

"Identify yourself!" barks Vern.

"Gladly," I say. "Uh—what name did Captain Flynn give
you?"

"You don't know!" cries Vince, hurling his beer can to the
floor. "Sonuvabitch, you are a phony! I'll tear you apart!"

I crack, "No, you won't, chum! Even *you* ain't dumb enough
to ruin your only chance—*me*—of getting free and clear of
a perjury rap!"

"Let's—see—your wallet," says Vern softly.

I shrug, but I am dripping streams of salt water. I have no
out. . . . I hand him my wallet. He finds my I.D. and looks
at it. He shows it to Vince. They both compare the mugg shot
to my face.

"Sonuva*bitch*," says Vern. *"That's* the name the Captain gave
me! Pincus. He's on the level. Sidney Pincus."

I'm free and clear. My heart resumes beating. "You should
be ashamed of your 2 selfs!" I act hurt.

"Jeez, we almost screwed this up bad," says Vern.

"Very bad," I concur.

"Wanna beer?" asks Vince.

"A Coke?" asks Vern.

"Not when I'm on police business. Let's just get a full statement about who you sold that license to." I pause. "You're *pretty* lucky I'll carry the ball after that."

So—after all this, a cliffhanger with triple twists that have me almost peeing in my pants, and it looking for a minute like I will be carved into a jigsaw puzzle, you would think my brilliant ingenuity and Mike's wonderful malarkey would be rewarded by Vern giving me the true name and address I was after: the blackjacker from Trinidad. Nuts.

You know what I got? The exact words? I will quote them from the facts the twins gave and I polished up and wrote down and got these stupid slobs to sign—once I could stop them from kissing my feet:

On or about March 20, I, Vernon Matrobe, in the presence and with the approval of my twin brother, Vincent Matrobe, both residing on Woodland Drive in Yonkers, did sell my N.Y. auto driver's license in the back office of the Lester Kranz Pawn Shop on West 42nd St. to a party who gave his name as Boris Horace.

This man is a genuine Caucasian, 5'8" or 5'9", around 150 pounds, 30–33 years old, with a scar on his right temple, going from the temple almost to his ear, which said party mentioned he got in a rumble in Philadelphia when he was a mere teen-ager.

For my driver's license, the said Boris Horace gave me $100 in 10-dollar bills.

Private Investigator Sidney Pincus, who is taking this affidavit for the N.Y. Police Department, has fully informed me of my legal rights before taking down this confession.

He was also kind enough to remind me that under Section 43-A of the U.S. False Sale of Driver's License Code, if the money obtained from such a sale is contributed to a recognized charity, all criminal charges will be dropped.

I hereby give Mr. Pincus $70, plus $30 from my brother—which $100 I want him to deliver to the United Jewish Appeal.

So help me God.

(signed) *Vernon Matrobe*

Witnessed:
Vincent Matrobe
Sidney Pincus, P.I.

11

20 DOGS IN THE OFFICE

Back to H.Q.—breathing clover from Devil's Island.

In the lobby I hear Original Louey singing "Flying u-up!" in a new key.

"Hel*lo*, Mr. Pincus!" he greets me.

"Hi, Louey."

Up we soar, the chains clanking.

"That was a *very* beauti-ful lady I took down from your office yesterday," he beams. His teeth look like a piano: white keys against black.

Yesterday? My God, it's like a month ago. "Very beautiful. Any company waiting?"

"Just Mr. Goldberg." Louey laughs. He just loves that name. "Fourth floor! Polar bears, antique transistors, ladies' step-ins . . ."

The "step-ins" date Louey. He is a fan of Betty Grable. "Ha, ha, ha," I laugh: Louey expects it.

I enter Watson and Holmes, Inc.

"Silky!" gasps Herschel, like I am back from Alcatraz. "You are very *late.*"

"I had to give a karate lesson. Is Mr. Clancy in?"

"No, he had to go to Paramus—that's in New Jersey."

"*Thank* you: I thought Paramus was in Persia. . . . I'm starved. Call Solly's Deli—"

"This late the service is terrible. What am *I* here f-for? I'll go, Uncle. . . . The usual?"

"The usual. *Don't* call me 'Uncle'!"

"Roger!" Herschel loves to say Roger! It gives bystanders

the idea he was a hero in the Air Force, when he wasn't even in the Hot Air Squad.

In my office, Mr. Goldberg gives me a very nasty glance, for my absence and neglect, then yawns and stretches out and closes his eyes.

"Izzy . . ." I say.

He deliberately opens 1 eye to advertise how mad he is at me, then shuts it. This says a feud is on.

This leaves me with no option. The book of Proverbs tells you a gentle answer turns away wrath, but Mr. Goldberg never read that. He can keep a mad going 16–17 hours. My nerves have been tortured so much I don't need extra heartache.

So I reach under my middle drawer. When I feel button number 3, I press. At once 20 bloodthirsty dogs begin barking— the most horrible barking and snarling you ever heard. The *tararom* comes out of the old-fashioned clock near the door.

Isadore jumps up like someone gave him the hotfoot and he starts *"Woof—woof!"*-ing and runs around the outer edges of the office like a shot out of hell and he is at the dogtrack in Miami. I never can figure out if Izzy knows the ferocious barking comes from a tape I recorded at the Harlem pound before a lunchtime, and installed, along with several other re- markable reels, inside the big clock. Or whether he thinks invisible monsters from outer space have invaded Watson and Holmes. The mutt will run around like that as long as the tape goes.

Enter Herschel. He waves a brown bag and puts a container of coffee and a pastrami-on-rye plus a baked apple on my desk. "Eat, eat." He nods to the lunatic running around like a mad Cocker. "I could hear him in the lobby."

"Then you must of left the outside door open!"

"The neighbors will be hollering soon," he predicts.

Soon is exactly when the hollering starts. "Chain up those fuggin' hounds!"

"Shut 'em up, goddam you!"

"Call the S.P.C.A.! Call the S.P.C.A.!"

I know that is a funny thing to holler, but I can't imagine anyone on the spur of the moment hollering, "Call the Society for the Prevention of Cruelty to Dumb Animals!"

I trip the lever on the panel. The demented menagerie stops cold. So Mr. Goldberg stops, panting like he's set a world's record for asthma, cocking his head at me, like asking, "What kind of *mishegoss* is going on around here, Pincus?"

I bite into the pastrami. Nothing's better for a boy from the Bronx.

Herschel goes to the clock, opens the lower panel and pushes the rewind control. This makes the taped dogs "wickety-wack-wackety"— backwards. Now Mr. Goldberg howls like he's all alone on the moon—until silence stills the Cabinet of Dr. Caligari.

"Herschel," I say, "when Mr. Clancy comes in, tell him I have a 6 o'clock date. With Mr. D. C."

"You going to Washington?!" he gasps.

"I said *Mister* D. C."

"How do you spell it?"

I fume, "Are you trying to bug me? Ulcers I don't need—"

"I only w-want to spell it right!" he complains. "Whoever heard a name like Decee? Maybe in *France*—"

"It's not a name, it's two initials! You don't *spell* initials. D and C. Is that so goddam complicated?"

"You don't trust me with the whole name?!" he pop-eyes.

There is only 1 way to answer an out-and-out *nudnick*. With a poker. "Hersch, the reason I do not give you the full name is because I don't want when you are kidnapped and being tortured with bacon being forced down your throat to have that name to squeal to the *bonditten* who are trying to put the owner of that name in a cement mixer and he will end up as part of the Long Island Expressway."

"Mobsters? Killers?" He prepares to faint. "Silky, remember the family!"

"If you don't shut up I will send you back to Gimbels' basement."

"Roger!" he shouts. "I will tell Mr. Clancy you are going to see Mr. D. like in 'Dragnet' and C. like in 'Cantor.' Where? Did you say?"

"You didn't let me. I will see him at—the Factory. And if you ask me, 'Which factory?' may all your teeth fall out except 1! You know why I say, 'Except 1'?"

"So I should have a permanent toothache!"

"Roger."

"There ain't a s-single curse from of old I do not know!" he brags.

"You have put a trolley car in my stomach," I say. 1 thing I am ready to grant you about Herschel. He can hike my circulation up faster than if I'm skipping rope in a cold shower.

"I will wait here until you r-return!" cries Herschel.

I did some paperwork until 4:45. Then I called A.B.C. Radio Cabs. I couldn't risk being a victim of the N.Y. taxi scramble during rush hour. The dispatcher tells me Cab 52 will be in front in 8 minutes.

Suddenly, I remember the 100 bucks I finagled from the Brothers Matrobe. That could be the peak of my career. I get a stamped envelope and refer to the Manhattan directory to choose a charity I want the Matrobe boys should really appreciate. I sure found it:

American Jewish Mental Health Center
146 East 41st Street
New York, N.Y.

I write that on the envelope and put the money in, plus a note:

Please send receipt to:

Vernon Matrobe
Kosher Fish, Inc.
Woodland Drive
Yonkers, N.Y.

I drop the envelope in the mail chute near the elevator.

I hope you realize that giving to charity is 1 of the basic

mitzvahs of my faith. It made me feel noble and generous to donate 100 boffos to such a worthy cause. . . .

I ride down with Julio, Louey's replacement (Louey goes off at 4). "Hulio" is a true eager beaver from Chile who says "chess" for "yes." He can't say "do you"—but "Jew." This offends many customers.

A.B.C. Cab 52 is waiting at the curb.

The driver is no comedian, for a change, but a very tired "Al Navodny," it says on the placard. Pictures of his hideous grandchildren are pasted on the dashboard.

"Mott Street," I say.

"Mott Street in *China*town?" he amazes.

"You know any other?"

He pulls down his flag. "I been driving a hack thirty-two years and in all that time not once does a fare ask for Mott Street!"

"This is your lucky day." When I think of Donny Chu, I hope it's mine.

He reaches to kiss the crucifix dangling from his rear-view mirror. "Buckle your seat belt. Here we go."

I will not say Mr. Navodny was a bad driver. He was very good, in fact. He just drove like he had to make Mount Rushmore before 7.

"Ain't you gonna take the F.D.R. south?" I dare to inquire.

"At *this* hour?" He looks at me like I'm from out of town. "One conked motor ahead of us and we're a turtle."

He makes it down and around the truck convoys on 2nd and takes a couple of shortcuts I don't know, including a sidewalk. . . .

I tell him to hold off the accident until we get to Mott and Canal. But Speed is in this Hunky's blood. So is "Emergency Entrance."

At last, Canal and Mott come up on my Tarot cards. I give the hot-rod ace 6 simoleons.

"My pleasure," he says.

I do not groan. "Those your kids?"

"Where?"

"On your dashboard."

"Naw." Navodny blows his nose. "They're my partner's."

"Tell them they won't live long, driving with you."

"God forbid they *should* live long!" he hollers. "Vlata—that's the big one—ran away with a Spic who robs churches—only Protestant churches, him being religious. And Anton—the punk with the broccoli ears—is number nine on the FBI's Most Wanted—"

I raise both my hands in apology. "Forget it, Al. Excuse me, forget it!"

No wonder they call it Fun City.

12
FOO MOY'S

The main street of Chinatown is bustling and noisy, as usual, with many male natives in black pajamas, even though they wear American-type hats, and Chinese ladies with their long, sleek, shiny, braided black hair.

A big Greyline Rubberneck Wagon is crawling along at the corner. The customers will pile out, gawking, like they are visiting a freak-show. They will go into an Opium Den cellar, and they will buy paper parasols and *shlock* jewelry, and incense and joss-sticks when they go into the Temple.

I scan this colorful scene and spot Donny Chu's big maroon Continental. I stroll toward the gold-and-red sign over a wriggling dragon, that in Chinese-type letters say "Foo Moy" in English.

2 cannons, wearing black hats, are sitting on folding chairs in front of the pretty brass door to the restaurant. *These* soldiers in Donny's artillery are Orientals, to blend into the scenery. The 1st watchdog is a very skinny type, a cougher, who is smoking a brown cigarette; and the other is a bruiser, who is picking his teeth with a solid gold toothpick—the type Donny gives his trusted help when they complete 5 years of service and can still take nourishment.

"Good morning, gentlemen," I smile.

"Who you?" asks Toothpick.

"Pincus. Confucius Pincus."

The 2 of them look me over like I am wearing cellophane. I mean they look right through my suit to spot any weapons on my person. Then the skinny sentinel stands up and nods into the restaurant. He must of got a signal back, on account of he coughs, "Very well. You are expected." He has a strong accent. From Harvard.

The brass handle of the door is shaped like the Chinese sign for good luck. I put 2 fingers to my lips, then touch the handle. It don't hurt to play percentages. The 1 day my Uncle Yussel didn't kiss the *mezuzah* on his door jamb, he fell down the stairs and broke 2 of his elbows.

The interior of Foo Moy's is very attractive, with gold-leaf on all the walls, splashy paper chrysanthemums, a dandy fire-spitting dragon over the bar, and soothing stuff like that.

There are a few Chinese swingers drinking on bar-stools— young and real *chic*—but only a handful of customers are eating this early: some Orientals, a couple of Germans (squares), and a few tired tourists. It is too early for the high-rollers. . . .

Out of the kitchen comes a veteran waiter in a red jacket. He walks like a camel. "You Mr. P.?"

"Bingo."

"You want, uh, Chinee- or Amelican-style bleakfast?"

"Breakfast?" I echo.

"Mr. C.—he just wake up. Amelican or Chinee?"

"Amelican," I say.

"How you rike eggs?"

"Over. Easy."

"Bacon? Ham?"

"None." (I promised my mother on her death-bed.)

"Fly potato?"

"No."

The Camel mourns, "Evelyone on diet. . . . So. Boss waiting."

I have been to the Factory before, so I know where Donny will be. I go to and up the stairs at the back, to the mezzanine. I nod to a tough, freckled Mick, who from the bulge in his nubby silk suit is warming an oversize heater in the armpit. He surveys me. "You got hardware?"

"Do I look loco?"

He frisks me—and is smart enough to do a knee bend and check out for an ankle holster. "Okay."

A gorgeous screen shows a poetic scene of old-time warriors in armor hacking their heads off each other in a cherry-blossom garden, while ladies with rice-powder faces and huge hairdos clog around on a bridge in fear, fluttering pearly fans.

Behind the screen is a door. A plaque hangs on it:

SINO-U.S. SOCIAL CLUB
MEMBERS ONLY

Under that is the same message, I suppose, in Chinese—because it looks like a rooster with his feet dipped in ink ran across it.

Another door reads: OFFICE.

In front of this door, so help me, is another bulldog, true Italian in looks, so I say *"Ciao"* to test him, and he passes with *"Ciao."* He knocks on the office door twice and opens it for me like he is a butler instead of a goon.

I tell you I could bust the C.I.A. Map Room easier than any place I ever found Donny Chu waiting. Another thing you have guessed is that Donny has an international staff. The reasons are there—once you get an idea of the different types razzle-dazzle he has going for him.

"Silky, *Sil*ky, my old friend!" It is Donny's sweet croak— gravel hitting barbed wire. He is at a big desk, nicely carved with snakes and crocodiles. He stands up and comes around, his thick arms wide open, his shiny lemon-color skin busting in a smile like the joker in the subway ads: "You don't have to be Chinese to love Levy's Jewish Rye Bread."

We embrace like we are Russians, in a bear hug, only I don't get my arms all the way around Donny on account of he must weigh like 320. Over his shoulder, through an open door that shows a very long room, I see red-and-gold lacquer panels showing storks and mountains where old men with canes are *shlepping* theirselves up them. In front of that is a big roulette wheel, 2 green crap installations, and 3 blackjack counters with high stools in front of them and green lamps over them low. . . . The action don't start 'til 8, if my memory is right.

Donny holds me away at arm's lenth—his arm's lenth, which is pretty far—so he can enjoy the handsome arrangement of my features.

He is bald for real now, and has a slick Fu Manchu drooper on his upper lip that trails down to his chin. His brown eyes are definitely lip-shaped. He has no eyebrows. No eyebrows at all. He gleams like old amber in the soft light. . . . He wears his usual pongee suit. If not for the pongee, he could play Attila the Hun.

"You look *healthy,* my friend! This pleases me. . . . And how is the charming Mrs. Pincus?"

"I haven't met her yet."

"What? What?"

"Donny, I'm not married."

His 2 eyes slit, but he makes a shrewd recovery and slaps his thigh and busts out yakking: "How d'you like that?! He thinks Donald Chang Chu has lost his goddam marbles! . . . The reason I ask is, who knows?—maybe you took the lotus walk since the happy day we last met. In Boca . . . remember Boca?" He is flashing teeth galore.

"I was never in Boca Raton, *bubie.*"

What little opening there was for his eyes screwed closed, and he laughed and heaved until his jowls shook like Jell-O. "Testing, testing again! Trying to fake you out. . . . Don't *I* know we never met in Boca?! A dum-dum would play along with Donny Chu, flatter him up, always agreeing, and the stupe would say, 'Boca, Donny? *Me* remember Boca?! Great time we had in Boca!' . . . Not you. Always honest! . . . That, I like about you." He pushed my chin playfully with the heel of his hand. If it wasn't playful, I'd be on Canal Street. "C'mon, sit down, pal. You ordered?"

"Yes."

"So have some tea 'til it comes." The Canton Chopper sits

down in an ornate mahogany throne. He sinks down in layers. . . . Then he lifts a blue pot and pours tea into beautiful
small green cups that have no handles. He is shooting me
amused looks all the time. Like a kid playing "I know something
you don't know . . ."

He sips tea and sighs, "Well, sport. How's business?"

"Picking up."

"Too bad. . . ." He leans over and asks confidentially, "Why
you never come to work for me? . . . Silky, good help is very
hard to find these days. I need talent. Your type. Brains, moxie,
afraid of nothing . . . "

"You read me wrong, Donny. There's plenty I'm afraid of."

"Yeah? Like who?"

"You."

I don't know if he likes that. His eyes drill me. "Bullshit.
You never have to chicken out regarding Donny Chu. Not
so long as you stay my friend. . . . I *like* you, kid. You want
I should prove it? I repeat my offer: Come into my organiza-
tion."

"That," I say, "is an offer I can refuse."

That, he loves. He throws his head back like a seal, and his
moon-face wrinkles up like a webbed lantern, and he howls,
"Sonvabitch, he *kills* me! This guy *kills* me. 'That's an offer I
can refuse.' . . . Hey, that was some goddam good movie, huh?
I was sure glad it was about Dagos. A flick like that used to
be about slant-eye, treacherous 'Chinks.' *Pee*oo! Tong wars,
pulling out fingernails, water torture—terrible crap like that.
Gave us a bad image. . . ." He sighs. "Times are better. The
American Way is best. Do not lean on race, color or breed. . . .
Did you know my Number One Son is engaged?"

"Congratulations."

"You know to who? Sarah Skolnick. . . . How d'ya like that?"

"Mazel tov."

He don't crack a smile. "His mother and me throw the best
Chinese girls you ever seen at his feet. Girls from high-type

families, college grads. Nothing. . . . But he meets this paleface chick and goes ape. . . . Sarah Skolnick." He shakes his hairless dome in amazement.

"Are you against it?"

He clears his throat like it's a bowling alley. "I tell you my feeling: East is East and West is West . . . but love is love. Sure Sarah looks funny, not being Chinese. But imagine the *kids* they gonna have!" He taps his temple. "Jewish is almost as smart as Chinese. . . . I just hope her folks change. Silky, they are very prejudiced," he mourns. "They don't approve their daughter marrying a Methodist."

He pours me more tea. It wasn't bad for green water sprinkled with perfume.

I wonder when Donny will drop the smoke-screen and get down to the nitty-gritty.

There is a ring—pause—ring from the gleamy lacquer door of the office, which I note is padded real thick inside.

Donny presses a buzzer and barks out the Chinese for "Come in!"—I think. (I do not understand 20 words in that foreign gab.)

The Camel enters. He is carrying an enormous tray shining with silver domes. He sets out places fast, puts a tray in front of me and another in front of Donny. My tray has orange juice, eggs, toast. Donny's has an omelette as flat as a pizza, and a heap of rice and shredded noodles. I do not fail to note that the Camel provides me with fork and knife, but Donny with chopsticks made of ivory—which make a nice sound as Donny, who has tucked a big napkin in his pongee collar, clack-clacks them. He sure can eat with his mouth full. He is not a mandarin.

He points the clackers into the rice to re-create the Pyramid and says, "How you doing on the Marsh job?"

I breathe deep. "For openers, I'm breaking my ass and flying blind."

"I figured," he says, slurping his rice. Among Chinese of this type it is considered very classy to slurp and burp—that shows the cuisine is great.

"How did you get in this?" I ask.

Donny grins and makes his elephant paw into a fist and pushes it soft against my cheek, fondly. "I am just helping out the family—overseas. . . . What I want to know is, who hired you: Kenneth Marsh?"

I let that hang in the air to dry. "Since when did I ever name a client?"

He slaps the table. "Ya! That's another thing I like about you. Confidential is confidential. The blood of business. . . . The way I figure is, you have to be working for one of three scared cookies: Kenneth Marsh, or his sister, or his stepfather."

I lift the tablecloth and peek under the table.

"What the hell you *do*ing?" he amazes.

"I'm looking for the crystal ball you keep next to your abacus."

He gives me a sigh so long it has to come from his *kishkas*. And he winks.

So now I am in the cat-and-mouse bit with a master—a Chinese *Litvak*. I ask, "How did you figure out I have to be working for—"

"Don't *rush* it," he complains. "Confucius said, 'The longest journey begins with a step.'"

"And my Uncle Shmulke said, 'The man who blows the foam off his beer ain't really thirsty.'"

"Hey, that's good! I like that!"

I lift my wrist and analyze the time. "In 1 hour I have to be in the Police Commissioner's office . . ."

He gives me the shrewd version of his autumn line of smiles. "You won't leave here 'til you know why the goddam coon tried to bust your skull open." Chuckle, chuckle.

I stand up and stick out my hand. "So long, Charlie Chan."

"God*dam*mit, you know I hate that type ribbing!" He wags me a finger as thick as a knockwurst. "I hate to break a friend in many sections. Sit down. . . . How good d'ya know Mr. Kenneth Marsh?"

I waffled, "I don't have to tell *you*, do I?"

"That fancy Dan is in trouble, Silky. He is a bad boy. . . . He used to be a good boy—he last year paid 200 thou' on his gambling markers. . . . But now he owes a *big* one. And he's rattin'. . . . Or maybe he don't have that type heavy bread no more. . . ." He ogles me, kind of sly, waiting.

"How heavy?"

"Five hundred—big ones . . ."

There's hair in my throat. "Half a *mil*-lion—"

"If you quote me, you will lose an eye."

"I'm glad you trust me. How come he owes you?"

"Not *me*, sport! My family. . . . You ever seen Port-of-Spain?"

"I never been in Europe."

"It ain't even in Asia!" Donny is always disgusted by ignorance. "That's the big town in Trinidad. *Man*, that is some crossroads of the world: Hindus, Mexes, Turks, West Indies, Brazilios, Japs . . . and the pussy! Oh, them tomatoes! They make Paris look like a dog swamp. You never in your life seen such gorgeous muff as the Chee-chees."

"The who-chees?"

"Half-Europe, half-Asiatics. Plus every other combo in the whole fuckin' world. And do they do *that!*" He heaves so much bliss it makes the sweat bust out on his dome. "That Trinidad hangs just off South America. A perfect market for gash. Plus a dandy 'drop'—for opium and cocaine runners."

"Ah. So your uncle . . . "

"Don't jag off! He hates dope. That's a stinkin', rotten way to earn a buck! Who *needs* it? Up our alley is the gambling. . . . Our Casino in Port-of-Spain is like Monte Carlo West. Plus the tropical scenery and bimbos and night stuff . . . "

"Sign me up for the package tour."

He scowls. "The Casino is where Kenneth Marsh goes whenever the fever grabs him." Donny gazes soulfuly to where he believes Heaven is located. "Has that moke got the fever! Blackjack, Poker, Craps, the Wheel. . . . Man, that playboy will bet on cockaroaches! . . ."

Light begins to dawn on yours truly.

"And that punk is a loser. A born expert loser. He draws to inside straights! In Faro, he bucks the tiger. The roulette wheel there has a double zero—so the house percentage is murder, right? Does he care? Up a pig's ass." Now Donny sighs, which is like a rhino getting mushy. "Man, if that rich Jonah lived here in the Big Apple, my bookkeepers would send him presents on his every birthday!"

I feel like I am a Strasbourg goose getting fat stuffed down his pipe to balloon his liver before they wring his neck and make pâté. So I toss him a teaser: "He must hit the sauce, too."

Donny observes, "A canary don't get cured of birdseed."

"I hear he's on happy pills," I throw in. (It's free.)

He lets me suck egg. "The crum runs up this big marker—and takes a powder. Disappears right off the goddam scene. My relatives put out the flag on him—to me and every part of the family's tie-ins. But this skip don't show. No place. Not in one of them posh clubs in Mayfair, London, not in Vegas, not on that big gambling ship off L.A. . . . But there's a bigger problem. Real cute. Know what?"

"What?"

"My relatives cannot find a single goddam *picture* of Mr. Rich Rat! Only a description. Can you top that? . . . What good are *words* when you are hunting a smart rabbit? The skip dyes his hair, grows a beard, uses contact lenses to even change the color of his eyes! . . . But my cousin in Trinidad has a big ace up his sleeve—a very sharp bouncer in that casino, a bouncer who he has seen Mr. Kenneth Marsh like forty or fifty times. So my uncle in Port-of-Spain—"

"I thought he was your cousin."

He looks at me with pity. "My cousins run the Casino. Their father, who is my uncle, has the moxie. So *he* calls me and asks can he send over this bouncer—to New York, which is my territory—to locate his rabbit. . . . I am glad to do that. . . . Also, I dasn't refuse. Also, I stand to pick me up a nice piece of collection money." Yuk-yuk.

I do not assent to much selfish sentiment.

"We figure the Marsh boy—did you know his middle name is *Ardway?!—has* to show in N.Y. To his sister or stepfather. They got barrels and barrels of scratch. . . . Sooner or later, Kenny boy has to put the bite on his dear ones. Right?"

"So you put the Trinidad tail on him?"

"Naw. How can you put a shadow on nothing? . . . I put the bouncer on his sister."

"Crash!" It hits me like a hammer. She was the thread, not the needle.

"I don't even give that black bum *wheels*, understand? You know how easy the cops can trace a license. One of my birds gives Kid Trinidad cash. To buy a used heap." He winks. "How's that for cover?"

"Nice, Donny." I put a poisoned worm on his hook. "You know what type wheels he chose?"

"Who cares?"

"A white Cadillac."

His eyes bug out. "A *what?!*"

"A . . . white . . . Caddie . . ."

He begins to cough and choke on his chestnuts. "W-*white?* Sonvabitch! For *tailing?* It stands out like a hard-on in a nudist colony!"

Who would not appreciate that image? "That's why Kimberley Marsh caught him spooking her," I say.

He's still flummergasted. "What kind horse's ass buys a white Cad to—"

"His kind. Hungry for fizz and jazz. It's an *old* buggy, Donny, so he must of got a bargain. And what cowboy from the Caribbean could resist showing off? Hell, he's probly sent a ton of snapshots back to his buddies. . . . Say, how'd he get a driver's license?"

Donny strokes his long lip muffs, admiring hisself again. "Any day of the week I find you two hundred on sale—lost, fences, or from muggers . . ."

"Neat, Donald, very neat. . . . What's the clown's real name?"

He goes Buddha. "Next question."

"Has he nailed Kenneth Marsh yet. In New York?"

Donny's eyes twinkle like fake stars. "That is classified information."

"So he didn't."

"I didn't say that!"

"You didn't deny it. . . . How come you tail only the sister? Maybe you could find Marsh through another lead. . . ."

The Rising Sun leaves Japan to appear behind Donald Chu like a halo. "Oh, wow. You are on top of everything."

I try to look modest, which is hard for anyone except a *shmegegge*, who looks modest because he has to. (Any expression except egg on a *shmegegge*'s features is like a pickle on strudel.)

"The Trinidad tom," grins Donny, "is not the only bloodhound in my kennel."

"So you're tagging Howard Rodenbaker."

"Natch."

"I will give you another name." I figure there is no reason Donny shouldn't take some of the load off my shoulders. "Shelby Maiterloo."

He looks disappointed in me. "You mean Shelby Maitland."

"Heavens to Betsy."

I know fun and games are over because Mr. Chu's soft brown eyes have gone unfriendly. "Talk, Silky."

"I suppose the Trinidad creep also telephoned Kimberley Marsh every night—with deep breathing?"

"Yah!" Donny bangs the table like he hit the jackpot. "You gave it away! So *she* is your client! Has to be! *Who else could tell you about them phone calls?*"

"You are too smart for me, Donny," I mourn. (Ha!)

"Agreed!"

"But why did he do it? The telephoning, I mean. . . . To scare her?"

"No, no, no. *I* told him to make them calls! But I don't want the spade to talk to *her!* I hope her brother is in that apartment and will answer! . . . Screw the hair dyes, wigs, fake eyes. He can't change one thing—*his voice!* . . . If my bouncer once hears his voice, which he knows real good, we know Kenny is in town! And where." His orbs are gleaming like a tiger before a leap for the kill.

"Very sharp, Donny. Very, very sharp."

"Thanks, Silky."

Having stroked his ego, I feel entitled to tap his game plan. "But how come your bouncer don't ask her, when she answers the phone, 'Can I talk to your brother?' . . . If she puts Kenny on the phone, or says he's expected Friday . . ."

The stubby finger wags again. "I order that bouncer to never say one goddam word! With *his* accent?! Christ, she would never forget that tony voice. . . . You realize how much trouble a shakedown can get in from recognizing a voice? This is a subject on which I am very sensitive."

"Who can blame you?" I choke up with *rachmones.*

"Anyway," he confides, "all I have to do is wait."

"Okay. Sooner or later you nail Kenneth. Then?"

"Silky," he sighs, "you think I am so dumb I think *you* don't know what happens to a skip on a six-figure marker? . . ." He makes a what-can-you-do face. "In this business you can't let a nark get away with that. It would run around like lightning that the Chu family has lost its balls. Every gung-ho in the U.S. would hustle over to one of our stores without they are afraid that if they lose they have to pay up. . . . Also, our competition! They'd send in ringers—to break us. What can they lose? Either the ringers win like crazy, or they lose but leave us holding toilet paper!"

I nod gravely. "Sound thinking. I know that when you nab Marsh you will give him the same educational lecture."

"No! Him we do not try to educate. He knows not paying debts is a serious cop-out. He has to learn 'Crime Don't Pay.' "

"How will you teach him?"

"First, we rough him up. If that don't make him cough up, we explain how inconvenient it is to play tennis with one foot. . . . Or how Society broads do not go for a dude whose puss resembles a map of Romania." He sighs, the picture of pious. "I have tried to teach all my help the principles of Christian charity. But there is so much greed and hate and desire for revenge in this lousy world, Silky. . . . *You* know how I hate rough stuff. . . ."

"I know, Donny. At heart, you are an artist."

"Thank you. And knowing my weakness, some of my associates finally convince me that the best way to bring this cream puff to cut the custard is"—his blink is right out of Orphan Annie—"through his sister. . . . Suppose the sister stands to lose some looks—say in a—uh—car crash . . ."

I know people their blood would run cold on hearing those horrible words. Not me. I just feel I will keel over in a *khallish*.

I make myself retain my cool, and keep busy to hold on to it. I wipe my mouth with my napkin, fold it neat, fold it again, lay it down.

"Do you get the moral of my sermon?" Donny asks politely.

"I didn't fall asleep once—even during the commercial."

"Silky," says the king of the jungle, putting a lead paw on my arm, "that black jerk didn't know you from Mary Poppins, but remember: You 'made' him, so he panics. Goddam amateur bangs you with a sap. . . . It's all the fault of TV! It encourages violence. These hired clowns see three installments of a cop series and they begin acting like—Baretta. . . . I took the creep off this job. Did I tell you? I'm sending him back to my uncle."

I finish my tea. "Donny, I don't want you and me to ever have a cloud darken our beautiful friendship."

"Likewise."

"1 enemy is too many," I declaim, "and 1,000 friends are too few! . . . That's from the Talmud."

He goes to his rapture mood. "Friendship is next only to kinship! Lao-tse."

I push my chair back. "You want me to convince Miss Marsh to give her brother half a million clams?"

"My God, Silky, you are one of the greats! . . . . You think you can fix that? . . ." His grin could be off a hyena. "Plus, of course, 10 percent interest . . ."

"Interest?" I gasp.

He blinks, so innocent. "A marker is a *loan,* sport. Chrissake, even banks charge interest!"

I stand up for good (I hope). "You won't be mad on me if Kenneth Marsh gets the pesos from someone not his sister? Like from Rodenbaker? Or Maitland? Or Moishe Kapoyr?"

"Who is *Moishe Kapoyr?*"

"1 of the richest diamonds in Palm Springs."

"I don't give a fart in a bottle *who* gives that fink the money!" snaps Donny with Oriental elegance. "Just so my family gets paid!"

"And you get your commission."

He spreads his arms out. Shanghai Mostel. "Baby, you gonna deny I am entitled to a fair and square commission?"

"Never. . . . Now, what about me?" I flash many teeth.

"Come again?"

"Me. What's *my* cut? . . . If I put this big bite on the sister, or Rodenbaker, maybe both—"

His jaw drops like a lock in the Panama Canal.

"How's a 10 percent for me, Donny?"

"You sonva*bitch!*" he murmurs. "You trying to chisel me?!"

"So make it 8 percent."

He assembles his tonnage to erect. "I don't give you 8 green stamps, you mockey! You don't even have a shine on your shoes!"

"Tell you what: I'll do the whole *shmeer* for a lousy 5 grand."

The beady eyes are working overtime. "How's 2?"

"Wahoo."

He puts out his hand. "You got a deal."

I look at his mitt like it has leprosy. "Stuff it, Donny. . . . This time I was testin' *you.*"

"Goddam! You are my boy—a natural!" He howls and rubs

his hands together. "I knew you would go along!"

"All the way."

"That's my Silky!"

"Except 1 part."

"Huh?"

"Kimberley Marsh. I never yet sold out a client, Donny. So if she won't roll over on this deal, or if she just can't dig up so much lettuce to bail out her brother—"

"Don't even *think* that!" he cries. "You have to sell her!"

It got so damn quiet in that room I could hear my pulse on the trap drums. "She will not ever 'lose' any looks, Donny. . . . If 1 of your gunsels puts a finger on her—a *finger*, man, not a hand, an arm, a fist—just 1 lousy finger—"

He is breathing like 1 of the dragons on his desk.

"—I will rape your daughter."

Green goes his skin. Red go his eyes. He begins to shake like a paint mixer.

"That is exactly what I will do, Donald. And I'll have Polaroid shots to prove it—to show every clan in Chinatown."

He foams around the mouth and his hoarseness is like a worn-out bowling alley. "You fuckin' crazy . . . *crazy*. . . . I will cut your balls off!"

"Not yet, Dad. Later, maybe. But not yet."

"No?" He pounds such a fist on the desk, the plates and silver make "Jingle Bells." "Who the hell will stop me?"

"A safety deposit box. In the vault of a Chemical Bank. If anything happens to me—my partner and my mouthpiece have keys. They open that tin box. *And what do you think they'll find?*"

He is wax yellow and breathing strange, which is not unusual when your whole body is shaking like a paint mixer. No words come out.

"You know what they'll find, Donny. . . . And in half an hour lieutenants from Narcotics and Immigration and Homicide will be jumping down your throat!" I put out my hand. "Better we stay friends, huh?"

His eyes are dead. The Fu Manchu lip fuzz is quivering.

The bald head is showing beads. He wipes it with his palm. He is so shook up and confused, he takes my hand—like in a dream. His fat palm is spongy. . . .

When I retreat out through the padded door, Donny Chu is wrinkling his brow, his head to 1 side, like a doped-up monkey in a maze.

The Italian enforcer who let me in says, *"Arrivederci."*

"You should live so long." I take the stairs fast and move through the restaurant and pass the 2 chairs outside with the cannons on them. Toothpick touches the brim of his chapeau.

All this time I am traveling on cold *chutzpah.* I would not be surprised to feel a bullet or shiv enter my back.

But my full terror don't really break out until I'm in a cab, when I bust out so wet I could be wearing sprinklers for underwear.

"Where to?" asks the well-groomed driver.

"Grogan's Bar and Grill." That's nearest.

I am so damn scared of what I done at Foo Moy's that in Grogan's I go to the bar and order a scotch straight. I start to sip it and almost throw up.

So I go next door, to Nosh at Nathan's.

I take a table and call my waiter. "Ike."

"Hi, Mr. Pincus. The usual?"

"The usual."

The minute I bite into that pastrami on rye, I feel my blood return from cold storage.

13
GUESS WHAT?

The truth is: *I have nothing on Donny Chu.* In no safety deposit box, in no bank vault . . . but he don't know that! He will fill my box up *in his mind*—with 20–30 capers he'll move heaven and earth to keep buried in a vault.

I had tossed him, off the top of my head, "Narcotics . . . Immigration . . . Homicide . . ." Those were only starters. Think of other P.D. bureaus, like Safe and Loft, Stolen Property, Missing Persons!!! Donny will.

Like it says in the Midrash: "A guilty man flees when no one's chasing him."

You might object that an operator as hep as Donny Chu would never fall for so hairy a bluff as mine—a threat that is pure phony. You might say he would want a piece of proof, some sample . . . but you forget the gut point: Donny knows I have very good connections in the police force, and if I start asking around about him, I not only pick up a thing or 2— but I suddenly revive interest Downtown in certain files not stamped CLOSED. So Donny will have to make a lot of new trips to the Interrogation Room, which is not an ice-cream parlor. From that he faces only possible trouble—a slip-up in his memory of what he said before; a boo-boo by 1 of his uncouth lieutenants; a new trace on a guilty-of-something Chu choirboy. . . .

My other answer to you is more simple:

1) Donny put me up against a hot wall, and I *had* to do something—something to get the Syndicate to lay off Kimberley Marsh (at least for a while).

2) Rods and rocks could bust my bones, but words (like those I tossed out) can be reopened for arguing.

3) The door to success has 2 signs: PUSH and PULL. What did it hurt to make a grab at both?

4) The most important thing: *It worked!* Donny bought it. Do not argue with success.

5) You know why it worked? Because even if the odds are 100 to 1 that I was faking, *there's still that Number 1 chance haunting Donny!* Any man who's been around racetracks knows that the most amazing thing about a long shot is that the horse comes in. . . .

I also have to confess something. My saying I would rape Donny's daughter. I did not enjoy that. It was a lousy, crummy thing to do. A terrible trick. But the way Donny was leaning on me, the awful threat about Kimberley—those were terrible, too.

I was ashamed of myself, I admit, tossing him that Polaroid-shot bomb. But Donny had thrown the lowest punch in the book: ripping up an innocent party—a girl, yet—to shake down her brother.

Did I pull "an eye for an eye"? No. I put on an arm for an arm. . . .

With all this off my conscience, of which a guilty 1 hisses like a snake in the heart, let's get on with my troubles.

I got back to the office around 7:40. Sure enough, Herschel has kept his word. He is waiting, rocking in his chair like Grampa Walton.

When he sees me, he gasps like I just been released from a torture tank in Uganda. "Mr. Clancy c-can't wait to see you!" he hollers.

"Unless you open the window," I observe, "they won't hear you in Brooklyn."

I go into Mike's chamber. He is nursing a drink. He stares at me. "At least your puss looks undamaged."

"My nerves ain't." I pour myself a shot. "Hold your hat, chum. You know who put the tail on our client? Donny Chu.

To try to find—her brother. He owes the Chu Chus a bundle of big ones—and skipped."

"Oh, Jasus!"

The whiskey was very consoling. "Your phone call to Yonkers saved me from having my parts distributed to a class in anatomy. Mikeleh, you are the king of Blarney and Malarkey."

He grins. "Did you even the score with Black Beauty?"

"A *shvartz yohr* on him! His driver's license was a swipe. The real Matrobe is white. In fact, there are 2 of them. Twins, yet. Slobs."

"So . . . how will you find the spade now?"

I shrug. "Donny Chu is sending him back to Trinidad. . . . There'll be a new boy, I guess, tailing our client."

"Ah, 'our' client. . . ." He sighs. "I'd like to get a look at her. How often does a Mick from Yorkville get to breathe on a piece of royal fluff like that?" He just loves this. "By the way, how is she?" He says it lazy, but those baby blue globes don't miss a move or a twitch.

"Okay, I guess."

"Don't guess, *bubeleh,*" he croons. "You hurtin' from her?"

I study my booze. It don't surprise me to see her face floating in the glass. "I'll be damned if I can figure myself out, Mike. . . . She's smart, and she's screwed up—"

"She's on your back—"

"Yep."

"—when you want her on hers!" He busts out laughing, but stops smack in the middle. "Look, am I out of line? For Chrissake, don't tell me you're itching for more than a nice *shtup.*"

"You are a sordid animal, Michael. . . . I'm—call it fascinated. Call it intrigued."

"That's for the birds. You've got it. Bad. . . . So? What's to knock?"

"How's Kathy?" I ask.

"There you go, there you go!" He jumps up, annoyed. "I can't even daydream about a chick without you bring up my true love. . . . She's gettin' better, I hope. Slept good last night

. . . but don't fake me out. You still get the juiciest cases in our shop."

"This 1 could involve hemstiching my throat."

"Hey, bucko!" Mike hesitates. "I hope Donny Chu likes you."

"He wants me to get Miss Marsh to cough up half a million simoleons. . . ."

"Half a—" Mike whistles. "Are you gonna do that?"

"I'm going to let her decide. . . . Hell, I don't even know her brother."

"I have every confidence in you." Mike is dry-cleaning me. He sits down and leans back and crosses his long legs on the desk. "But if you weren't so goddam stubborn—you know how tough Donny Chu can play—you'd hire yourself some armor. Add the expense to her bill, for Chrissake! She's loaded. . . . How about taking on Duster McKee, with his brass knuckles? . . . Or Bull-Bull Kraus? I once used Kraus on a brawl and he saved half my profile, I swear!"

"Thank you, Michael. . . . Believe me, I'm playing custard-and-cream with Donny. If I need muscle, you'll be the first to know."

"Okay." He stands up. "Good luck." He finishes his drink. "Be sure to tell Herschel where I should send flowers."

Out he goes.

I tell Herschel, "Call it a day."

"You mean call it a night," he pops. (Every time that *shmendrick* can top me, he is in heaven.) "I left some letters on your desk. You want I should get you something? I don't mind."

"You have a heart of gold," I say.

"That's true. And when you give me a compliment, even with an *utz,* I celebrate. *Shalom.*"

He's out of there like a shot.

My own office is dark—but Isadore's yip-yip welcomes me back. I pat him.

Then I snap on my desk light and get my notebook and dial Howard Rodenbaker's number in Gramercy Park, where

Kimberley said she would be. . . . The number is busy.

I read the letters Herschel left on my desk. A report from Dolores Czernik on the kid-snatch in the custody hassle between Logan and Beatrice Detweiler. Dolores has checked into the Goshen Inn, in Elbridge, Mass., right near the old mansion where she is sure Mr. Detweiler has taken 9-year-old Walter. . . . A bill from Noodles Samuels for 1275 bucks (a bargain) to locate James Ledeker; his mother hired us to find him: Ledeker is in a drying-out sanitarium for boozers near Cos Cob, which is in Connecticut. . . . A flier from Stoke and Alby, our L.A. contact, about—

The outer door, from the hall, opens. "Mike?" I call.

I move my chair around, and a large dark shadow—very quiet, very fast—sails through my doorway. I can't see a face— but I am looking into the ugly front hole of a silencer, plugged on a .38 pointed right between my eyes so that the lousiest shot in the world would blow out my brains.

I do not utter 1 single sound. I can't. My heart is a hammer, and "O mi*god!*" stays unshouted, because it is stuck—paralyzed—in the big, hard vise that is squeezing my throat. . . .

It took real willpower for me to pull my popped peepers away from that murderous barrel-hole—up to the face of my executioner, who has stepped into the circle of light from my desk lamp.

It is the man from Trinidad.

14
THE HIAWATHA GAMBIT

His black skin is shiny—from sweat; and he is breathing fast and hard, and the gun is shaking the way his hand is.

"That's funny!" bangs through my mind. Not funny "ha-ha" but funny "not kosher." Why? Well, in such a horrible setup, according to all the movies I ever seen, the triggerman who has you covered like a rabbit in a straitjacket is *smiling*, grinning, real nasty—in sadistic anticipation; and his marble eyes are glittering with the meanness of forthcoming triumph. . . . Mr. Trinidad's eyes are drilling into me all right—but he is not smiling. In fact, he is so *hutzed* up he is shaking.

Aha! That's my only ray of hope. His anger. Anger blinds. Even if it don't blind, it crowds out other valuable emotions— like caution, judgment, balance. . . . My Uncle Fischel used to say, "Anger is a fool." I grab onto that thought like a drowner to a stick.

"Which are you, mon, Watson or Holmes?" That elegant voice is plenty sarcastic.

I do not say a word.

"Too frigh-tonned to onswer?!"

"N-no, sir." I force a smile, trying to stay as calm as a cucumber—only in this case the cucumber is scared stiff on account of it's about to be turned into a dead pickle.

"You should be frightonned! " He quivers with hate.

It is very dangerous to let a jittery guy with a gun up your nose-holes think you are scared—because that heats up his tensions—and his finger might jump from the pressure of his nerves. So I add layers of cool as I lie, "Faith is stronger than fear, brother. Whenever I prepare to meet my Maker—"

"You goddam flotfoot! I hov been sacked—because of you!"

"Oh, *no*, sir," I say politely (what can it hurt?). "You received the shaft, if I may be permitted to express an informal opinion, because you struck me on the back of my head with a very blunt object. . . . Did you not know that Mr. Donald Chu is a true Christian? A pacifist? It is well known throughout the circles in which he moves that he strongly disapproves of rough behavior amongst his personnel."

"You must be os stupid os you are repulsive! That domn honky has ordered me home!"

"Oh, *no*, sir! I do not believe Mr. Chu is a honky. All the evidence points to his being of Oriental descent—and courteous upbringing."

Are you wrinkling your brow? Are you wondering why I am talking in such a puffed-up and cockamamy manner? *To stretch out time!* That's why. To stretch the little seconds out so the bloodthirsty weirdo before me gets trapped in my conversation, no matter how peculiar it is. In fact, he has to get more hooked the more peculiar it is! If I knew a way of dragging in "Hiawatha," by H. W. Longfellow, I would recite it word for word! "By the shores of Gitche Gumee . . ." I used to be able to go through that like it was the batting averages of Willie Mays for his entire career.

And all the time I am talking—and stalling—I am shifting my position in my goddam chair—very, very minutely— sweating buckets, trying to lean closer so I can drop my right hand—

"Stop!" he snaps.

"I was just itching . . ."

"So om I. To kill you! . . . I shall be on thot plane home long before your body is found."

I do not say, *"Bon voyage."* Instead, I say, "May I ask you, in the most friendly fashion, to consider the fact that our elevator operator has a remarkable memory for faces? . . . He—"

His smirk does not soothe me. "But he did not *see* my face,

Charley. Nor any part of me. I took the precaution of using the stairway. And thot is how I shall leave! I tell you this to rob you of any lahst hope you may enjoy thot I shall be caught. . . ."

"That sure does rob me of the 1 pleasure left in my life. *Hold* it, sir! Don't squeeze . . . I am about to die. I accept that. The least you can do—in the eyes of our Lord—and your Savior—is let me make 1 last sacred prayer."

He frowns.

"For *your* eternal peace of soul, too," I add.

What hopped-up creep don't want eternal peace of soul? "Take 5 seconds. . . . One . . ."

I close my eyes and bring my left hand up to my brow, praying. What am I praying? That his bloodshot eyes follow that movement of my left hand—while I drop my right out of sight.

"Two . . ."

I now sing-song in the cadence of my fathers: *"Zaulst brennen, paskudnyak. Boorkess zollen vaksn in dein boech. A shvartz yohr zol dir khappen . . ."*

"Three . . ."

The fingers on my right hand have been sliding fast across the buttons on the panel on the side of the kneehole of my desk. *"Gai in drerd . . ."*

"Four . . ."

I press the button. And 20 crazy, howling dogs smash the air—furious, ferocious, barking. Isadore, who has been snoozing like an idiot throughout my awful travail, leaps into the air like he is into electricity.

The goon automaticaly spins around—to protect hisself from the horde of mad dogs or wolfs behind him, and the sight of leaping Isadore makes him gobble in terror as it confirms the fearful image in his brain—so he screams and pulls his goddam trigger. *Plunk! Plunk!* go two muffled shots.

He don't hit Mr. Goldberg. 1 glop of lead goes into the wall and the other hits the carpet—because inside the first split-second of that tape in my clock busting out in crazed dogs on a rampage, I have leaped across the desk and slammed my left arm around his throat in a brutal *V*, and locked my right hand on his wrist, smashing his fist on the desk again and again with wild but delicious delirium. All this time I squeeze his Adam's apple and he begins to choke and gurgle, and drops the .38 on the desk.

Mr. Goldberg looks absolutely amazed by all this, his never having seen violence except on TV, and he stares at me for instructions on how should he behave. That, at a time like this, really bugs me. I bare my teeth and snarl, *Grrrr!* in sarcasm. It is like giving a pissing lesson to a skunk.

I will say 1 thing for Isadore: He is a quick learner. That mutt bares his fangs and rumbles a vicious *"Grrrr!"* like I never heard out of his throat before, and he points right at the hustler from Trinidad like he will jump at his throat and tear out free samples.

"No-no!" the goon gasps, with the wet pouring down his features and on my arm. "Call—him—off! . . ."

I pick up his gun and release my hold on the sucker's neck. *"Shtay azoy!"* I command, and Isadore sure does stay *azoy* in that position, growling, bare-toothed and tensed-up, like ready to spring into action—*if* he knew what to do next, which he don't, being raised by a gentle rabbi in a law-abiding home.

"He'll tear you to pieces if I give him the go!" I growl.

The gunsel is blubbering and coughing, mucked up like a trapped pig, backing away from Mr. Goldberg in true terror and bewilderment. In other circumstances, I might feel sorry for him. But the bump on the back of my head is throbbing, and that ugly .38 with the awful silencer is itching in my hand. . . .

"Give me your sap," I say.

I keep the rod pointed.

He reaches around to his back and tugs and pulls out an object which he clutters on the desk. It is a billy—a blackjack with a spring inside the handle.

"Now empty your pockets."

He is glomming me with double hate, but he gets his billfold out of his inner breast pocket and drops it on the blotter, then a passport from Trinidad, then a B.I.W.A. split envelope. . . . Then his pants pockets provide a change-purse, European style, a bunch of keys, a fancy handkerchief.

Isodore growls louder, enjoying his new role as a killer.

"Shoyn genug," I say.

I flip open the passport. The picture matches him. Then I open the wallet and remove the bills and spread them on the blotter. Over 600 U.S.—and a number of Trinidad notes. I also find the "Vernon Matrobe" driver's license. Then I find an identification card with his picture—for the Clover Casino, Port-of-Spain.

"Is this your real name?" I ask.

His throat is parched. "Yes."

"Tell it to me."

"Stowbridge," he croaks. "Anson Stowbridge."

That name checks with the passport.

He sinks into the chair.

"What's your job, Mr. Stowbridge?"

"Where?"

"In Trinidad."

"I om a guard—at the Casino."

"You mean a bouncer?"

"All right."

"Are you good at it?"

He don't reply.

I wiggle the gun.

"Yes, I om good at it."

"How many people you beaten up on?"

He goes sullen. "I just follow ordors."

"If you get an order to chop a chick's fingers off, do you chop them off?"

"I—follow orders. I do not give them."

"Have you ever iced people?"

Pause. "We do not use thot expression bock home."

"How about 'murdered'?"

He wets his lips. "I decline to onswer thot."

"I don't blame you. . . . Now, Mr. Stowbridge. You used this billy to hit me on the back of my head. Right?"

He don't know what to answer, but his eyes tell me enough: They dart to the blackjack.

"Stand up," I say.

He does it—slowly, and shaking.

"Turn around—your back to me."

He does it—uneasy, watching Mr. Goldberg out of the corner of his eye.

"Are you religious, Mr. Stowbridge?"

Pause. "Sometimes."

"*I'll* let you say your prayers." I ram the muzzle of the heater into the small of his back.

"Oh, God!" he cries. "You con't shoot a mon in the bock!"

"Sure I can."

"Don't! Please!"

"You smashed my skull when *my* back was turned. . . . Pray, Mr. Stowbridge."

He closes his eyes and mumbles. His pipes are clogged. I can't hear what he is saying. I don't want to. I wait.

But I do hear "Amen," and that's when I lift the blackjack and bring it down on the back of his head—just as he had done to me. An eye for an eye, a *k'nock* for a *k'nock*.

He makes a sickening gasp and gurgles, and he slips down to the floor like he is sliding out of a burlap sack.

I am surprised to hear how husky I am breathing. I am also perspiring like I am back in the old Luxor *shvitzbud*.

I study the stuff on my desk. I put the money back in the

billfold and tuck it back in the jacket of the butcher on the
floor. Ditto for the plane ticket, the keys, the fancy hanky.
But I keep the .38 and the silencer, and Vernon Matrobe's
license.

I dial 911. "Emergency . . . I need an ambulance."

It was a slow night, I guess, on account of I got action in a
couple of minutes. "Unconscious man at 1-3-9-0 1st Avenue.
4th floor. . . . No, it's not a heart attack. He fell. Maybe a
concussion. . . . He's breathing okay. . . . Is there color in his
cheeks? Man, there's nothing *but* color in his cheeks. This case
is black. . . . Send a stretcher. The man is big."

I pat Isadore on the head. *"Er vet zein besser bahld."* That
dog has compassion for *everyone.*

Now I dial 472-9711. That's Precinct 19 on East 67th Street,
and I know that number by heart. A toughie growls: "19th
Precinct. Sergeant Orens."

"Stuffy?"

"Yeah?"

"Silky Pincus."

"Hey-*hey*, how you goin'?"

I have made his day. "Who's on deck, Stuffy?"

"Lieutenant Hildebrand."

"Put me through."

I didn't know Hildebrand. "Lieutenant, I'm a P.I.," I say,
"a friend of Captain Korby. I was on the Force. . . . I have
an unconscious man in my office. A black gentleman whose
passport says—"

"Hold it, *hold* it!" he complains. "Who are you again?"

"Sidney Pincus. P.I." I give him my license number.

"And how did the unconscious man in your office get unconscious?"

"He fell," I say. "Hit his head on the desk."

"How come he fell?" suspicions the Lieutenant.

"High blood pressure. He fainted." Now I make it sad. "Poor
guy, he just keeled over . . ."

"What," gripes Hildebrand, "was he doing in your office?"

"He come up to hire me—to find his true-blue love, a Creole girl from Haiti who he cannot find for over 2 weeks now. So he is very depressed, as who wouldn't be in such a romantic hoo-ha? So he asks me—"

I can practicly see Hildebrand's cheeks puffing out in outrage. "What the *hell* are you calling *me* for? You damn fool—"

"Gee whiz, Lieutenant. I'm sorry, gol-*ly*. What should I of done?"

"Call an *ambulance*, for Chrissake! Stop wasting time, dummy! Get him to a hospital! Since when is it a crime for a man to fall against a desk? What's the *matter* with you, Pinsky? You think I got nothin' better to do than play nurse?" He slams the phone down with great sincerity.

I hang up with pleasure.

I hope you understand why I didn't tell him everything— about the goon, the gun, why the strong-arm really came to the office, the slug on the head I performed. . . . If I told all that, it would of been a case of Attempted Homicide with a firearm—and no sensible Lieutenant would ever let it pass, or let me go on with my business. Man, I'd have a real *tsimmes* on my hands—an official arrest, plus formal charges, plus a long statement at the stationhouse, plus maybe hours tomorrow waiting for an arraignment . . . et cetera galore.

I figure I am a better citizen for sparing our overworked police unnecessary work. The gunsel will soon depart from our shores. Let the Trinidad cops handle him, if necessary. . . .

I open my top drawer and put the billy and the .38 and the silencer inside. Tomorrow I'll take the gun down to Headquarters.

You can't get a decent fingerprint off a gun in 1 out of 1,000 times (in case you don't know that) on account of the oil and the smudge you make when you hold tight and squeeze. Still, the rod has a serial number, and they'll fire some bullets through it for "lands and grooves" markings, maybe to match up with some others. . . . Who knows what that piece has done? . . .

When I hear the siren of the ambulance, I feel better. Real humane.

Stowbridge stirs, moaning.

"Stay there," I say. "I want you to get top medical attention. . . . You should get your skull X-rayed—"

You think I am being Good-Deed Joe? . . . Don't judge the contents by the wrapper. If Anson Stowbridge is really hurt, I will have to answer some nasty questions. For *my* sake, he should be okay.

He is mumbling. "I . . . the plane . . ."

"So you'll be a day late. . . . Listen. I *covered* for you, Anson. You never came in here carrying a piece, you hear? No billy neither. . . . I'm not filing an Intent to Kill with the cops. So I save you 10 years in the clanger! Be grateful. You grateful? . . . Okay, just tell me: Has Kenneth Marsh showed yet— in New York?"

His eyes are bloodshot and don't focus so good.

I repeat, louder: "Did—you—find—Marsh?"

He moans—nothing, but his orbs now glare at me like hot beads.

I start to shake him—when 2 juvenile white-coats rush in. 1 of them carries a rolled-up stretcher. The other has a portable oxygen tank and mask. Gung-ho boys, working hard.

"You need an ambulance?" yells Intern Number 1.

"Not me." I indicate the muttering lump on the floor. "He's going to have a baby."

"Oh, brother!" groans Number 2. "A wisenheimer."

Stowbridge wobbles half up on an elbow. "Must . . . airport."

I tap my temple significantly to the future Drs. Kildaire. "His banana's split."

So they kneel and give Stowbridge the standard spot-check, patting his cheek, pulling down a lower eyelid, asking him what day of the week it is . . .

"Feel the back of his attic," I disgust, "before his marbles roll out."

Medic 1 feels. "Oh-oh."

Medic 2 says, "Easy does it."

So they bend down to Stowbridge, who is rolling his eyeballs like roulette balls, and the paratroopers in white lift him just enough to stretch him out on the canvas.

As they pick up the stretcher, I lean over him and bark, "Anson! Don't take the rap! . . . Kenny Marsh! Did—that—skip—*show*—yet?"

He is bobbing toward the door on the stretcher, staring at me, blinking, maybe stunned, maybe murderous, gurgles, shakes his head a notch, and croaks: "No . . . nor—his—yella—chippy . . ."

15
A YAWN ON THE LINE

After the ambulance jockeys remove the unhappy bouncer from romantic Trinidad, I start to dial the Rodenbaker home again. I am not surprised that my hand is still shaky from the tango with the goon. That iron in my face scared all the chow mein out of me. . . . The line is busy.

I stop and light a cigarette and take a long, deep drag. Cancer-shmancer, at this point I am a network of nerves that need stroking.

I dial again, and this time the ding-a-ling works. No "busy" bleep. Pick up.

The butler, I guess, answers—like he is in Canterbury Cathedral, which does not employ cantors: "Roden-bakuh residence . . ."

"Kimberley Marsh, please. Mr. Pincus calling."

"*What* is that name agayn?"

That snob *shtick* always bugs me. "Pin-cus."

"*Pin*-cus?" He pronounces it like he is lifting it out of a laundry vat with tweezers. "One moment. I shall see—"

"Sir!" I crack.

"I beg your pardon?"

"I said, 'Sir'! You're suppose to say that! To me."

He gasps.

"And don't give me that 'I'll-see-if-she's-here' jazz, Arthur Treacher. I *know* she's there."

A pause. "Y-yes . . . sir."

It takes like 193 moments before an extension is picked up. "Mr. Pincus?"

"In person."

"This is Howard Rodenbaker."

Well, well. It's time I met him. I throw him a slider. "What's that name again?"

"Howard Rodenbaker."

"Congratulations. I want to talk to Miss—"

"Yes, yes, I know. May I ask who you are?"

"You may ask," I fume. "Now how's about you put Miss Marsh on?"

The throat clears. "I happen to be her stepfather. I think I have a right to know—"

I create a snort of disgust, disgust being the best response to snobs or snots. (The next best is sarcasm—if they don't trump you in that department, which these types are experts at.) "If you want to know who I am, Mr. Rodenhooker—"

"Rodenbaker!"

"Sorry." (This type goes nuts if you screw up their name, showing you never even heard it before.) "Miss Marsh can tell you who I am. That's up to her. What's up to you, sir, is not to waste time futzin' around—"

"*Must* you be unpleasant?" he snaps.

"I'm following your example. We are not playing for peanuts, Mr. R. If you will peek out of your window, to Gramercy Square, I bet you will see a car parked—not more than 1–200 yards away. 2 men are probly in it—not gentlemen, on account of they wear square-shoulder suits plus firearms you can't see, but they're there, believe me. If you think I'm throwing you a load of bull—"

He must of seen a Donny Chu car and soldiers out there now, because I hear a sound that is hard to describe, unless you work in a hospital.

"I'll call the police!"

"Don't. The cops can only make those bulldogs move along. So their boss will send out a new team. Smarter, this time."

Silence. "Hold on."

"I'm nailed to the floor."

He covers the mouthpiece with his hand, so I know he is discussing my message with someone. His voice has a slight case of the shakes when he says, "Can you—come right over?"

"I can. But I want to hear it from her."

A pause. His voice goes sarcastic. "Don't you trust me?"

"What's to trust? I don't even know you. Did you put up a bond? Did you lay down a deposit? And do I know you're really Rodenlaker—"

"Rodenbaker!"

"—and not some 4-flusher? How do I know this ain't a setup— with me walking into a buzz saw?"

He rumbles, "You certainly have a lurid imagination!"

"That's why I'm not dead." I let my watch tick.

Blop. Silence. Then: "One moment . . ."

"Take 2."

The clack tells me the phone is being laid down, and then— after some strange sounds and a click—picked up.

"Hello . . ."

It is Her voice. Man. Very soft. But Her voice.

I do not answer. You know why? Because I want to hear how she says "Hello? . . . hello? . . . Are you there?" A normal person would say that fast; someone hopped up couldn't. So I wait. . . .

"Hel-lo? . . . Hel-lo . . ." Her pace is very slow. "Mis-ter Pin-cus? . . ."

I wish I could lubricate my throat, which is in the Sahara. "Hello. Do we have company? Is someone on this line?"

"Mmh? . . . What?"

"Tell them to—get—off—the—line . . ."

She hesitates. "Oh . . . yes . . . Shelby? . . . Howard? . . ." I hear muffled sounds. "Please . . ."

A click. Another click. I was right. . . . "Are you okay?" I ask.

A yawn. Jesus! A yawn.

"Do you need me?" I ask.

Hesitation.

"Listen, lady. This morning you asked me to phone you—right after my important meeting with the Chinese gentleman. . . . Remember?"

"Yes . . ."

"Well, I've seen the Chinese gentleman. He is a forceful type. I have news. Plenty. Bad . . . but this is a helluva way to report it. . . . Can you get away from there?"

"N-no. . . . Better not."

I don't hardly know what to say, so I say the obvious: "Are you on daffy pills?"

Laugh, low in the box.

"Are you high or low?"

"Oh, high . . ." Giggles.

I wonder where to move now, so I shoot in the dark. "Is anyone giving you a hard time?"

Chuckles. "Oh, no. . . . How-ard says—he'd *love* you—to come over. . . . He's a lamb."

"Chop or cutlet?" I hate to hear her bombed.

"He is—longing to—to meet—Silky. . . . So is . . . she."

"Who?"

"The tramp . . . I hate her . . . every . . . inch . . . of . . . her! . . . Come over, Sher-lock . . . darling . . ."

16
GRAMERCY PARK

The west side of Gramercy Park is right out of New Orleans, with its lacy ironwork and frilly balconies and fancy balustrades; the fenced-in square and the mansions on the south side could be London. There's not a niftier part of Manhattan to call home, for my money. Sure, it's out of the way for taxis, but if you live there you don't use them. . . .

As I get out of mine, I fall into a wholesome hygienic habit: I case the environment. I am not surprised to see a big Chrysler parked in a shadow of a tree across the street. It is occupied, I guess from their outlines, by 2 honchos in the front seat. And there is an antenna for a telephone in the car sticking out of the roof. I give no sign I have made Donny Chu's choir-boys. . . . He sure wasted no time getting subs for Anson Stow-bridge—and that means they tailed Kimberley right to Roden-baker's house. . . .

I go through a fancy arched gate and up a flight of stone steps to the front door, which has a gorgeous fanlight over it. There are old carriage lamps on both sides of the door, polished so strong they gleam warm. And the mahogany door is paneled and waxed and has a big lion's-head knocker and looks 40 feet high. To the right of the door is a white button, set in a brass plate that someone must shine once an hour. I am so impressed I push it with my pinky.

I hear a distant ring. . . .

When the portal opens, I meet Arthur Treacher's short brother, a very stiff butler in a wing collar and a monkey suit: a swallow-tail coat with 2 rows of brass buttons, and a short

striped gold vest where the stripes go crosswise, not up and
down. Over his starched wings, the Jeeves sniffs, "Mr. *Pincus?*" You would think I was applying for a job in the Egyptian
secret service.

"Sir!" I growl. (All I need after what I've just been through
is a snotty sniffer.)

"Sir," he echoes. His expression you could cut into ice-cubes.

"And what do I call you?"

He is taken aback, as they say, but recovers: "Chambers,
sir."

"Invite me in, Chambers."

Gulp. "Do come in, sir."

I do come in.

So Cholmondeley Chambers, Central Casting's model butler,
leads me past a Venetian mirror that is so high it could provide
solar heat, and past a fancy curled rack on which 2 hats are
hanging—a crumpled brown 1 and a hard English-type bowler;
plus, hanging from a bentwood swirl is an airline bag with a
yellow-and-orange "Air Sunshine." Dangling from the strap
is a tag: "Key West." And another: "Eastern."

"Whoopsy do," I conclude.

The funky flunkey stops before 2 tall mahogany doors with
ornate brass handles—not knobs. Chambers now uses his both
hands—sliding 1 door to the right and the other to the left.
(I should tell you I admired this type door before, in the Dakota,
the apartment fortress on Central Park West and 72nd Street,
when I executed an informal Lost Property search, for All-
Star of Hartford, on the premises of a certain famous actress,
who, the minute a play she was in folded, would put in a claim
for stolen bangles. I opened them doors myself, no one being
on the premises at that time. I actually "broke and entered,"
which is against the law—though I never broke a thing, using
the small plastic calendar my savings bank mails out each Xmas,
to slip the catch on the front door. . . .)

The Marsh-Rodenbaker parlor reeks Class: shining parquet
floors; a marble fireplace with a painting of a young old ancestor

over it; an Aubusson rug, if there ever was 1; two creamy punch-button chairs; a long sofa with roll arms. The draperies are green silk and thickly fringed. . . . Every table gleams and has silver on it: cigarette box, pictures in heavy frames, ashtrays. It is a sterling room.

A sparkling chandelier hangs from the middle of the ceiling like a waterfall of glass. And to top it all off, so's it looks like *The Forsyte Saga,* a log fire is burning, altho the air outside is far from cold enough to inconvenience the nuts of a brass chimpanzee.

"Mister Pin-cus!" booms Swallowtails. I could practicly be the ambassador from Saudi Arabia.

"Thank you *so* much for coming." I recognize Rodenbaker's voice. He is a big, burly, jolly (to my surprise) man, maybe 60, in black tie and a snazzy maroon velvet smoking jacket with satin lapels, plus he is wearing red slippers with silk bows. He is ruddy in complexion and wears horn-rim glasses and stylish dry long gray hair. Around his eyes are the crinkly lines of beaucoup laughter. His pot belly did not come from hunger. His handshake is good and solid, which surprises me: You expect flab with fat. "I'm Howard Rodenbaker," he smiles. "Delighted . . ." He don't say about what.

"What will you drink?" asks the butler from BBC. I know he dropped the "sir" on purpose. 1 thing I hate is *Alrightnik* manners.

"Dr. Brown's."

He has to do a take. "I beg your pardon?"

"Celery Tonic."

He flinches.

"You mean you don't have it?" I amaze.

"No—sir."

"I'm aghast, Chambers. Positively aghast. Dr. Brown's Celery Tonic comes from a secret formula, guarded for centuries by *Galitzianer* monks who only converse during a monsoon."

Rodenbaker is taking this all in like it's Noel Coward. "I take it you do not want alcohol?" he chuckles.

"Not when I'm going to play poker."

"A Tab, sir?" asks Brass Buttons. "Pep-si Cola?" He pronounces that like it's the name of an opera.

"Pepsi. I own 10,000 shares of stock in the company."

Exit Chambers.

For a reason I won't explain, I ask Rodenbaker, "How much money is tied up in the Marsh Foundation?"

"The what?"

"The—uh—Josiah Something Marsh Foundation for Psychiatric Research. You must be on the board of trustees."

"I never heard of it," he says. "Let me explain the—um—confusion on the phone when you called. . . . We were surprised by a visitor, who flew in just in time for dinner—"

A snort comes out of the chair I'm standing behind. Then a hand reaches out and takes a lo-ball, full of booze and ice, from the end table. Out of the chair rises a tall blond sunburned Adonis with a helluva build—and a costume that in this scene is as duffy as a clown's suit at a Bar Mitzvah. I am positively dumboozled to behold his denim shirt, unbuttoned down to the *pupik,* a pair of white Levi's with slash pockets, and navy sneakers. This jock looks like he just jumped off a yawl to a pier—and I don't know the difference between a yawl and a *yenta.*

"This," says Rodenbaker, "is Kenneth Marsh."

"Ra-ta-ta-*ta!"* the bugle in my head blares. Oh, no. Not Kenneth Ardway Marsh! At this point all Donny Chu needs is the Target, in person, in Manhattan. . . . I squeeze air into my lungs. . . . Then I double my thoughts back: Wait! Him in New York takes Her off the hot seat—if he, or she or they cough up the dough for his markers.

Marsh could be an ad for Brut: very handsome, tanned, with the washed-out blue eyes that make admirals. But I am glad to observe that his peepers are set too close together to give the true-blue integrity look his other features aim at. His jaw is solid, but his lips are curved a shade too cute. And I notice a thin gold necklace dangling down to his manly nipples. . . .

Rodenbaker is studying me in an amused but shrewd manner.

Kenneth Marsh does not offer to shake my hand, which is not in the *Social Register*. Both his mitts grip the squat glass of booze he is swishing around so the ice-cubes tinkle like a Swiss music box.

We size each other up. I bet he knows that sooner or later this whole thing will boil down to just him and me, and he will have to go up against me. Enemies give off a smell to each other. His—even without the booze—is sour. I don't know about mine, because I am too busy trying to hide my shock and figure my play.

Golden Boy says to Rodenbaker, "I assume he"—nodding at me like I'm an Armenian lamppost—"is the 'detective' Kim hired?"

"Right."

He surveys me, slow, hair to heels, like I'm on exhibit at the American Museum of Unnatural History. "I adore my sister. But she's stupid."

Rodenbaker says, "Kenneth, we have—"

I cut in, "What made you say she's stupid?"

"Hiring a type like you." He downs some *shnapps*. "Damn waste of money, if you ask me."

"But I didn't."

He blinks, "You didn't what?"

"Ask you."

He turns pink and starts for me, but Rodenbaker says, "Kenneth! There *is* a car watching this house!"

Apollo snickers, "So what?"

"So those beagles," I say, "have by now reported your presence to a very tough gent named Donny Chu, whose relatives in sunny Trinidad are out to get you. . . . If you step out of here, they'll clobber you cold, toss you into their buggy, and take you to some garage where uncouth hoods specialize in extracting teeth and money—" I keep my gaze glued every second to this cocky cookie: His type goes wild very fast, even without firewater. I rarely met anyone (since Futzy Grubnick) I got a hate on so quick. (Okay, okay, say it's because of my yen for his sister. Look it up in Freud.)

And what does Golden Boy do? He leans against the mantel on his elbow, very la-de-da, sipping his drink. "Those hoodlums don't frighten me."

"Then you're a horse's ass. They scare the spit out of me."

"I'm not surprised." He smirks. "Do you still sleep with your Teddy Bear?"

Oh, brother. It's only a matter of time before dukes and teeth fly. I hold on to my thirsty temper. "Look, sonny," I say in a few well-frozen words. "Less than an hour ago a son-ofabitch put a loaded gun between my eyes—because of you. And I've been through a hairy hassle with Donny Chu, who wants to beat you into fertilizer. About all that, I couldn't care less. *But you've thrown your sister into a nutcracker!* And I'm working for her. So if I have to do it, to save her, I'll clap-hands-here-comes-Kenny as I hand you over to Donny Chu's plastic surgeons myself. With pleasure. . . . Tell your swishy flight instructor I don't like you. You rat on your debts. You are spoiled and snotty and a lush. If you weren't a Marsh, you'd be a run-of-the-mill punk."

His cheeks turn extremely red. "You want your goddam nose broken?!" (Rodenbaker puts a restraining fin on Marsh's arm, but the *shtarker* flings it away.) "It will improve your profile, which I do not like. In fact I do not like any members of your tribe hanging around my kid sister!"

Rodenbaker groans, "Kenneth!"

This is an insult situation I have faced before, so you don't have to catch your breath in admiration when I tell you what I did. "Mr. Shmuck," I say, "I am slightly hard of hearing, since my recent victories in Tokyo at the International Karate Tournament and Flower Show. So I give you 3 seconds to apolo-gize—I bet you can count to 3, if you use your fingers."

"Kenneth was being facetious," soothes Rodenbaker.

"He was being a shit-heel." I lift a fancy cushion off the

sofa—not to admire the needlework, but because you'll see why in a minute.

The bare-chested Rich Boy plops his glass on the mantel and dives right at me, his face purple, his fists up in the classic position they teach Princeton boys in what is called "the art of self-defense," his left shooting out in a jab and his powerhouse cocked to break my jaw. To me, it's taking candy from a bed-wetter. My right forearm swings his left out of the action and with my left I jam the pillow smack into his puss. He gasps and staggers back, bewildered plus smothering, so I smash the heel of my right shoe onto his unsuspecting left foot. His yowl proves that a canvas sneaker is no protection against a hard leather heel, especially when the latter is aimed at a 90-degree angle by an expert in dirty tactics, which I am.

As the gargling dummy staggers back, I jam the cushion right along after him, so he is struggling between groans of agony and gasps of smothering and grabbing franticly to pull the pillow off his oxygen source.

I let go, and he swallows a gallon of air and starts hopping on one leg as he raises his other to massage his throbbing toes. "You—dirty—rotten—bastard!" he hoarses. "Can't—you—fight—*fair?!*"

"As fair as you talk."

Glamour Boy is heaving in pain and expelling feathers in humiliation. "Howard!" he shouts. "Get this lousy—"

"Your Pepsi, sir," comes the voice of Jeeves, who appears with a tall glass on a silver salver. He acts so deaf and blind to Goldilocks's convulsions I give him "A+" for poise.

"Thank you, Chambers." ("Upstairs, Downstairs" would hire me on the spot.) I sip the cool cola.

Marsh hobbles to the mantel for a slug of whiskey, still coughing and cursing in various phrases.

Even with his broad back turned to me, I hate this guy's guts so much I inform him, "I didn't need the pillow, sonny. I could of nailed you senseless with my right. But I didn't want to knock you into all that expensive glassware, plus it could cut up your puss so bad what would you use for sex bait? You would still be splashing blood over the Pulitzer Prize carpet." To Rodenbaker, who all through this oration showed the kind of awe you expect at sunset over the Grand Canyon, I disgust, "I don't owe this idiot the sweat from my armpit. The only reason I came here is that Miss Marsh—"

As if on cue, Kimberley and Shelby Maitland float in from the adjoining room—and I do mean float. They are holding thin-stem champagne glasses, and beaming like they are on a joy ride. He is Mr. After Six, in black bowtie and cummerbund and patent-leather pumps; she is in a pink cloud of gauze. A cluster of pearls adorns that honey hair. . . . Call it my emotions, or the torch I carry, but I could swear she stepped out of a Gainsborough, who, I think, changed his name from Ginsberg.

Maitland says, "You certainly got here fast."

"My middle name is Swifty."

"Silky Swifty got here fast"— Kim flutters her lashes in mock elocution —"because we need an all-star cast. . . . That's a poem." She raises her bubbly to me. "Good evening, Mr. Holmes. Welcome to the old family manor. I see you have met my favorite brother."

"Are you two hitting it off?" beams Maitland.

"You sure have a way with words," I say.

"What on earth is the pillow doing on the floor?" asks Kimberley.

I pick it up. "Your brother was demonstrating a Yogi headstand—he flopped."

Marsh turns. He has not grown friendly.

I tuck the pillow back neatly on the sofa.

The stalwart sailor has managed to resume normal breathing, altho his tan has an undertone of nausea. To Kim, he announces, "Dirty Dick is—just about to leave."

" 'Dirty'—?"

"We were reenacting the Muhammad Ali–Sonny Liston bout," I explain. "I took the part of Ali."

"Good-bye, Pincus!" he seethes.

"No, no," Kim reminds him. "He came over to tell us something important. Am I right?"

"My clients," I declare, "are always right."

She smiles. But all this time she acts like I'm some square she met a year ago at Maxwell's Plum. *Makkes!* . . . Is this how she really feels? Or is she putting it on for the benefit of the others? Or is she on a trip? Or—oh, hell. How can I *tell* with her? She's as changeable as quicksilver.

Marsh regards me like I'm the Abdominal Snowman. "He's already spoken his piece, pet. I got the message. Forget it. . . . If you'll excuse me, I think I'll take a shower."

He starts out, but Kimberley says, "No!"

She's not as flaky as she's been pretending. She and her brother swap glances. And once more I get the feeling that she has always known—or suspected—a lot more than she ever told me. . . . She asks me, "What did your Chinese friend tell you?"

"Do you want it alone, or is this the hour for Group Therapy?"

She rolls the sound of delight deep in her throat. "I want everyone to hear it."

"I'll settle the whole damn thing tomorrow!" blurts Kenneth.

Again he starts out, the gold links glinting on his chest, and again she stops him. "What—'thing'?"

"Ask your boyfriend!"

"Me?" blinks Shelby. "I—"

"I didn't mean you," says Kenneth. "I meant her cozy-cozy private eye."

I itch to belt him good, but I'm not exactly the right type to declaim: "How dare you insult the girl of my dreams, sir, your own dear sister!"

Kimberley kisses him on the cheek. "It's 'private investigator,' dear. 'Private eye' is passé—utterly out. . . . You seem nervous. . . . Silky has that effect on many people. He has a horrid habit of telling people things they'd rather not hear." Now, brisk and unkidding, she says, "I've gone through a hellishly scary time, Kenneth. And I want to end it, once and for all. . . . Silky, what did your Chinese friend tell you?"

"Your brother," I say, "owes the Chu clan a bundle of money."

"For what?"

"Gambling."

She stares her sense of betrayal at Kenneth. "How much?"

I drop the bomb. "500,000 dollars."

The color drains out of her cheeks.

"Half a *mil*—"Maitland has melted into a chair. "Kenneth!" he complains. "You told me—" He puts his face in his hands, ready to bawl.

Rodenbaker drawls, "Go on, Mr. Pincus."

"The Chus intend to collect every dime. Plus 10 percent interest. They don't care from who the money comes. They put a tail on you, Miss Marsh—the black man, the one I thought was named Matrobe, but have since learned it's Strawbridge"—(yeah, yeah, I screwed up the name—on purpose)—"because they figured your dear brother would show up here, sooner or later. He'd have to. To get the dough. They think he hasn't enough to cover his markers." I figure this a strategic point to act puzzled. "That threw me, Marsh. I thought you're loaded. That fancy spread—"

"Mortgaged to the hilt," sighs Rodenbaker, blowing a ring of blue smoke from his cigar. "The Casino has you over a barrel, Kenneth. You're in trouble. Considerable trouble. You can't raise another dollar—"

"Not even in Tel Aviv?" he smirks. (I enter that shot in my memory bank, under "Future Settlement.")

"Don't be rude!" says Kimberley.

Now Kenneth changes from mouse to cat. "You must be feeling very smug, Howard."

"True."

"Don't be. I'll have a carload of cash within—an hour."

"Really?" Rodenbaker, with that comfy paunch and cherub's face, sitting in that chair with a cigar and a snifter of brandy, reminds me of Churchill. "Half a million dollars is not gum-drops. Especially"—he burns Kenneth—"after your sister and I took you off the spot for 200,000 a year ago."

"You promised me you'd never gamble again!" she cries.

"—Two hundred thousand dollars," repeats Rodenbaker. "Of which you have yet to repay her—or me—one penny. . . ."

"But I will, Howard." Kenneth is pouring out charm like it's malted milk. He twists a boyish grin at Kimberley. "*Very* soon, pet. You have my word."

Rodenbaker raises his hulk out of the chair. He must of been a powerful gent in his prime. His glasses glitter and his beautiful long gray hair could go under Uncle Sam's hat. But the words he now fires are hammered out of steel. "You're damn right you'll pay off. You will put the Trinidad property up for sale. At once. House, plantation—all of it. You'll settle the mortgage. Then you'll pay the 500,000 you stupidly lost at the Casino. Then you'll repay Kimberley her 100,000—"

"And 100,000 to you?!" The Boy Scout's sneer exposes conceited teeth.

"Yes."

"Like hell I will."

"Kenneth!"

"*He* never put up 100,000, pet!" Kenneth snaps. "That was Mother's money!"

Rodenbaker examines the red tip of his cigar like he's deciding whether he should stub it out on Kenneth's kisser. "No," he says. "It was my money. Your mother's is in an airtight trust—"

"But you administer it!"

"Meticulously. If you don't believe that, take me to court. I'll give you a lesson in bankruptcy. Your legal fees will eat up everything you'll have left."

I feel I have stumbled into *The Little Foxes*.

Suddenly Marsh busts out laughing. "What's the *matter* with all of you? What's all this jazz about selling Divahli? Didn't

you hear me say I'd pay off all the debts? Don't you understand
why I came here? What I brought?"

To my surprise, Kimberley says, "I'm afraid I do." The way
she says it, she could be at a funeral.

Rodenbaker curses. "You damn fool! . . . To this house?! Is
that what's going on upstairs?"

And me, with my billion brain-cells working at top speed,
am lost on the road to *Shnippishok,* which is the sarcastic name
my people use for noplace or "Where the hell is that?"

Kenneth gets a long, thin cigar and Shelby, who all this time
has been ignored, which is an easy thing to do, even though
he has been sniffing and *krechtzing* and quivering like a bowl
of terrified Jell-O, jumps up to light it.

Rodenbaker says, "Do you realize you're committing a felo-
ny?!"

"Howard," sighs Kenneth, "one of these days I may have
to kill you."

"Oh, God!" wails Shelby. "Don't even *talk* that way!"

"Kenneth"—I never saw Kimberley this way—"have you de-
cided whether to kill me, too?"

The athletic idol goes Clifton Webb, very blasé. "Never, dearest. I adore you. I always have." To me he says, "Tell your
Chinese Shylock I'll take care of the marker."

"Where do you keep your printing press?"

"Upstairs." He smiles. "I brought it with me. . . ."

From the way Rodenbaker and Kim swap glances, you'd
have to be very dumb not to know they know what Kenneth
means. I don't.

"I do *not* want that discussed!" says Rodenbaker sharply.

"By the way," Golden Boy asks me, "the man they had shadowing Kim—is he the same nasty who put the gun between
your eyes?"

I don naïve. "Which man?"

"Stowbridge."

Man, oh, *man!* The cheese-head didn't know what he'd let

out of the bag! He had to be swacked to make a boo-boo like that. I am triple glad I turned down the hard stuff. In a rumble, booze can bury you. (Like it says in the Talmud: "When whiskey enters, judgment exits.")

"So you know him," I murmur.

"Mmh?" Marsh arches an already arched eyebrow. "I didn't say I knew him. Never heard of him before."

"Stop blowing bubbles! *I* called him 'Strawbridge.' But you just gave his right name: Stowbridge. So you know him. . . ."

Marsh's cheeks go bloodless. He is so flim-flammed he is glassy.

Kimberley looks like she's been hit with an auto jack.

Shelby has lowered his head; it hits me that Marsh's giveaway was no news to the éclair. So he must of known Stowbridge's name, too! (How? Why?)

Rodenbaker, who does not miss a mohair, throws 1 crisp question to Apollo: "How *did* you know his name?"

"I—suppose—sure, I heard it at the Casino." The family scion is snatching at splinters. "I think he's on the staff there. . . . Hell, Howard, I've heard a *lot* of names on the island. Who hasn't? . . . Let's not make a big deal out of it."

"But it is a big deal," I knife him. "The guy was sending your sister up the wall. She told you the whole story at dinner, didn't she? . . . Why didn't you tell her you knew him?"

And as Kimberley stares at him, unbelieving, and Kenneth flushes and fumbles for an answer, a very peculiar event intervenes: From the open sliding doors a man's voice calls, "Mr. Marsh . . ."

In the doorway, we behold a short, squirrel-type man, in rumpled clothes with dandruff powdering the shoulders. He is carrying a doctor's black satchel. It must be heavy, he is so *shlumped* over. He don't nod to any of us, or make with a polite "Hello" or "Good evening."

Kenneth heads for him like a shot out of hell. "Yes, Doctor?"

The doctor whispers a few words.

Kenneth's face lights up. "Great!" He shakes the man's hand. "Great!"

The medical mouse walks out of our line of sight, toward the front door.

And I observe some strange reactions. Tears hang in Kimberley's eyes. Rodenbaker looks furious. Shelby slumps on the sofa like a wet jock-strap, which he probly has.

When Kenny comes back to us, he is practicly jumping with joy. "Done! *Fini!* Here's a toast!" He grabs the bottle of Chivas Regal and pours it out like it's for 2-cents plain, or this is V-J Day.

I do not think you will gasp in astonishment if I tell you that this whole bit, from the moment the grubby doctor called Marsh's name from the doorway to Goldilocks's sudden ecstasy, stinks in my nose. Is that how a doctor would leave after a house call? Without saying, "She'll be all right now," or "I gave him a sedative," or "Call me in the morning"? Did you ever hear of a doctor going away without making *1 single comment about his patient?!?* . . . This guy left like he just delivered groceries.

And his clothes! Is that the type suit a Society doctor would wear on a house call? Baggy pants? Shoes not shined since *Purim? Shmontzes!* Clothes like that you pick out of a barrel. . . . I feel like I'm on the panel for "What's My Secret?"

I ask, "Who's sick?"

"A—servant," grins Kenneth.

"That's a lie," says Kimberley.

"It's nothing s-serious," stammers Shelby.

"It's damned serious!" ices Rodenbaker.

Kenneth laughs. "Such ingratitude! Here I am, bailing you all out, and you act like sourpusses."

I drift over to Kim. In a low key I ask, "Who's the doctor?"

Pause. "You don't miss a thing, do you?"

"Only my Mommy and Daddy. . . . What's his name?"

"I don't know."

"A doctor makes a house call and you don't know his *name?* Where's he from? Medicaid?"

"Ask Kenneth," she says.

"I didn't notice the Doc taking Sonny's temperature."

"They were upstairs for an hour, before you arrived." ·

Rodenbaker comes over.

I ask, "Was the pill peddler delivering or collecting?"

Pause. "What?"

"Like cocaine. . . . That satchel could hold a lot."

Pause. "It could."

"So he bought the stuff upstairs."

Shrug. "I was not upstairs."

"But the satchel wasn't that heavy when he came in?"

Mr. R. examines me for signs of jungle fever. "No comment."

"Thanks. . . . Incidentaly, why are you being so frank?"

"Because you're my witness," smiles Rodenbaker. "That I was down here—and not party to any transaction in this house tonight!"

We hear Chambers in the hall, butlering, "Good night, sir," and we hear the front door open and the doctor grunting something and the door shuts.

I cruise to the high window and inch a drape away for a peep.

The *zhlub* with the heavy black satchel is clumping down the stone steps. He is wearing the greasy brown hat that was hanging on the bentwood rack. He goes through the iron gate to the curb, and there he stops.

Now Dr. *Gurnisht* does a very strange thing for a doctor. He sticks his left hand inside his jacket. He stands there, at the curb, his left hand stuck inside his jacket. I ask you: Does it take genius to surmise that this geezer has a gun in a shoulder holster?

Soon he pulls his hand out and pushes it forward so the sleeve of his coat is pushed away from his shirt-cuff so's he can look at his wristwatch. Back goes the paw to the heater. He looks to his left. . . .

Sure enough, the lights of a car appear, and a long, shiny Mercedes-Benz pulls into sight and stops at the curb. But the chauffeur don't cut his motor or get out to open a door. Oh, no. The back door opens fast. The inside dome-light automaticly goes on—long enough for me to glimpse a man in the back: a classy type with a Homburg and a topcoat that has velvet half-lapels in the style called Chesterfield, altho not after the cigarette.

The Doc hops into the luxurious buggy and the door slams shut, and before you can say, "Ish Kabibble," the Mercedes roars away like a hornet in a hurry.

I scan across the street. The big Chrysler don't move. It's not the Doc or the Mercedes that Donny Chu's boys are staking out. Obviously.

Gramercy Park is very peaceful.

I turn from the window. "Kenny, how much snow did you bring up here?"

" 'Snow'?" he echoes. "Whoever heard of snow in Trinidad?"

"Some people call it cocaine."

His brow darkens. "Go see a shrink."

"You *sailed* to Key West—outsmarting the Chu family's bloodhounds. You took Air Sunshine to Miami. Then Eastern for N.Y. . . . How much white dust were you carrying? Up here, big 'C' brings like—3,000 bucks an ounce."

"My, my! I must be very rich again. Where did you say all this treasure was?"

"In the Doctor's bag. The *shnook* was bending under the weight. . . . You and he were upstairs for an hour before I got here, right? I don't think he was testing your sinuses. I think you were negotiating price. Then you come down. He stays up there to analyze the quality of the dope, and weigh it—down to a fraction of an ounce—with the scale in his satchel.—"

"You mean I left a buyer *alone,* with a fortune?!" he mocks.

I kill a minute on that. My cheek itches. Then I get it: "No. Someone was up there, watching him. While the Doctor ran his batch of tests on the angel dust, you were down here . . ."

Rodenbaker lets out a long, fake yawn. "So sorry." (Yawn.) "I must have dozed off. Too much brandy. I haven't heard a *word* of the conversation." He covers another counterfeit yawn with his fingers.

And then I see something glinting, glittering, coming down those long stairs from the 2nd floor. And into the room—very confident, as sleek as a plump Burmese cat, in a tight lamé gown that leaves 1 shoulder bare and is slit up the legs (like Chinese chicks wear) up to the thigh, her bracelets jingling and gold earrings tinkling like tiny musical pagodas—glides a teakwood goddess.

"Melody," murmurs Kim.

17
MELODY NAVARRE

She is magnificent: a queen from Indonesia, with those up-swing, almond-shape eyes. Her coal-black hair, very sleek, is coiled in a swirl that drops down on a slant to 1 ear, and has a spectacular jeweled comb stuck in it. Her lips are ripe as cherries and glisten with silvery lipstick. . . . And her Saran Wrap gown makes my blood bubble. And that bare skin! Amber . . . with the radiance of light shining under the flesh. I saw luminous buff like that on the baby-doll girls when I was on leave in Thailand (which used to be Siam when I was in school). A chain necklace is around her throat—and I'll be damned if I don't see a tiny silver spoon dangling from it. That spoon is for sniffing dust. (Hell, you can buy them spoons at fine jewelers in N.Y., L.A., L.V., Palm B., and et cetera.)

The only surprising thing about this dazzling cross between Myrna Loy and Dorothy Lamour is that her nose is straight, not broad, and tilted up, not squashed; and she is not chic slim, the way most Eurasian ("Chee-chee!" pops into my head) beauties are, but balloon curvy. Suzy Knickerbocker calls that type "svelte." In my circles, we call it *zaftig*. This exotic broad has a slim waist but luscious thighs—like 1 of the maidens in those erotic sculptures of old on certain temples in India. And, this looker either wears gorgeous falsies or is naturally endowed with cantaloupes you itch to get your hands on. (Maybe you don't; I do.)

The sequins on her lamé gown send slivers of reflected light around the room as she sashays in. She could be the hostess for the family tea, nodding casualy to Rodenbaker, Maitland

and Kimberley (only what the 2 dames exchange is politeness laced with poison).

When the teakwood *tchotchke* lamps me, her sloe eyes slow down, then hang around. "I," she croons, in a delicious contralto, "om Melody Navarre."

I try not to whistle: that name: And that accent! Anson Stowbridge had it. (His words from the stretcher replay on memory's cassette: ". . . his—yella—chippy. . . .")

"I assume you are Kimberley's gollont protector," she salves me.

I bow. I *like* to bow to knockout ladies, especially when I don't know what to say, and I never yet met a foreign broad who ain't flattered by the waist-bend.

"Gawd," Kim breathes into my ear. "Next, you'll kiss her hand."

"Why that low?"

"Melody," chirps Shelby Maitland, "is from Bangkok."

"Don't pun!" Kimberley mutters.

"But I wos raised in T. and T.," says Miss Navarre.

"The phone company?" I amaze.

"You'd roll them in the aisles at an Elks' smoker," snorts Kenneth.

"T. and T.," explains Rodenbaker, "means Trinidad and Tobago."

"Two *beau*tiful islonds," purrs the sepia special, "but won nation. . . . Howard, dahling, *could* I have some chompagne?"

"Your throat must be very dry," I say.

*"Ra*lly? Why?" The seductive cat is pulling out all the sex stops. She sure knows her hormones (as who, seeing her, don't?).

"From your long gab upstairs," I coo, "with the Doctor from dreamland."

Kenneth scowls, "You're cute, boy. Very cute."

Melody gives me a mock curtsy, steps to Kenneth, and puts both arms around his neck. I notice she is clutching a big beaded bag I doubt costs more than a Toyota. "I don't mind, lohve." She presses her cheek against his.

(I remember Rudy Korvo, the most successful gash-hound in our outfit, telling me how Oriental dames hate to be kissed on the mouth in public; in fact, some even hate lip-lather in private, on account of they regard smooching as unsanitary, plus low class.)

Rodenbaker hands La Navarre a crystal glass of bubbly. "Dear . . ."

"Angel," she breathes.

I get my pack of cigarettes and hold it out to Kimberley. "Take 1," I say softly.

She takes 1.

As I light it, I whisper, "How can you 'hate—every—damn—inch' of that dear, sweet lollipop from T. and T.?"

She blows smoke in my eyes. "Do you want to lay her?"

"I might have to. Research."

"Make a pass at that bitch and I'll fire you."

I look at the ceiling like I'm weighing the deal. "I'd rather lay you."

She gives me the Brearley brush-off. "She's Kenneth's whore."

"I'd never of guessed."

"And sometimes"—she inhales very deep—"Howard's."

The goddam lighter fell out of my flipper. I had to bend down to get it. When I straighten up, I let fly: "Miss Navarre, where's the money?"

This creates a boom of silence. . . .

"*Mon*ey?" Her almond-shape cheaters lose the lure of the East and harden into the cold of a pawnbroker from the West Side. "What 'money'?"

"The cash the dealer gave you. Upstairs."

Kenneth moves his lady-love aside. "Hawkshaw, you never saw that man give her one goddam quarter!"

"That's why I need a story. True or false. I need a cover!"

"Why?"

"In case the Narcotics Squad gets wind of what went on here tonight."

Kenneth flips. "They won't."

"Don't bet on that, buster. If I get a call from Headquarters, or a goddam summons, I talk. If I don't, my license is lifted. . . . So I've *got* to have a bedtime story!"

"You mean you'd commit perjury?" asks Rodenbaker. (The crock puts it so casual he could be asking, "You mean you salute the flag?")

"What's perjury?" I humor him.

"Lying under oath."

"I *never* lie—under oath. I'll tell the cops *exactly what I'm told.* Not what I suspect, or what I damn well believe—but what I hear from the lips of the only person in this squirrel-cage who was upstairs—alone—with the 'Doctor.' Why should I doubt her? I'm sure Miss Navarre will tell me the truth. . . ."

Her chocolate lamps change to panther yellow.

Rodenbaker chuckles, "Mr. Pincus, where did you study law?"

"With my Uncle Muttel. He used to say, 'You shouldn't lie, but you don't *have* to blab more than you're asked.' "

"My compliments to your uncle."

"I'll kiss his grave for you. . . . So now, Miss Navarre, tell me something the boys in blue will buy without shining lights in my eyes."

"Up yours!" says Kenneth.

Rodenbaker chastises him: "He's right, Kenneth."

The amber princess waits for the nod from bronze Ulysses, who, having a brain that works slow—but stupid—says sarcasticly, "The doctor—uh—examined Melody's sprained ankle!"

"*Damn* you, Kenneth!" explodes Rodenbaker. "Don't you have any sense at all?! Don't you know the spot we're all on if this thing leaks?"

"You're a big wheel in this town," Kenny sneers, "and you've got enough money—"

"I'm not fool enough to try to bribe the police," cracks Rodenbaker. "I don't intend to wreck my reputation, or spend three years in prison, to protect you."

Panic sweeps that room like leaping lockjaw. You can hear the atoms collide in such silence. Kenny gapes. Melody gawks. Shelby shivers. Rodenbaker is an icicle.

"Silky . . ." Kim whispers.

God is good to his prodigy son. "Jewels!" I pop. "Emeralds. Diamonds. Rubies. . . . Kenneth and Melody brought the goodies up from Key West. Sold them here—to the gem scout for some of the best-heeled buyers on 47th Street."

The corpses come to life. Kimberley smiles, "How clever. Perfect. Melody's father was one of the richest men in Paris. When he moved to the island, he brought along the priceless family heirlooms."

Any *shmo* could tell this is news to Melody Navarre, whose old man was probly a pimp from Marseille, but Rodenbaker could put the king of *shmoes* at ease the way he chortles, "Superb! Kenneth and Melody went upstairs at six forty-five, or was it seven? . . ."

"Six forty-eight," says Kimberley.

"The Doctor, you should excuse the expression, arrived a few minutes later," I say. "The 3 were together for a while, then Kenneth came down. Melody and the dealer took a careful inventory—"

Madame Navarre is glomming me with an admiration that under other circumstances could have led to gorgeous gropings.

"Where's the money?" I ask again.

Kenneth fields that: "In a safe place."

"You have a safe upstairs?"

"No."

"Then it's not in a safe place."

He swears, then thinks, then bitches, "What the hell business is that of yours?"

"It's what-the-hell business of my client!"

"Oh, Christ," sulks Kenneth. "Stop grandstanding. I told you—I'll get the money to the Chinaman."

"I'd rather do it myself."

"You mean you don't trust me?" That tan is getting purple as sage.

"Marsh," I observe, "I wouldn't trust you in a barrel of rice with your lips sewed up."

He practicly came out of a cannon at me—with a heavy ashtray in his hand.

I have no pillow now, no time, no plan, so I duck and the blow crosses my cheek. I feel a sharp pain, plus blood trickles down. . . . So out of instinct (and practice) I bring my knee up fast—into his balls.

How much harm I did future generations of Marshes I do not know, but at the moment I am not interested in eugenics. His shriek of pain does not flood me with regret; but it brings rapid reactions from the congregation.

"You filthy swine!" spits Melody Navarre.

"He deserved it," snaps Rodenbaker.

Maitland, driven to a gibbering frenzy by what he has seen happen to his dream-boy, is so crazy he grabs a fireplace poker and swings at me from the floor.

Gottenyu! I have not got a club to hit against that speeding spike, or pepper to throw in the cupcake's eyes, so I make a wild grab at the homicidal iron. My palm almost splits from thumb to wrist, but I own the poker, which even Herschel, who is short on muscle, could twist like a lever and yank out of Maitland's grip. His shriek of dismay could qualify him for a chorus line.

He and Kenneth are both blue in the face, but Shelby is sobbing.

I wipe the blood off my cheek and raise the poker, and through clenched temper announce, "Once more, boys, and I will split open your both heads."

"And *me?*" shouts Melody Navarre, pushing her sizable body between me and moaning Maitland and gargling Kenny. "Will you strike *me?*"

I lower the poker—to press the point against her stomach.

"Stay cool, *dah*ling. . . . Just hand—me—your—bag."

The Chee-chee's peepers go from brown to murder. "Why?"
"My uncle, Sebastian Kaminsky, makes ladies' bags like that.
I want to see if it's one of his." I extend my free hand.

"No!" The no comes from Kenneth, not Melody Navarre.

All this time, Kimberley has been smoking calmly, observing
the brawl like she is at ringside in Madison Square Garden,
with the utmost confidence I can handle a very strong and
hotheaded jock, a hefty and hotter-blooded Chee-chee, plus
her brother's gay pal, who may be great on a squash court
but is a *Kuni Lemmel* when it comes to a fight-in.

Miss Navarre has put the beaded bag behind her, heaving
hate, and I am so sick of this whole charade I lean the poker
into the lady's belly and reach behind her, grab the beaded
bag, pull it into view, open the snap, and turn the thing upside
down.

As astonishing sight greets all our eyes: From the oversize
pouch falls a paper torrent: crisp green bills. Bills. Not the
kind you pay. The kind you get at the cashier's cage in a bank
when you say, "Can I please have 50,000 fresh new dollars?"

Silence falls on 1 and all like a very heavy blanket.

Finally, Rodenbaker's voice slices the ozone: "Nobody move!
Not—one inch."

"Howard!" cries Maitland in terror.

The cause of his terror becomes clear: Mine host's merry
blue peepers have turned to narrow cold marbles, and those
friendly jowls are stretched tight over muscles that have gone
hard as rocks.

And he is holding a big pearl-handled revolver.

18

THE GREEN, GREEN FISH
ON THE FLOOR

We are all hypnotized by that big pearly shooter. Especially
as the bad news is being held in the clutch of the man voted
"Least Likely to Commit Murder" by his class at Harvard—a
rating I revise, facts being what they are.

Rodenbaker says, "I will shoot anyone who is fool enough
to test me."

Anyone who doubts this man's capacity to make holes in
the head or other parts of the body is eligible for embalming.

"Are you crazy?!" hollers Kenneth Marsh.

"O mi*god,*"moans Maitland for the 10th time and with the
same success. He looks ready to faint.

Kimberley lights a fresh Parliament. A cucumber would envy
her.

Melody Navarre mobilizes her most seductive smile, to which
Rodenbaker responds by signaling her to move away from the
cash to a chair. She scowls, but does that.

Me, the man gives an order: "Pick up the money."

Picking lettuce off a floor—even (as I notice) in denomina-
tions like 10,000 and 5,000 and 1,000 and not a number
smaller—is something I can do without getting a hernia.

"Put them on the coffee table," says Mr. R.

That involves no heavy lifting.

"Kimberley," says Rodenbaker, "arrange the bills in piles
of 50,000. . . ."

Kimberley does her job, kind of amused. A pile of 10,000's

builds up fast. A pile of 5,000's don't take much longer. The combination of 1's *and* 5's *and* 10's takes a little more time. But in my opinion it is not 4 minutes (which when you consider how many seconds that is, and the fact it don't take 2 seconds to spot a number and add it in a running count) before the coffee table contains an arrangement of the green that would be pleasing to the eye of an auditor for the U.S. Treasury.

"Stand over there, Kenneth," says Rodenbaker. "I don't want another display of your stupid temper. . . . Hand me 100,000 dollars, Kimberley. . . . *Thank* you, Kenneth, for repaying your loan. Late, but commendable. . . . Take 100,000, Kim, for *your* loan. . . ."

Kenneth cries, "You're skimming 200,000 off the top!"

Rodenbaker reaches behind hisself and takes an attaché case off a writing desk. "Put 500,000 in this"—he tosses me the leather—"for delivery to Mr. Chu."

I start stuffing the money into the bag. "Peachy," I say. "But do you expect me to walk out of here with half a million bucks cash? Without a Brink's truck?"

"Your ingenuity is up to that challenge," he says.

"I could head for the border."

"You won't."

"Your faith is touching."

"Not faith. That 500,000 will take Kim 'off the hook,' as you so picturesquely put it. . . . And you love her."

I would rather not describe the expression on Kenneth Ardway Marsh's face: It belongs on a hangman who loves his work. "You left only 50,000, Howard," he says hoarsely. "That's what I paid for the coke!"

Rodenbaker says, "An excellent investment."

"You bastard! You're *robbing* me of—"

Charlemagne Chambers appears in the doorway, clearing his pipes. "Excuse me, but there seems to be an urgent call for Mr. Pincus."

Kimberley lifts an ivory phone out of its cradle and hands it to me. "Give my love to Isadore."

I wait until I hear Chambers click off his extension. Into the talker, I say, "Pincus."

I hear a double whistle. . . . Traffic noises—and that short, sharp, double whistle. . . . *"Bong!"* goes my ticker.

19
THE QUAKER PLOY

I return the recognition signal with 2 short shrill blasts.

"What *are* you doing?" ogles Madame Navarre.

I cover the mouthpiece. "It's my parakeet. He won't sleep 'til I whistle his lullaby."

Kenneth curses.

Chinatown's chief rabbi growls: "They're fryin' in Vegas."

I reply, "They're stiff in Siberia."

Kim's mouth makes a circle. Shelby aims a bewildered frown at his heart throb, Kenny, who uses another bad word. . . . And Rodenbaker—his eyes could be question-marks in a cartoon strip.

"This line clean?" comes the gravel of Donny Chu.

"I think so."

"You know why I'm calling?"

"You want to sing 'Happy Birthday.' "

"Not to you, friend. To the skip."

I let that bounce down to silence. Then I rib: "What took your soldiers so long to call you from the Chrysler?"

"I been on the move. . . . Let's cut the mustard. Is the family gonna erase the markers?"

I hesitate. "Most of them."

"What the hell does that mean?"

"I'm getting flak. . . . How does half the tab grab you?"

"Half? *Half?!*" Donny is a candidate for a stroke. "Tell the rat he takes *one* step out of there and we tear out his guts—"

"Make it 400 big ones."

"Drop dead, *shamus!* That fuckin' family can pony up another 100—plus 10 per—"

"Donny," I sigh, "I—"

"No *names*, goddammit!"

"I will level with you, man to Chan. Maybe I can swing that last 100—but these people are very religious types. Uh—Quakers! You heard about them types? Wow. The idea of shelling out *interest*, which they call 'usury,' is absolutely against their whole religion! This has made them real hard-ass. They don't give an inch! . . . So I'm up the creek, friend! Give me a paddle. Just 1 lousy little paddle! . . ."

Donny gargles, a sure sign he is thinking. "You pullin' a fastie?"

"Me? For Chrissake, pal, you think after all the business you and me done I have a cauliflower brain?! . . . I done the best I could! . . . I think I maybe can nail down the 500—but they say go-to-hell and kiss-their-ass and drop-*dead* when it comes to *per annum* and *percent!*"

He swears, which is bad. Then he croaks, which is good. Then he sighs, which is Bingo. "Sonsabitches. Rich finks. They got clout Downtown. . . ."

"Heavy. Very, very heavy."

Pause. Panting. Gravel rattles. Then a blurt: "The 500 G's?"

"Yeah."

"I don't want no goddam paper!"

"Would I be *shmuck* enough to offer a man like you something needs to be *endorsed?!*"

Sinuses blow. "Naa . . . *cash*, big shot. Green?"

"Yo!"

Dr. Fu Manchu makes the line shake with victory. "Great, kid. *Great!* I knew you could bust it! You will make my family on that certain island very happy. . . . I will now call my boys in the car. They will drive up to your entrance. You just give them the loot—"

"Hold it, Daddy-O. I'm not passing out half a million to strangers."

"They will give you a receipt!" he hollers.

"So what? Receipt-shmeceipt—they can grab the scratch and head for the Holland Tunnel!"

"My help?" he amazes. "You lost your friggin' flywheel? You don't trust my best boys, been with me 5–6 years?"

"I don't trust anyone but you. You want the dough, chum? I give it to you. In person."

Pause. "You're not goin' nark on me all of a sudden? Suckerin' me into a rip-off?" Cunning is in flower.

I produce a groan for top effect. "Oh, sweetheart. . . . You don't trust me? *Me?* . . . Okay. So *you* name the place!"

Chuckles show we are back on good terms. "Keep talkin'."

"I'll be carrying all this green. I need *protection,* man. Solid protection. So tell your soldiers to pull up to the house, and I get in your buggy, and they take me to meet you—wherever you want."

"Hey, that's sharp!"

"Only—don't tell them what I'm carrying!"

Cackles. "You scared they'll heist you?"

"You're damn right I am. 500,000 green fish can change muscles to hijackers. Remember 'Molly' Preston?"

"Okay, *okay!"* Quick as a flash. There's not a mob king in America who don't remember what happened to Martin "Molly" Preston: A team of his most trusted lieutenants was suppose to transport a lawyer from the Waldorf to Molly's warehouse on Avenue B, with 2 million in ransom for the Billy Strickland (age 8) snatch, and on the way down, Molly's guardsmen grabbed the briefcase, dumped the blindfolded mouthpiece out on Houston Street, and tore away to parts still unknown. The grapevine says that Fatso Bolinsky, who was Molly's buddy as well as Numero Uno, made it to Rio, after he canceled Nels Edwards, the 2nd gun, by running over his body in a deserted parking lot like 9 times, thus keeping all of the 2 million for his own self.

"I read you," says the king of the Chus.

"Where do we meet?"

"Oh, no. *Dat* I tell only my boys!" Donny is so pleased with that bright idea he practicly breaks the wire with ha-ha-has. "See you soon, Silky. . . . Hey, you not nuts enough to come heeled?"

I snort, "You boys would shoot me into a popcorn shaker."

"You are some smart."

"Tell your torpedoes to honk twice when they reach the curb."

"For that kind of scratch they'll play 'God Bless America.'"

I put the phone down. I note my hand is shaking. My lips are salty. I guess I lost 10 pounds in the last hour.

To the ga-ga, waiting assembly I sigh, "Okay. It's fixed."

Kimberley is studying me with the kind of admiration I figure advances me to Boardwalk.

20
ME, THE COWARD

"If I ever want to negotiate a loan at zero percent interest," says Rodenbaker, "you're my man."

I start to close the fancy staples on the attaché case, then stop. What the hell am I doing? "Your incriminating initials are on this Gucci," I say. "Better not go into a career of crime, Mr. R."

I look around. On the library table I see some neatly stacked magazines. I pick up 3 of them and take the money out of the attaché case and stick bills—5 and 6 at a time—between the pages. One of the magazines is called *Fortune,* which is not a bad place to stick 150,000 clams.

I put the magazines, spines down, under my left arm. "Ladies . . ." I wiggle fingers. "You're coming with me."

The mouth of Melody Navarre opens like for a dentist.

"I want a body on each side of me. The 3 of us are going down the front stairs together—into a nice, big car with 2 bodyguards." I grip my right hand around the plump arm of Madame Navarre. Kim comes around to my magazine side. "Good night, gentlemen."

Kenneth Marsh seethes, "I'm going to get you, Pincus."

"You kill me."

"I will!"

I give him the kind of look designed to describe gallstones. "You're still a horse's ass—advertising a murder threat in front of 4 witnesses."

Now comes a corker. Oh-*oh.* Rodenbaker has stepped between me and the door, very flushed, and his pistol has grown a lot bigger. "You leave without—hostages!"

"Hostages?" I do not hide my disgust. (In fact, I lay it on, disgust being less liable to send him around the bend than anger.) I also smell danger signals, so I put the magazines on a table. "You disappoint me, Mr. R. The ladies will be my witness, to you, for every move I make 'til I deliver the money."

"You are endangering their lives!" He shoves the gun into my belly, just like I hoped he would.

"It's less dangerous," I tell Rodenbaker, "than leaving the ladies in this nuthouse—with that hopped-up brother, his nervous-Nellie valentine, and an old man dumb enough to poke a gun right in my belly—" I demonstrate what I mean by "dumb" with the simplest, quickest move they teach you at Quantico: I swing my left elbow against his gun arm, sending it away from my stomach, grab his wrist with my right hand and twist him around by bending his elbow fast and hard (he yells with hurt). So now his back is to me, my left hand is around his throat, and my right hand pries the shooter out of his hold.

Why was there no shot? Because it takes more time for an assailant's brain to send the signal to his finger and his finger to squeeze the trigger than for a trained commando to execute a maneuver he has practiced like 800 times, with a stop-watch sergeant who brings the time for this whole dazzling maneuver down to under 2 seconds. (If you don't believe me, ask the next F.B.I. agent you run into.) With an old futz like Rodenbaker, my risk was zilch.

I ram the gun into the middle of Rodenbaker's back. "Kim, the magazines. . . . Melody . . ." I invite her towards me with a motion of my head.

The 3 of us have no trouble getting to the front door, where Arthur Treacher, Jr., stands, stiff as a Royal Guardsman, with an expression of awe he has not used since he witnessed the Charge of the Light Brigade. "Excuse me, sir, but I *must* ask: Are you actually going to use *women* as *shields?!*"

"Gladly." (I give him time to make like a flounder.) "Because

I'm dealing with pros. No hit man will risk a shot at a thin little target, Me, squeezed in behind two females. Juries are rough as hell on any ape hits a lady."

"How comforting," says Kimberley.

"But you're taking the money to Chu!" rasps Melody. "Who are you afraid of?"

"The party who gave it to you," I educate her. "And his boss—in a Mercedes—who maybe wants it back. What is this: a seminar?!" I break Rodenbaker's gun open and spill 6 cartridges out of the chamber. "Are those flowers in water?" I ask Kimberley.

She peeks into a huge vase. "Only up to their knees."

"Toss in the bullets."

She does that, saying, "Plop, plop, ploppety, plop."

"Give the gun to Jeeves."

She is puzzled.

"I'm not dumb enough to step out of here with a howitzer. Donny's dummies could read me wrong."

She takes the piece, holding it between her thumb and forefinger like it's a chicken with a broken neck, and hands it to the bug-eyed Yohoman of the Guard.

"Once we're moving," I say, "give it to Mr. R."

"But it contains no *pellets*, sir!"

"What does he know from pellets? It's his security blanket. . . . If *I* had to spend overnight with those 2 fruitcakes, I'd want anything that looks like a pacifier."

"That's *most* thoughtful of you, sir!" blurts young Treacher.

"Now open the door. . . . Girls? Laugh it up. We're having a swinging party. . . . A little night music, please."

Out we step, laughing merrily. But my knees are shaking like baby rattles.

21
NIGHT MUSIC

The Chrysler is waiting.

We come down the steps, with a double fortune (sure it's a pun) under my arm, laughing it up and throwing in a giggle or hiccup to add flavor to the act. Kimberley does it great, but Melody Navarre, who is smoldering, needs my pressure on her arm to play along.

I will confess that those 12 stone steps, plus the gate, plus the 14 feet of concrete to the Chrysler, with half a million bucks clutched in my armpit, was 1 of the hairiest trips I ever made. My throat is jammed with emery sticks.

The Chrysler is purring pretty, and since Donny Chu employs very savvy hoods, the driver is glued to the wheel while his stage-coach rider is standing outside, his hands in his pockets, which I give you 100 to 5 contain hardware and not potato *latkes*. He frisks me with his eyes—not a complete job, but enough for an open street. All I have to tell you about this character is that he is wearing a velour hat.

The girls and me jackknife in—and onto the back seat—fast.

Mr. Velour, the outside cannon, slams the back door, which makes that solid 2-stage clack you only get in luxury conveyances, and he hops in the front seat, and we tool away.

I survey outside—back, side, front, other side—and, spotting no Mercedes, or any reasonable facsimile of a deputy car, I slouch down between my 2 health preservers.

Kim says, "There's blood on your cheek."

"Not enough," spits Melody.

Kim wets a lacy handkerchief and wipes her brother's souvenir away.

To the front line I ask, "Where we goin'?"

The driver, who has a flat head and all the emotion of a manhole cover, thins my blood just with the glance he caroms off the rear-view mirror.

But Velour Hat regards my question as so funny he gives me, "No spikka da Engalish."

"No?" doubts Kim. "I spikka Italiana. *Dove, amico?*"

"Sheddup, lady!" scowls the fake foreigner.

Manners are never a gorilla's best side.

Suddenly, Melody Navarre hauls off and bangs me on the mouth. "You are *kidnopping* me! I sholl tell the police—"

I grab her. "Do that! And *I'll* tell them the type snuff you sell—and did you enter the U.S. legally?"

She turns lavender.

Kimberley says, "Don't try to outsmart him, darling." (Sarcasm drips off that "darling.") "His mother's milk was full of brains."

Navarre really blows up, cursing in some dialect I don't dig, and starts a clutching, hitting, scratching tussle, which forces me to put my open hand across her face with the advice: "If you don't stop, I'll push your nose through your head. You'll sneeze backwards."

This unappetizing possibility registers. The bitch wrenches away, backs into a corner, her big balloons heaving, her blinkers wide with rage. Her beautifuly coiled hair has come uncoiled, and the jeweled comb is reeling askew like a bent weathervane, and sweat beads form around her lips, which she licks.

"You look *love*ly," coos Kim.

"Drop dead," puffs Melody.

"Whore."

"Tramp."

"Slut!"

"Floozy!!"

"Trollop!!"

"Leg-spreader!"

"Fa Chris*sake!*" yells the astonished manhole cover. "Ain't rich broads got *no* sense of refinement?!"

I congratulate him.

So a sullen silence falls upon the unfriendly girls—and the next thing I know we are rolling down the Bowery and suddenly turn into Bayard, then Pell, and we have to move slow through parked cars and throngs of tourists and native Chinese . . .

I'll be damned if we don't stop in front of an old nickelodeon-type theater! The posters are full of slant-eye soldiers about to rape round-eye virgins. What the name of the feature is I can't tell, but over the entrance is the name of this temple of cinema—in Chinese:

THE YELLOW DRAGON

I know that's what the Chinese characters mean, because "The Yellow Dragon" is printed right underneath, in English.

Velour Hat grins at me. "You ast where we're goin'?"

Flathead cackles, "To the movies, short-pants. To the movies."

22

THE YELLOW DRAGON

"I hope it's a double feature," says Kim.

"I'm not that lucky," I say.

"I hope they kill you," says Miss Navarre.

I start to open the back door, but it's locked, from the driver's panel, and the *holdupnik* in the front seat grunts, "Wait," on account of Velour Hat has picked up a phone and is getting instructions. He answers in a voice so low I can't make out more than a word here and there. ". . . and two dames . . . sure . . . okay."

He hands me the talker. "The Man."

Before I can even say, "Hello," Donny Chu's voice rattles my eardrums: "*Crazy* or somep'n, you punk, bringing 2 tomatoes?!"

"I never travel without 2 girls."

"Listen, horny. Don't make with jokes. I don' wan' *no* broads around on a business deal!"

"1 of them is Miss Marsh, Donald. Remember? The plum in the whole fruitcake. The 1 you put your spook on."

"Oh, Je-*zus!*" he croaks. "I don' wan' *her* anywhere! *You* c'min', goddammit. *She* stays in the car. The boys will drive your 2 bimbos home. Now move your dumb ass outa there. Fast!"

As I give the phone back, Flathead flips a dingus that makes the door click, and Velour Hat hops out and opens the back door from the outside.

"Good night, pussy," I toss Navarre.

In true, poetic Bangkok tradition, she replies, "I hope he cuts out your tong." Some pun.

To Kim I say, "They'll take you home."

She takes my face between her 2 hands and kisses me— on the lips! "Thank you—for everything."

"Wait'll you see my bill."

"Call me—as soon as you're done."

I hesitate. "And you be ready to tell me why the hell you never leveled with me." (She pales.) "Why you sent me blind into this goddam skimble-scamble."

"Silky . . ."

"Practice up first, ma'am. A mess of pieces don't fit."

I get out and the velour cannon takes my place in the back seat, saying, "I hate to see blood," between the two pulchritudes. (I have been wanting to use that word ever since I learned what it meant.)

The Chrysler spurts away.

So I push through some very curious pedestrians and gaping spectators from the United Nations and go to the glass box— where the Oriyenta mother of Shelley Winters is selling tickets. She has had her orders: She waves me in.

The ticket collector is in brocade pajamas and has his orders, too, waving me in with a guttural, "Go up! Reft side, prease."

So I enter The Yellow Dragon. It is more like the Black Hole of Calcutta. Your ears could bust from the boom-boom of a bombing, plus the squeals of fleeing sing-song girls, plus the carrying-on of 200 delirious customers bobbing up and down in their seats. I have come into the bloody climax of Bruce Lee's *The Glorious Rape of Peking*, or whatever-the-hell the stinker is called.

I wait for my eyes to adjust to the darkness, and when the whole theater is lit up by a burst of Technicolor red showing Shanghai on fire, I spot the stairs at the left and ascend. I hug my magazines until I come to a door with a sign:

PROJECTION ROOM
STAY OUT!

Before I can enjoy the pretty hen-tracks that repeat this message in the local lingo, the door is opened.

The looming cliff-in-human-form can only be Donny Chu.
The ham that serves as his so-called hand sticks out and I take
it and it yanks me inside the projection booth like I am attached
to a yo-yo string.

Donny turns a gadget on 1 of the projectors and the sound
of the movie goes off in the booth. He grumbles an order to
the projectionist, who kowtows like to a warlord and paddles
out.

"You own this flea-bag?" I ask.

Donny nods, grinning. His beady blinkers give all of me the
once-over, which, finished, wipes out his grinning. "Where the
hell's the dough?! No satchel, no bag, not even a violin case—!"

I plop the 3 magazines on a steel worktable, under overhead
stacks where cans of film are lined up.

He looks like I'm showing him a card trick. "What the fuck
you come up for? *Readin'?* You think this is a goddam libary?"

I raise a reassuring hand. It always tickles me to see Donny
buffaloed. "Do not underestimate the power of print."

I take *Fortune* and, holding the spine, flutter it—and 10,000
and 5,000 bills fall out like leaves from a tree in the fall in a
wind.

Donny's blinkers make saucers. Then I pick up and shake
the 2nd magazine. And the 3rd . . .

"Sonva*bitch!*" pops Donny. "All 500 thou?"

"Count them."

Don't think he don't, beaming and chuckling all the time
he puts the bills in piles of 25,000 each. "Hey!"

My ears hear the tune of ". . . and then my heart stood
still"—even though no one is playing that immortal number.

"You holdin' 10,000 bucks out on me, *shamus?* You takin'
that percentage cut—and think you get outa here in 1
piece?!" He starts for me like King Kong, bald.

In steaming sweat I shake *Fortune* again, and no U.S. Treasury notes fall out! I gulp and quick shake the 2nd magazine—
and the sweetest 10 grand I ever seen floats down to the table
like a Walt Disney nymph in *Fantasia.* Breathing resumes.

"Bingo!" yells Donny. "Bingo, boy, bin*go!*" He is cackling

like a hen who just laid the biggest egg in the history of Rhode Island. "You are some *gonif!* I got to hand it to you! You came through!" He pumps my hand like he's trying to bring water out of a well.

"What about the fink's markers?" I idle.

The oaf gives me a playful jab in the jaw. "Don't lose your hard-on, sweetheart." Out of his pocket he pulls an envelope, and out of that he pulls maybe 20 paper chits reading:

CASINO CLUB

PORT-OF-SPAIN

TRINIDAD

Each I.O.U. is for thousands of U.S. currency, and is signed "Kenneth A. Marsh."

I add them up in my head. They come to half a million simoleons.

I say, "How about you write 'PAID,' plus your name—across them?"

Chuckles. "Anything for a pal!" Chuck-chuck. And as he's writing, he asks, like he just thought of it, "Hey, tough guy, who was the second tomato you had in the car?"

"A Chee-chee."

"Do I know her?"

"How would I know?"

"Okay, so does she know *me?* I mean, my name?"

I scratch my cheek. "You know something, Donny? I mentioned it 4–5 times tonight, but she did not even once clap her hands in glee, crying, 'Donny *Chu!*' . . . Why should that muff know you?"

"No reason." He puts the canceled markers back in the envelope real neat and hands it to me.

I feel like Shea Stadium has moved off my back to New Jersey.

Donny smiles, "What's her name?"

"Melody Navarre."

Oh, wow. That smile slid off the Man's lips like I cleaned

it off a blackboard with an eraser. He goggles me like I just revealed the secret password that will blow up the world. "Melody Navarre *what?*"

"Come again?"

"That was her maiden name, f'Chrissake! Don't you know her married name?!"

"I didn't know she was married."

He glares, "They shouldn't let you out without a hearing-aid! I bet you take an hour to cook Minute Rice! Why in hell didn't you tell me *she's* in this transaction?!" From his breathing you would think he is wrestling a bull.

To calm him up, I shrug, "She's in it only on account of her john."

"Which one? She'll screw wallpaper."

"Kenny."

"God*dam.* But what's she doing *in town?*" He hits the metal table with his fist and it's an Arthur Rank production again. "What'samatter with my family down there? Not once they let on that hot-pants broad ain't where she oughta be! At home! Singin' in the Casino. Melody Navarre, my bare ass! That's her *stage* name. You know her married name, f'Chrissake?"

"Du Pontski?"

"Don't try smart, you crum. It's Stowbridge. That's right. Mrs. Anson Stowbridge."

My head cracks in 2, without the help of a hatchet.

23

DRINKS IN A ROLLS

Donny Chu does not offer me a ride back to my humble dwelling; he is too damn busy eating up the money with his eyes whilst jabbering Long Distance to one of his family in Port-of-Spain.

I split without good-bye.

I make the stairs like a sleepwalker, my mind bobbling from this fantastic twist. The theater has a Cherry Blossom theme on the soundtrack now. . . . I push open a FIRE door. I find myself on the sidewalk, jostled and kowtowed by various joss-stick tossers on the main stem of Chinatown.

To say I am pooped, considering the long day of thrills, chills, fights, horrors and surprises I have had to go through, is like saying that the Greek kid who ran 26 miles from Marathon to Athens without stopping for air got there a little tired. If I remember my high school history, that guy dropped dead. At this moment, I would welcome 2 weeks at Grossinger's instead.

I feel wiped out—like I never before felt in my whole 32 years, even including my time in S.E. Asia in the glorious service of our country.

I look for a lit-up "Taxi" light on the roof of a public carrier, when a *"honk-beep-honk"* cuts through my confusion and a shiny long gray Rolls leaves the No Parking zone and pulls up alongside me. It stops.

The back door opens. A blonde head leans forward, with a halo from the dome-light like a bright moon behind her. She looks like an angel on the ceiling in an Italian palace. "Going my way?"

I get in without a word and a no-doubt unfriendly manner, and collapse into soft upholstery.

The Rolls starts moving.

Kim says, "I turned on enough charm to persuade Flathead to call my apartment. Gunnar, thank goodness, was still up. . . . *Voilà.*" She cuddles me, squeezing my bicep. "Where shall I tell him to go?"

"*Hotzeplotz.*"

"What's that, a nightclub?"

"A funeral parlor. Right next to *Shnippishok.* Forget it."

"You need a drink."

"*You* need a shrink."

"I had one." She sighs.

"When did he cut his throat?"

She leans forward. "Home, Gunnar."

I close my eyes. "Why can't his name be James?! Gunnar. Yech! Don't you know it's classier if a passenger hears, 'Home, James'?"

"Gunnar is his name, Silky. I told you that."

"Then it's 1 of the few true things you ever told me."

She ducks that. "How did it go?"

I hand her the envelope in which Donny Chu stashed the markers.

When she sees the canceled chits, that 1-in-a-million face lights up.

"Keep them in your vault. Give Kenneth Xerox copies."

"You don't trust him?" Sarcasm struggles to stay off her features.

"I trust him like I trust my own brother."

"I didn't know you had a brother."

"I don't."

She says, "You look terrible."

"I wonder why. You've had me on a crazy merry-go-wrong

from the minute you walked in my office with that Sassoon hair-job and your 700-buck Givenchy."

"It wasn't Sassoon, it was Cinandré. And it wasn't Givenchy, but St. Laurent."

Wouldn't you know?! A woman will forget the number of her 20-year-old bank account, but talk Fashion and she remembers what she wore to the opera 8 years ago.

"Smarty," she's saying. "You're always so damn *sure* of yourself."

"Douché." I bow my head in shame.

"Do you trust Howard?"

"A man with 2 faces has 2 hearts."

"You're really revved up. . . . How about Shelby?"

"Shelby," I say, "will make someone a good wife."

She winces. "Do you think he's smart?"

"That *tim-tum* couldn't find the notches in a saw."

"What's a *tim-tum?*"

"My Uncle Yankel's word for little boys who like to dress up in little girls' clothes."

"You have more uncles and aunts than anyone who ever lived!"

"That's because I add a new 1 whenever I wish I had a large *meshpoche.*"

"Why," she complains, "do you always toss me—foreign words?"

That cut. I dribbled the ball a bit before I took the shot. "Maybe I want to remind you that you're a true-blue Wasp."

Pause. "I think you do it to remind me that you're not."

"Whiff!" . . . Right across the strike zone. "Tell Gunnar to stop at the nearest bar."

"He doesn't have to." She rummages in her purse. "The nearest bar is"—she puts a key in the lock of a walnut panel on the back of the driver's seat—"here."

The panel drops down on 2 hinges and hangs there, horizontal, and I am staring at bottles of scotch, vodka, brandy. There is cut-glass, too, and stirrers, and a bottle of soda and a decanter marked "water."

"What, sir, is your pleasure?"

"Humping."

She makes with a sidelong Bacall glom. "Do you *have* to be vulgar?"

"You call that vulgar? You should catch my late, late show. If you play your cards right, Miss Marsh, I'll—"

"*Try* to be subtle. What do you want to drink?"

I have to scratch my cheek to reduce my admiration of How to Live It Up in Spite of the Income Tax. My throat has gotten even drier, so what I hear cross my cotton lips thickly is, "Scotch. For the love of mercy, *belle dame sans* same."

"Straight or soda?"

"With morphine."

She gets a lo-ball glass. "Your French is dreadful."

"I was a dropout from Berlitz."

The bottle gurgles like a church organ. My lips are moving before the glass leaves her hand. I toss my head back and dispose of a slug.

She does a take. "We're not snowbound!"

"Leave us not discuss the weather." I hold the glass out.

She makes a refill, and for herself pours a ladylike 2 fingers of gold. She raises her glass, "To you."

"To me." I drink and I note with satisfaction that my hand has won the battle with the shakes. Booze defrosts the remnants of fear.

So now I take a nice long optic trip from her gorgeous ankle up—up across the graceful curve of her gams. "You ever read Omar Khayyám?"

"Mnh."

"Drink to me only with thy thighs."

"God," she groans, but her mouth is music. "Is that all you ever think of?"

"Frequently." My voice is harsher than I expected. "Give

me some answers, pussycat. . . . You said dear old Howard gets into Melody, too. How often?"

"I'm not there to count."

"Does your brother know?"

Pause. "I doubt it."

"Then how come you do?"

"Melody told me. That creature loves to make me furious."

I spread sugar on my next words. "Did you know Melody is married?"

"She was."

"You mean she's divorced?"

"Separated. She says she and her husband get together— every so often."

"Despite Kenneth?"

Shrug. "I *don't* think her husband knows he's sharing her hot goodies with my brother."

I lob, very casual, "What's her husband's name?"

"I never asked. Does it matter?"

Lord! I'm about to pull the pin on that grenade, but instinct stops me. If I tell her the connection to Stowbridge, the scare she faced before would multiply by 1,000.

The Rolls stops. Geography has come to my rescue. I leer, "We're home, doll."

24
CONFESSIONS

"Home" means the Cloverly Chateau on 5th Avenue.

Gunnar touches the visor of his gray cap. "I be up in few minoots, Miss Kimberley." He sure is from Vikings, age maybe 63½.

The car door is opened by an exiled potentate from Persia. *"Good* evening, Miss Marsh."

"Good evening, Toller."

"Good evening, sir."

"Ta-ta," I laze.

We dosey-doe to the gilt-braided portal, which is opened from inside by a stiff-collar with a striped vest and blinding white gloves. "Good evening, Miss Marsh."

"Good evening, Edward."

To me: "Sir . . ."

From me: "Absolutely."

Kimberley does a queen's walk down the marble, and across the royal rug runner, under the gilded rotunda, around the splashing fountain, to the bank of bronze Art Deco elevator doors. I pull a blasé half-yawn, genteelly touching my lips with my fingers. The more hi-class, the more you should strangle a yawn. Things are too, *too* terribly boring these days.

"When did you last eat?" Kim has the brilliance to ask.

"1906."

"You fool."

The white-tie-and-tails admiral of the elevator says, "Good evening, Miss Marsh," and she says, "Good evening, Eddington." And he nods at me like it's Orphans Day, free admission when accompanied by an adult.

We enter a peacock sanctuary. It lifts off once the feathered doors close.

Since Eddington leads a sheltered life and has his ears pricked up for dropping eaves, I proclaim: "When I'm on a U.S. Secret Service assignment like this, Miss Marsh, food means nothing to me. In Ranjapur, where I had to rescue the Rajah from a band of Thugees who wanted a ransom of his weight in sturgeon, I went 16 days without so much as a spoonful of caviar."

She parodies Carol Channing. "How *ever* did you survive?"

"Chicken soup."

A mothball must of gotten inside Eddington's gullet.

The spiffy elevator stops on 9.

"Smooth ride," I commend Eddington. "Congratulations. And my compliments to Westinghouse."

His expression will sour the milk surrounding his ulcer.

Kim is fumbling for her key when her door is opened by a spotless though overweight maid from Sweden. (She could be a spotless old maid, for all I know.)

"Christina, Mr. Pincus is starving," says Kimberley. "Do be a dear and fix him a cold plate. Gunnar should be up soon."

"Ya, Miss Kimberley."

"And a bottle of champagne. . . . Two glasses."

Never argue with your hostess.

The living room is nowhere as large as Carnegie Hall, altho more cozy. The rug is so thick, I feel I am slogging through a rice paddy, and the furniture I glimpse would of brought 6 figures at the Sotheby Parke Bernet auction on a slow night.

I observe a painting over the mantel that looks like 2 women are eating each other in a color vat. I ask, "Picasso?"

"No. Braque."

I close 1 eye to peer through the other, like a *maven*, at a landscape. "Surely Cézanne? That quiltwork—"

"No. Vlaminck."

"Nonsense. . . . The still life? You can practicly feel the fungus. That's Andy Warhol."

She shudders. "It's Fantin-Latour. . . . How do you happen to know so little about art?"

"I was on guard duty for a week at Wildenstein's."

"Couldn't you at least read the painters' names on the little plates?"

"They don't let you read whilst on duty."

She says, "Admire the view. I must change."

"Don't forget my slippers."

She pauses in the doorway, the teasing half-smile adorning her lips. "What is that word you once used for gall?"

"Chutzpah."

"You've got it."

"So sue me."

I admire the smasheroo view of Central Park. The trees are Japanesey branched and beautiful, the lighted paths like necklaces of light, the skyline south a smash shot of Essex House, the Park Lane and the R.C.A. building beyond. Across the park, C.P. West is strung out in fortresses, with the twin towers of the Beresford a high castle. "It's not a bad way to live," I announce, "if you like luxury."

No answer.

"I bet you don't get flies this far up."

No answer.

"Pigeons? I have to say I hate pigeons."

No answer. There's no percentage in a conversation with nobody. The reason there were no answers is nobody else was in the room.

I study a photograph in a huge silver-encrusted frame, on the table behind the sofa: a man with thin lips and a jaw like a refined Moose Mancusi, and a lady of true elegance, aristocratic in bearing, with a low-cut gown and a choker of pearls.

"My parents," comes Kim's voice.

She has changed into a loungy chiffony kaftan of soft green. It is so large and loose that it don't reveal every luscious curve of the receiving set underneath, but it reveals every aspect of the transmitters.

A knock on some door precedes the entrance of Christina the Fair. She is holding the handles of a huge silvery tray, which she sets down on a table as she gets a folding tray, opens it, puts it between the sofa and the fire (when you're that rich you can turn on the air-conditioning and have a cheerful fire, too). Then she puts the tray on the table.

My mouth waters enough so I don't need to wash the cold roast duck down. That bird is very crisp and with orange slices around it. I attack the dead duck with King George III's knife and fork.

"Why don't you use your fingers?" asks Kimberley.

"Good thinking, ma'am."

Now Gunnar enters—with a bucket-stand in which the neck of a champagne bottle, draped with a napkin, sticks out of packed ice. He positions 2 gleaming champagne glasses on the saw-buck butler's stand.

I reach for the bottle, but Kim says, "Eat on, soldier. I'll do that."

She untwists the wire and twists the tinfoil like an expert, but just as she starts to thumb up the cork, I take the bottle away from her, wincing, "You're pointing it at me. Do you work for the Eye Bank?"

I put the bottle under the butler's tray and pry the cork and it pops up with enough force to dent the underside of the table.

She says, "You learned that at Maxim's, I suppose?"

"No. From Bogey Nayfack. He said to always protect your loved ones."

She slow-smiles as of yore. "Am I one of your loved ones?"

I pour the bubbly into the glasses. You can hear it singing. I give her a glass and raise the other. "I do not intend to repeat the affidavit of my feelings about you."

She digs that. "Thank you."

We drink.

"Now, while I eat this *kotchke*—which is the old Nordic word for duck—start cleaning up all the phony-baloney you've given me."

She gets a cigarette and uses a big Ronson and inhales, very deep, and I smell that slight sweet scent of pot, but I say nothing, on account of I know how a joint strokes the nerves and loosens the tongue.

I dab my lips with a napkin that has an embroidered crest. You don't get linen like that in the Catskills.

She still has said nothing. She is trying to find reasons for all her lies, or maybe the true meaning of life—by staring into the fire.

"Don't talk so fast," I say.

"Sorry."

Sorry. That sure is eloquent response. "For openers, why didn't you tell me that Shelby Maitland knew you were coming to Watson and Holmes? He was even waiting for you in the lobby—with his bumberella . . ."

"Shelby did *not* know I was going to your office!" she flashes. "I told him I was going to the dentist. Raymond Otway. I saw the name on the lobby directory when I was looking up your office number."

Surprise #204 in this mish-mosh of a case.

"Neat," I give her. "But why didn't you want Shelby to know where you were going?"

"To hire a detective? Oh, no. How could I be absolutely sure *he* wasn't making those freaky calls to me? . . . And maybe he was involved some way in the car shadowing. . . . I like Shelby, but still . . . I know Kenneth can wrap him around his finger."

I do not conceal my admiration. "You are not lacking in moxie."

"A compliment? From you?" She flutters her lashes in mockery. "The shock has paralyzed me."

"Then get set for another. Why did you tell me that if you kick off, your money goes to a Foundation that don't exist?"

She is reddening to the color of the flags in a Red Square parade. "You were so *damn* relentless with me. You were pushing too hard . . . and so conceited . . . I wanted to take you down a peg." Tears well up in the emerald eyes. "And I was in panic. I'd been living on Valium to calm down, and smoking pot to feel safe, and gobbling Dalmane to sleep. When those wore off, I went on uppers and downers and red pills and yellows. I was popping bennies like peanuts. . . . By the time I *made* myself go to you, I was half freaked-out. . . . *You* saw that. . . . How could I tell a total stranger that I thought, with no real evidence, that my own brother was—trying to kill me?!" She sinks to the hassock and puts her head on my knee. "I'm so tired . . ."

I touch her hair. "So where does the M-O-N-E-Y go if you conk out?"

Pause for station identification.

"If you tell me now," I bribe her, "I'll take you to the circus."

"That's a bore."

"The aerial tram to Roosevelt Island?"

"The sway would make me throw up."

"I'll ride you up the Hudson on my Yamaha."

That impresses her. "Do you own a motorcycle?"

"So I'll buy one." I kiss her hair. "Give, baby, give."

"When I die," she murmurs, "half the Trust goes to Kenneth. Father had *some* guilt—or conscience—about his only son . . . no matter how much he despised him for going A.C.–D.C."

"And the other half?"

"To Mother."

That rings "Tilt" on my pinball machine. "But she's dead!"

"She transferred her rights to me—with the proviso that if I die before Howard—he gets 'the other half.' "

Make it #205.

Above the crackling log (and hum from the air-conditioner), I yammer, "So Kenny and Howard each pick up millions of smacks if you pass on to Paradise."

She shivers.

"Why the *hell* didn't you tell me that? Worse, why did you flat out *lie*—saying nobody stood to gain a dime from your demise?"

"Because I was ashamed. *Ashamed*. My suspicions seemed monstrous. . . . I prayed to God that you'd find out it was someone I never knew who was telephoning me, and following me. A weirdo, a thief planning to rip off my apartment, a nut with some obsession—*you* ticked off all those possibilities! I was so relieved—so grateful—that I pushed everything else into the back of my mind. Because if you were right, and did find some stranger bugging me—"

"Your conscience about your loved ones would be clear?"

"Yes, yes, yes!"

I take more time than needed to freshen our stemware. "Wasn't there—way back in your head—another reason for feeding me all that smart *shmaltz* about your sweet ones?"

She waits, on guard. "Like what?"

"You didn't want to give me stuff—to blackmail you? . . ."

I will not say she caught her breath in total surprise and consternation: I have to say she choked on the champagne.

"In the back of that confused but far from stupid head of yours, doll, was a red signal, warning you that if you told me the real truth, and then it turned out that neither Kenny boy nor Howard nor Shelby had a goddam thing to do with the creepy hocus-pocus—Silky Pincus could lean on you . . . for a bundle."

"I don't understand."

"That'll be the day. The smartest owls are those who act dumb. . . . That's wisdom from Guatemala." (So it ain't from Guatemala.)

"How could you—'lean' on me?" she asks. "And why would I pay you a 'bundle'?"

"To keep me from double-crossing you, by telling Kenny—then Howard—then Shelby—that you'd hired me to investigate them because you thought each 1 of them was out to drive you nuts—or bump you off."

She puts both hands to her head. "I should have known you'd figure out every single embarrassing angle!"

"You should be ashamed of yourself," I say. "To even *think* a lousy thought like that would cross my mind!"

"Oh, I am."

"Don't be." I swallow the lovely bubble water. "You really were savvy."

"What?!"

"You didn't know me from Adam. I mean Adam Weischaupt, who took on a case for a Society dame, then turned around and took her for 120 G's—to keep him from blabbing to her husband, about Patrick."

"Patrick?"

"Their chauffeur. A handsome honcho who was—and still is—her lover."

It dawns on her that Silky Pincus could never be such a low-life, and in a burst of relief and maybe gratitude she throws her arms around me. "You're wonderful! I swear to God, I *never* met anyone like you." She kisses me, *"smack-smack-smack,"* on my irresistible cheeks.

So I take her lovely face between my hands and gaze into her emotional eyes, sighing, "What hell you put yourself through, sweetheart. And all unnecessary! . . . If you had leveled with me, I could of told you something at the very beginning that would of erased all those 'monstrous' fears."

She blinks.

"Don't you realize, Little Miss Muffett, that a *murderer can't inherit a plugged nickel from a murderee?!"*

It's like I told her that Kenneth Ardway Marsh is the nicest brother any girl could hope to have, and Howard Rodenbaker a candidate for sainthood.

"Migod, migod," she murmurs, and the murmurs turn into little laughs of deliverance. "Oh, Silky! God bless you! You're right. I don't have a thing to be scared of now!"

I did not correct her. It would of been cruel to remind her that greedy, crazy relatives have been known to hire a killer, and God only knows how many do get away with murder.

She laughs, "What I adore about you, Silky, is how innocent you are."

"Innocent?!" I am outraged.

"If you weren't, you would have seen right through me! You would have figured out why I was lying—and we wouldn't be sitting here playing 20 Questions instead of heading for the bed in which we're both longing to go. . . . Oh, you are sweet and good and innocent. . . . How can I not love you?"

She gave me her lips, then, and they were so warm and soft and fragrant that I drowned among the teeming, singing lilies of my passion.

25
PARADISE

We floated into the bedroom, then, like drunken angels, with my arm around her shoulder and her arm around my waist. I pulled her to a stop to kiss her and hold her, and her body melted into mine, and the low, soft sounds she made were like pleas of desire. . . . No one ever called me "Darling . . ." "Oh, love . . ." "Oh, oh . . ." the way she did. Never before. Never.

Yes, I know: I broke every rule in the book, and every paragraph in the P.I. code, and everything in the Boy Scout manual except loving my country:

1. You are not suppose to ever, ever make love to a client—I mean, not while she is your client. (Later don't count, because human is human.)

2. Only a *shmegegge* will mix business with passions, on account of the former diminishes the latter and the latter makes a mess of the former.

3. I am suppose to be so glued to my duties that even the Queen of Sheba should not be able to take my mind off what I am being paid to do, and—what's worse—put that mind on what I sure am *not* being paid to do! . . .

But none of this mattered. How could it? "Love is a kind of madness." And "Those in love are deaf, dumb and blind."

I *was* deaf, I *was* dumb—but I was not blind. My eyes had never seen such glory as when, in the bedroom, I undressed her. With reverence. Letting her kaftan fall like Scheherezade's satin down those long, long Saratoga legs. And in the dim light her nakedness gleamed like 1,000 pearls, and her young breasts—pink nippled—are from the Song of Solomon; and her golden triangle of hair. . . . What did God ever make more beautiful than a girl?

I took off my clothes faster than any fireman ever put his on.

She kept murmuring, "Love me, oh, love me . . ." her face flushed and her lips parted, and she was breathing very deep before I laid the finger on her. When I did, she cried out, "Oh . . . yes . . . oh . . . there . . ."

The rest, you have to excuse me, is personal. I'm not 1 of those describe-every-sexy-detail writers, especially when it's kinky.

But I will tell you that the sheets were like ice cream when we slid into them, and her mouth went as wild as my hands, and she cried out again and again in the wilder music of ecstasy.

I suppose I should describe the moans she moaned, the way her hot body moved into me and trembled when I touched the little man in the rowboat, and her burning mouth as I opened my mouth and surrounded her lips and sucked in her sweet, sweet tongue, and her cries of "Oh! Oh! Lover! Yes, yes, yes!" and her flaming, pulsing wetness as I slid into her, faster and harder. . . . And when she came, she screamed and it was like a hundred Baked Alaskas exploded for us and lit up the blue dark of the room.

And I suppose I should describe my own passion, my body hot and sweating in a maniac code all its own, my almost choking as my heart pounded like a crew of hammers wrecking the walls of my body, my delight as I touched her thighs and moved up and up and she gasped and cried out, raining kisses on my cheeks and mouth and eyes as I slid the hard, tingling throbber deep and deep into her and we began the moving magic together until our ecstasies exploded and fireworks lit up the heaven in our hearts.

These things are too sacred to go into. Like I learned in Hebrew school: "Noble character is better than noble birth."

One thing I can tell you—for sure and forever: I'll never

forget that first time with Kimberley Marsh. Never. Never.

When they lay me in my grave, and my eyes are closed forever, there still will be locked in my mind the memory of her face beside me on the satin pillow: It was a face of such beauty as you imagine could be only on a dreaming angel.

26
NEXT MORNING

I found a new razor and a fresh tube of lather on the sink, and this message Scotch-taped to the mirror:

Christina has a scrumptious breakfast for you. No bacon.
Go out through the *guest room. Burn this note* . . .
Je t'adore. Like crazy.   **—K**

So I shaved and showered and dressed and, acting as groovy as I usualy do after a weekend at the White House, I strode with real *savvy-faire* into the breakfast room.

The table is set like for Louis the 14, and that tremendous view of the Park was made especialy for my mood. I am the King of all I survey, and more.

A little silver bell is on the table, so I tinkle it.

In comes Big Chris with orange juice and a pot of coffee. "Goot morening, sir."

"*Good* morning, Christina."

She puts the orange juice before me and fills my dainty coffee cup.

"How you like aggs, sir?"

"Your way."

"Ah, *takk, taak,*" it sounds like.

"I always did like Svenskas."

"Not me. Ay am Norvagian."

That's the way it is in life: You fall on your back and break your nose.

The eggs were poached. Super. So were the sweet rolls. So was the coffee. It feels great to be served a breakfast like that—

at home, yet, and without you have to leave a tip.

It is 9:20 when I go through the Taj Mahal lobby, ignoring the uniformed muckymucks of the Cloverly. The Crown Prince at the door couldn't flag a cab, so I hopped a 5th Ave. bus, transferred crosstown, and by 9:45 I am at the portals of Watson and Holmes, Inc.

Herschel is right on duty, wearing a green eyeshade like a mitt-man in Vegas, and he is hunched over the F.B.I.'s latest *Crime Report.* He is so lost in the rape column he don't hear me. I am confident that someday Herschel will get such hi marks on his exam for a P.I. license that he'll end up a guard at the sanitation depot in Flushing.

"Mr. Ta-*bach*-nik," I tenor, like in an opera.

He jumps up like the spring is not in the chair but in his *tuchus* and warbles, "Oh, Theodora, my uncle's on the floora!" It took Herschel 2 years to work that out.

He follows me into my office, waving his notebook and yakkety-yakking. "Mr. Clancy will be late. . . . The morning mail is on your desk. Nothing outstanding, in my professional opinion. Your dentnist"— that's right; Herschel also says "paintner" and "carpentner"—"called. Time for your checkup."

"You take it for me."

"A funny?! . . . Ha, ha . . . You don't say hello to Isadore?!" he astonishes. "I hope you realize he had to sleep in my place *all last night!*" He makes beady-eye.

If Herscheleh expects me to tell him where I spent last night, he should rush to Bellevue for a skull test.

Mr. Goldberg is whining. I say, "Hul-*lo, bubeleh,*" and pat him nice to make him smile.

"A man has a dog has a child!" Herschel declaims. "Isadore needs love and attention like your own flesh and blood!"

"How true," I regret. "Little children won't let you sleep; big children won't let you live."

Mr. Goldberg barks happily. That bark still sounds less like *"Woof! Woof!"* than *"Oy! Oy!"* This shows the power of early training.

"Has Miss Marsh called?" I ask, as casual as buttermilk.

"Y-you *expect* it?"

I rub my temples. "A fool can ask more questions in a minute than a sage can answer in a year."

"Aha!" cries Herschel. "I will match that quote from our forefathers: 'The right word at the right time is like a piece of bread in a famine'!"

"Go back to the rape stats."

I flip through my mail: bills, ads, a junk catalogue for "Order Your Bermuda Shorts by Mail." (I once ordered 6 carving knifes by mail and got a crummy L.P. called "Music for 2 by Candlelight"—but no candle came with it.)

My buzzer croaks. "Sh-*she's* calling!" gasps the Gasper.

"*Glp!*" goes my throat. I press my outside line. "Pincus."

"Marsh," the dream-girl murmurs, and laughs low. "How do you feel?"

"Do I have to tell you?"

"*I'm* still on Cloud Nine." Her voice is fudge. "*Please* don't— uh—do 'that' with any of your other clients. . . . Do you miss me?"

(Why do dames always pull that? They come up from the basement dryer, or you come back from the newsstand on the corner, and the little frail lays guilt on you with: "Did you miss me?")

"Miss you?" I echo. Oh, Lord. Just her voice has me aching again. "I miss you so damn much it hurts."

"Where?"

"Everywhere. Yeah, *there*, too."

"A good man's hard to find," she teases.

"A hard man's even harder."

Her laugh is milk and honey. "You *are* spoiled!"

"Why did you leave that darling bed so early?" I ask.

"Think of my reputation, sir. I messed up the sheets in the guest room so Christina would think you'd slept there."

"Anyone has a guest room has an alibi."

"It stops rumors."

"I would hate for anyone to even think we spent the night like normal people."

"Do you know any?" she laughs.

"Not in your family. By the way, has brother Ken tried to kill old Howard yet? Has jittery Shelby stuck a kitchen shiv into Melody? Has Howard dried the bullets for his heater? Has Melody wiped out her real competition—Shelby?"

"You make it sound like a soap opera. Or *Tobacco Road.*"

"I didn't read the picture; I saw the book."

"Oh, darling, darling, you *are* crazy." A sigh flutters out of her heart in long ribbons. "I wish I'd met you years ago."

Mr. Goldberg has his head in my lap and is mooning.

"Say something to my rival," I tell her and put the phone to Isadore's ear and the pooch gives her his love-call and I hear her laugh and go: "Woof, *woof!*"

Mr. Goldberg keels over, either in ecstasy or astonishment. Go analyze a dog.

"Silky . . . you there?"

"No."

"I'm still your client, you know." Pause. Her voice changes. Tight. "Tomorrow night. The ballet benefit—the State Theater. I'd like you—and Mr. Clancy—to be there."

"Why?"

Pause. "Why? For God's *sake,* that whole cast of kooks you just described will be there!"

"So will 200 security guards, detectives, and insurance company operatives," I remind her. "From what I see in the papers, a billion bucks of Hi-Society jewels will be on parade."

"I know. Still—" Stop.

"You scared?"

"Very."

I get a chill: I can't help it.

"You'll be there?" she asks.

"We charge double for night work."

"Bless you. I'll arrive with my party around nine. I'll leave two passes at the box office. . . . Oh—it's formal. . . . You do have a black tie?"

"How wide?"

She laughs, but not much. "Must dash. . . . Thank you, my love—thank you."

Pretty soon, Mike drifts in, holding a cup of coffee, a wicked grin across his puss. "Welcome home. You must be itching for a *shmooze.*"

"Oh, brother . . . I practicly closed the Marsh file. Only our client still has the jitters, and wants you and me to work— black tie, yet. A ball."

"*She* needs dancing partners?" he mocks.

"It's snake-pit time: her family. When you hear the setup, you won't blame her."

So I tell him what's happened.

There ain't a better audience for this type tale than Michael Xavier Clancy. His eyes bug out at the heavy parts, his shoulders heave at the comic relief, he chortles and slaps his thigh and sends oodles of admiration over my wavelength. He practicly *plotzes* with laughs when I tell him about Anson Stowbridge and the dogs in the clock.

And when I'm all done—saying not 1 word about where I went after I delivered the loot to Donny Chu in Chinatown, my buddy exclaims: "I'll be a son-of-a-bitch! You get the Clancy Star-of-David Award for guts plus smart. . . . We should report the coke delivery to Narcotics, you know."

"I know. . . ." To tell the God's honest, I hadn't thought of it. "So you'll come to Lincoln Center?"

"If it's okay with Kathy. I never take night work without her permission."

"It's double pay."

"She'll give permission." He bounces out like a boy with a ticket to the World Series.

In a minute, in comes Herschel, holding out a yellow envelope and jabbering, "J-just came!"

Across the top of the envelope is printed:

FLASH!—FLASH!—FLASH MESSENGERS

"Not by mail!" Herschel hollers. "B-by messenger! *I* signed!"
"Go to the head of the class."
The envelope has my name and "c/o Watson & Holmes"
and our address. I open it and lift out a check, and a slip of
deckled stationery embossed "K. M."
The check is for $5,000.
I will not pretend my heart don't somersault.
The slip reads:

Dearest Silky:
Thank you, thank you, thank you.*

—Kim

* I mean for your professional services. There isn't enough money
to thank you for—loving me.

—K

27
LINCOLN CENTER

Lincoln Center. Lincoln Center!

I don't care how much the limp-wrist critics panned it, calling it Pop Architecture or Square Chic or an Edifice Complex. I think it's great—super—beautiful, with the big fountain splashing and the three buildings lighted up and you see all the dressed-up people moving around on different floors as living parts of the design. If my father, of blessed memory, was here he would say, *"Ai-ai-ai,* America *gonif!"* that being the greatest compliment he could give this wonderful country in a lousy world.

I tell you 1 thing: If Lincoln Center was in Paris or Rome, the same have-to-gripe-about-New York smart-asses would be chirping, "Oh, how gorgeous! How brilliant in conception! What exquisite execution!" I would not mind if you execute them.

Whenever I go to Lincoln Center (so okay, maybe once a year) I feel kind of grateful. No 3 ways about it. Art is better than *borscht,* except when you're starving. Art can make a *mensh* out of a nothing. Art is a preview of heaven.

Why am I snowing you like this? Because as I stand there in the Plaza, full of *shmaltzy* feelings, I think, "Goddammit, Sidney Pincus from Bathgate Avenue, you could of wound up in a matzoball plant, or as a cannon for the Shaughnessy mob, or even managing a porno flick on 42nd Street. And instead, look where you are! In a tux, in Lincoln Center. Like any other millionaire. Rubbing shoulders with the Rockefellers, or even Merrill Lynch Kuhn and Loew."

Show me 5 places on the map turn you on like that!

Plus, I am getting paid.

The Plaza is mobbed with customers, gawkers, reporters, photographers. Huge lights burn for the TV cameras, on account of Channel 13 covers the whole blowout.

The limousines are pulling up like it's a memorial parade, and out of each chariot comes a face you have seen like 1,000 times in the movies, or on the 7 o'clock news, or even on Johnny Carson. Lights flash all over like it's Christmas, and cheers go up from the *hoi polio* whenever they glom a famous puss—of which there is no shortage, male or female, tonight. I tell you, if your *zayde* was to swing a chicken over his head in this scene, the feathers would hit more celebrities than you can shake a stick at.

Easing my way to the inside, I spot biggies like the Mayor, who is escorting the knockout widow of a just-died TV idol. A billionaire from Texas is drooling over some *tchotchke* from a Broadway musical. The Governor of the Umpire State is making nice to a star ballerina of City Center. The greatest pitcher the Dodgers ever had (who is now doing commercials for odorless shoe-liners) is with a look-alike for Marilyn Monroe. Rock groupers with poetic names like "The Bad Breath" or "Rotting Corpses" pose for the cameras, who ignore the mere *Alrightniks* from Park Avenue and Sutton Place. More swingers and Beautiful People have flown in than showed up for the Inauguration orgy for the President of the U.S. of A.

I snatch my waiting entrance pass and take the few steps up the vast Promenade floor. I am under the gigantic white marble statue of an enormous nude Mother of Humanity—1 of a pair, with her sister at the far, far end of this glorious, 5-storey-high Grand Promenade, which is jumping with a crowd of Socialites who sure ain't Socialists. The view I get—oh, man. All the fancy gowns and dazzling sparklers and chin-to-chin yakking makes me think MGM is shooting a remake of *The Great Ziegfeld*.

There is enough jewelry on the dames—diamond rocks and

ruby chokers and platinum do-dads—to finance a Rose Bowl parade with the floats decked in pearls instead of flowers. Even the men's shirts sprout gems instead of buttons, and their cuff links did not come from Ohrbach's. In my opinion, this bash will set a new high for showing off.

With so much political clout and Society glamour and Wall Street *gelt* on display, you can be sure there is no shortage of Security. The Lincoln Center guards are in their blue uniforms with the silver chest shield and shoulder patch. I spot some Pinkertons and Burns cops and some cops moonlighting in black bows and stiff collars. They look like pall-buriers.

But this is certainly not a bash of only Middle Ages or Senior Citizens in *Who's Who.* There are plenty of young discotheque regulars, plus steady customers allowed in at Regine's or Elaine's or Shepheard's, which are snooty watering-holes for the young rich or famous. So I behold a raft of bushy beards and Wild West mustaches, escorting long-stem beauties with hair drooping down their spines like plastic waterfalls—hair so smooth it has to be ironed, I mean really flattened on an ironing board. The Girls are in costumes out of Granny's attic, whilst the Boys wear red velvet bowties and colored ruffled shirts—plus slave bracelets and even moccasins instead of patent-leather pumps. These days, no poor *kobtzen* would dare to dress as lousy as a millionaire's kid does.

I am reminded of what my *Tante* Hinda used to say: "If you have silk in the closet, you can step out in *shmattes.*" A truer idea was never spoke.

"Silky, for the love of Malone!" This is Alma Bowley, in fancy lo-cut chiffon with fluffy layers of baby-blue panels in the skirt.

"Hi, Sergeant," I say. "Never saw you in party clothes before."

A squawk box crackles. And Alma just reaches under 1 of the pretty panels and pulls out the box and says "Bowley" into the perforated circle. Then she listens. . . .

"Okay. 10–4." She puts the squawker back. "Some rich Jane is freaking out in the powder room. . . . And I thought I'd have a ball at the ball!" She says a bad word of 4 letters and heads for an aisle down the right side of the bar.

Tony Calluci, who was once my buddy in a prowl car, winks at me. "Great night for the boys, huh? What's the scuttlebutt?"

I nod him to bend his head close to me. "If God lived on earth," I whisper, "people would knock out all his windows." That's the effect Tony Calluci always has on me.

He nods wisely—to hide he don't dig philosophy. He has the personality of a shoe-horn.

I suppose the *Daily News* will report the joint "was crawling with cops"—but not 1 of the crime-suppressors I see is in anything but an upright position.

I spy Mike Clancy, who in a tux, with that build and profile, looks like the blast is in his honor. We don't need more than a quick telegraph to agree he will patrol along the high windows with the shimmering metal-bead curtains, overlooking the Fountain, and I will take the bar side opposite him, where they are doing a bonanza biz in booze, with Champagne taking the lead.

At 9:10, Kimberley enters, the queen of a party of maybe 14, all chatting, sometimes laughing it up, and I see Kenneth Marsh, who looks like a Sulka model with that great tan over a fancy white shirt and tie, and Shelby Maitland, who's like a pale penguin wearing black tails, and Howard Rodenbaker, supremely cool, who's making small talk with big ladies, some of who are fluttering *fans*, for God's sake.

I signal to Mike. He sizes them all up and hi-signs me back.

There's no doubt who our client is. How does she look? Plain and simple, she is radiant. She is poured into a shimmering silk gown; it must have cocoons underneath to make it balloon out and swing like that.

She is sprouting diamonds like they fell down on her in a sugar storm: on her head a little crown; from her ears dangle blazers; and around her peach-color throat is an iceberg fandangle belongs in Van Cleef and Arpel's main window.

The music starts—and I mean real music, not castrated tomcats howling, "Yah-yah-yah!" and "Baby!"—them being the only words the idols of the Pimple Set know. It is a waltz! Can you tie that?

So couples stream out on the dance floor—which, to be exact, ain't a dance floor on account it's the lobby, not made of wood but Italian-type marble with measles. It is a pleasure to see dancing where males and females actualy touch each other, putting arms around a partner's shoulder or waist, nuzzling cheeks and even looking each other in the eyes instead of being in a hopped-up glaze as they jerk up and down like zombies in some savage tribe's ritual to the Voodoo who is in charge of infantile paralysis.

Of course, I have to give credit to the orchestra, which is not "Ledbelly Guts and His Sump Pumpers" but the Danny Danzig Delights (*"Everyone* dances to Dapper Dan Danzig"). For this type music, the men's wing collars and flapping tails are perfect, and the women's bare shoulders gleam like at Versailles, and their gowns swish out like the flapping flags on Shea Stadium. It's the first time I see dames outside of a movie wearing white gloves wrinkled up to their elbows, which is the ultimate in snob.

Kimberley's partner, I am glad to observe, is Howard Rodenbaker, oozing the charm. His twinkly eyes and long gray hair remind you of the happy Dad you see in life-insurance ads over: "I Protected My Loved Ones!"

The Far Out generation is so disgusted by the music, it is getting swacked at the bar.

I now perceive Lieutenant Ray Thirkell, in white tie and tails! Thirkell looks like a bartender out of the Gay Nineties, but he happens to be the best *maven* on jewel-dippers in the whole Manhattan force. He has to be at a shindig like this, casing the scene for the likes of Light-Finger Fred Farrell, who they say can lift a woman's bra out of her dress without she feels anything except grateful.

"Hi, Lieutenant," I say. "Long time no steal."

Being a patsy for puns, he knows how to wince. "That's terrible, Pincus."

"You look lovely in drag."

His phiz becomes chowder. "Every goddam comic in the joint has to take a cheap shot at me just because I'm working in soup-and-fish. What do you expect at a clambake like this—Boy Scout pants?"

"They wouldn't do a thing for your legs."

Chuck-chuck. "Okay, Pincus, you've had your quota. You working for Prudential?"

"No."

"You didn't happen to spot Gluey Horkheimer here, did you?"

"That snake? He's up the river."

"He *was*. The Syndicate helped him swim free."

All this *shmoozing* must of dried up Thirkell's sinuses, because he says, "Guess I get me some Irish on the rocks."

"On *duty?*" I fake horror.

He grins like there's wolf in his blood. "You report me, sweetheart, and you get a fast call to red-ball Downtown toot sweet for violating some sneaky clause in the P.I. code."

"I never laid an eye on you, Lieutenant."

"Likewise. My feet are killing me."

I pace to and fro. There are 10–12 black couples in the throng, including a borough chief and a smasheroo no-bust dancer. A no-doubt champ golfer becomes Kimberley's partner.

Rodenbaker now drifts over to my very side, his eyes twinkling. "Doesn't Kim look marvelous tonight? You have taken a great load off her mind. . . ."

I knit my brow, to show Mr. R. that I am thinking.

He searches for her among the dancers. "She's the daughter I always wish I'd had. . . . But I wonder—" His voice trails off and out.

"You shouldn't do that, Mr. Rodenbaker."

He glances up. "I beg your pardon?"

"You shouldn't say, 'I wonder'—then clam up. 1st, it makes me wonder what you were going to say. 2nd, it makes me wonder if you clammed up deliberately—to bait me into asking you what you were going to say. . . . Okay, I'll bite. What were you going to wonder?"

Those clear gray eyes show the admiration my remarks deserve. Chalk it up to Mark Twain: "If you tell the truth, you will please some people and astonish all the rest."

Mr. R. says, "I just wondered when Kimberley will marry Shelby Maitland. . . . They're engaged, you know."

The only effect this has on my tough, case-hardened heart is that a cleaver splits it in 2.

Off goes Rodenbaker, smiling. Foxy grampa is a lousy fink. I manage to detour the Brillo in my throat.

I hear Danny Danzig's clarinet swing into "Tea for Two," which is par for afternoon "dansants" at the Pierre, or Arbor Day in the Rainbow Room. Some jivey boys hold their noses.

Then—I hear Her voice. "May I have this dance?"

Man, if she isn't standing right in front of me, light splashing down her whipped-cream shoulders.

"I'm suppose to be working," I say.

"For me." She raises her arms, smiling.

I slip my right hand around her waist and take her right hand in my left, trying to stop my goddam trembling about what Rodenbaker told me; and with the masterful authority I learned at Harvest Moon balls, plus my natural grace, I glide her into the rhythm. It don't take 3 bars before she asks, *"Where* did you learn to dance?"

"Private tutors." I guide her a half-turn away and a half-turn back in a 1-2, 1-2. "The secret of the masters, Miss Marsh, is this." I press my right hand into the small of her back and bring her up against me. "Notice *this.*" I put the heel of my hand on her lumbar and pivot her away from me. "That right hand is the steering wheel, and 90 percent of all the guys on dance floors throughout the U.S.A. don't ever learn it."

I never met any female who was not astonished to have this secret of the ballroom revealed to them. Kimberley would of been astonished, except some jock from a water polo team slams hisself plus partner into us.

"Oh, sorry," he apologizes.

"Ken!"

It's Golden Boy, all right. He gives me a sarcastic wink. "Ah, the messenger from Chinatown."

"I only deliver pork and flied lice." I slip him a shaft: "How's your foot?"

"He does limp a bit," says his partner, who he has not had the good manners to introduce me. "A brick fell on his toes."

"You ought to see Dr. Scholl," I offer.

Suddenly, Dan Danzig's Delights are taking a stand-up bow and everyone claps politely.

"Where is Melody?" Kim asks her brother.

The answer comes from the M.C. through the loudspeakers: "And *now*, ladies and gentlemen, direct from Trinidad for this special occasion, the famous Calypso Band—featuring that *marvelous* singer, Miss Melody Na*varre!*"

Onto the stage, which has huge velvet columns for a backdrop, file like 10 cheerful black musicians from the faroff isle I have come to hate.

Two drumsticks hit the steel top of a sawed-off drum of oil, with little circles bent into the top in an arc, so the sound is like a throbbing xylophone. And a trumpet blares, and a bass fiddle "*bup-bup-bups*" from plucked strings, and the Caribbean Smilers shake the big chandeliers with an explosion of noise and beat, and the floor changes from dancing to epilepsy. Couples separate like their partners have leprosy, never touching as they do solo jumps and jives, hair and arms flying in all directions like they just been freed from straitjackets.

The young boys and girls at the bar stop pouring booze into theirselves and with bloodthirsty cries of "Ya-ya-ya!" invade the dance zone. Now I could be observing 100 witch-doctors celebrating their queen's pregnancy. They shoot arms and hands around in those throes of whatever disease they have in the Congo instead of St. Vitus. I tell you, it is mass lunacy that turns on these characters, plus the scat cries of "Yah-yah!" and "Wa-hoo bongalooga!" or something equally *meshuggah* almost drowns out the banging drums, the steel barrel-top xylophone and the deep bass fiddle and the frenzied brass. The men in the band's faces are shining with sweat, but the dancers merely look like they are having orgasms.

Kim is doing the Hustle, so I have to jerk around, too.

"Let it all hang out!" some punk advises me.

"My zipper's stuck," I reply.

Kim laughs. "I wish I had a picture of you."

Then the Calypso ends and the lights dim down, and a spot hits the microphone—where Melody Navarre has appeared out of the thin air (and God knows she is anything but thin). The gorgeous Chee-chee is dressed—well, let's say I doubt if there's anything between her costume and her amber flesh. She ain't naked, but looks it. Between her big black eyes and nipples you could mistake her for the 4 of spades.

But can that Tootsie Roll *sing!* "Island in the sun . . ." Her contralto rolls the words out in honey, of which I can't understand much, but it is not vocabulary that hypnotizes the mob, but that mellow, fruity voice. If Melody Navarre *shtups* like she sings, Kenneth and Howard have their selfs the best lay in the animal kingdom.

I can't hold it any longer. "What the hell gives with you and Maitland?"

"Oh-oh," Kim winces. She comes in close, her hair brushing my cheek, her own smell better than Channel No. 5. "Don't be cross with me."

"Why didn't you tell me—you're going to marry him?"

She stops dead in our tracks. *"Who* told you that?"

"Rodenbaker."

"Oh, gawd. Howard. He can be so *mean!"*

"What kind of cop-out is that?"

"It's not a cop-out."

"Then what the hell is it?"

"Bubble gum! I was just playing cute."

It's Guess What? time again, but I won't play. She can see I'm boiling.

"Oh, don't sulk," she says. "At my place, before we came here, in front of Shelby and Howard and everyone, Kenneth began teasing us, and he asked me, 'Why don't you marry Shelby?' Shelby went blue and stammered; and I laughed, 'He's never asked me.' So Kenneth leers, 'Okay, Shel, ask her. Go on. Now.' Shelby looks so flabbergasted, so *hurt*, by Kenny, that to spare the poor slave, *I* say, 'Marry you? How *sweet* of you to ask. . . . Darling, I'll think it over.' But Kenneth says, 'Hooray!' and Howard pats Shelby on the back, saying, 'Congratulations! Consider yourself engaged!' So the others applaud. . . . Just because I put on poor, mixed-up Shelby."

"The strain of your kidding"—I acid—"plus your happy pills could land you in Payne Whitney, which is not a florist but a clinic for what is politely called 'the emotionaly disturbed.' " The bitter stuff spills out of me. "I have to give Maitland 1 point: He's your social type."

"You're jealous."

"Jealous? My Cousin Sooky used to say, 'Love without jealousy ain't love.' "

She gives me the Mona Lisa smile. "I'm *not* engaged to him. . . . Do you love me?" she whispers.

"Oh, my aching back."

"Do you think I'm crazy?"

"Only on weekdays and weekends."

"Well," she pressed against me, "I might be crazy enough to marry *you.*"

Moishe Rebbaynu! She is dishing out chills and fever in the same breath. ". . . marry you." I go as hot and cold as an ice-pack in a sauna. My heart is pumping buckets.

God knows what I would of said if not for what happened. Only God could have timed it that way. And I tell you 1 thing: I'll never forgive Him.

28
MURDER, MURDER!

It happened so fast, it happened so unexpected, it exploded in such an uproar of drum bangs that it blew everyone's fuses. I mean the fuses that keep our eyes, ears, nose, brain working to constantly tell us where we are, who is where, what is how much, how much is too much, take it easy, run for your life, don't get excited, jump, run, dive, escape! But when something pops to make all your senses holler, *What the hell is going on, oh God, I can't understand a goddam thing!* that's when your control system blows all its fuses.

When this type crisis explodes, some people black out; and some run around in circles like raving lunatics; and some start screaming—just screaming and screaming; and some holler *"Gevald! Gevald!"* in whatever language their mothers used when they hollered *"Gevald! Gevald!"*

What let all Hell loose in the packed Promenade was—a scream. A high, shrill, long, shrieking woman's scream. Nothing I ever heard is more terrible than a high, shrill, long, shrieking woman's scream. This 1 electrified the dancing crowd—I mean it like electrocuted everyone on the floor, the way it paralyzed all motion and turned everyone to stone for a split-second, and the orchestra's music stopped like a blown L.P.

Then the mental currents switched back on, and at once people began hollering and gibbering, and some women gave out screams of their own to show how much more sensitive they are than others.

I grab Kim, in a reflex, and turn her away, wrapping my arms tight around her and bending her head down, and I curse.

I am more mad than scared. I am a veteran observer of hysterics, coming from the Bronx where the mothers held daily competitions in demonstrating pain or surprise with *"Ooooooy!"* and *"Gevaaald!"* and even their bodies fainting.

In the back of my head is a preview of the panic that seizes people when some *kochleffel* hollers, "Fire! Fire!" The day President Kennedy was killed, you could hear the screams race the lenth of Tremont Avenue, and female bodies were dropping like flies on the Lower East Side, and on upper Broadway many a man turned green and sank down on a bench without a word, before they cried.

Then I see (but Kim don't) what started the panic: a terrible, horrible sight: Melody Navarre. Her eyes burn white in the spotlight, rolled towards heaven, as blood pours out of her open, astonished mouth. *She has been shot!* Blown open. The mike stand hits the rail of the stage, but Melody falls over both in a gushing red lump and crashes to the floor with an awful thud—loud, flat, heavy—like a bag of cement hitting the marble.

This, most of the whole goddam throng sees—and pandemonium don't begin to describe what follows. The musicians stampede—yammering, knocking over chairs and music stands, and their instruments fly around like Frisbees. On the floor, ladies scream, and some throw up, and others keel over. I see a body hit Mike, and he goes down. The Promenade is a howling mob of zombies. Bodies stumbling over bodies. Men go as white and delirious as the females, fighting to escape what's unknown.

Kim is whimpering, bewildered, and I push her down, down, very low down, and I bend over her so my head is over hers and my back will protect her—and I will take a next shot, which could damn well be aimed at her. Or me. . . .

I hear another shot—*this time not drowned by drums!* . . . Panic, bedlam, madness.

I smash through the milling mob—dragging her, sobbing, crying—to the safest place I can think of—away, just away,

away, down a side aisle and past a stream of crazy broads pouring out of the LADIES, screaming like they're in a Monster
from Outer Space film.

I lift Kim up in my arms, to move faster, and like a little
girl drowning she throws her arms around my neck in a hammerlock, her eyes glazing like she is going under, and froth
starts bubbling on her bloodless lips.

I push open a big door. She is babbling, "Oh, God . . . don't
. . . let them kill me!"

I hurl myself through with her—and we are inside the big
dark auditorium.

Her lips are pressed on mine like it's her last conscious moment on earth, and in the passion of terror she moans: "Help
me, oh, I love you, please, *save* me!" then rivets her mouth
to mine, weeping, like we will die like that together. . . .

29
THE MOUSE IN THE DARK

I am soaking wet, and breathing so hard my chest hurts—things I notice only while my eyes are taking time to pierce the darkness, which turns out not to be pitch dark but dim, on account of the EXIT lights over many doors cast a reddish tint over rows and rows of empty seats, and the bare stage glows, strange, a greenish dimness from some light in the wings.

"It's all right," I whisper. "It's all over. Breathe deep . . . deep . . . easy . . ."

I carry her to a seat and gently lower her.

She is in a trance: "Don't—leave—me."

"Sure, doll. You know I follow orders."

"Oh, Silky . . ." Her arms leave my neck as she sinks into the seat, and as it slides forward she stretches out, limp.

"Good girl . . ." I kneel down next to her and take her face between my hands. "I always did want to take you to the theater."

I still hear the distant shouting and *tummel*, muffled by the doors, and I wonder how the hell I can tell her—what? . . . Melody is a goner. Who snuffed her? . . . Rodenbaker? Kenneth? Maitland? A maniac? . . . Maybe Mike is on top of it. . . . Mike? Holy mackerel, that lobby is swarming with guards and plainclothes men and insurance eyes—and I can't believe *no*body will nail the—

A mouse squeaks. A *mouse?!*

A sliver of light from outside slices the semidarkness—for a brief moment, and goes out. Mouse, hell! That squeak was a hinge. A door hinge. Someone has come in. . . .

Soft, quick footsteps pad down the aisle at the opposite side of the auditorium. It has to be the opposite end, because this place has no center aisle. My skin crawls.

I slide down deeper, taking Kim deeper down, too. I start to shush her, but I hear her breathing different. Her chin is on her collarbone. She has funked out.

I strain my ears to hear and my eyes to see, and I'll be damned if I don't hear a soft, sinister "Psst! Psst!"

Oh, Godalmighty. Whoever snuck in is trying to trick me into revealing where we are.

The foot-pads stop. "Psst! Psst!"

Under my shoe, I feel slick paper. I never was more quiet as I use my heel to slide the paper back, on the rug, towards me. I sink down to get it. It's a program.

I hear the soft padding quicken, and under the reddish glow of an EXIT sign I see a form. A human form, all right—plus a long thin stick or pole or—a *what?*

The form stops. Its head is scanning the seats. And lowering the pole to horizontal. Christ, that has to be a rifle! . . . A *rifle?* Who the hell could sneak a rifle past that carload of guards and cops? . . . And what the hell can I do now? . . . I just have to *con*—yes! It might work.

I roll up the program and get down on my knees and crawl out into the aisle, down the soft rug towards the stage, away from Kimberley. The main point is to *get away from her,* so if there's any shooting it should be at me, by whatever diversion I can create, but away from her—because that form shot Melody and now is gunning for—

A whisper wafts across that eerie scene. "Pincus? . . ."

Oh, God. The killer is gunning for *me!*

I freeze. My brain is pumping faster than my heart. Sweat comes down my brow so thick I have to wipe it off with my sleeve to keep my eyes from getting flooded.

Pad-pad, fast. Stop. "Psst . . . psst . . ."

I untie my black bow and wrap it around the ballet program, very tight, and tie a knot, hard. *The missile must not loosen up.* That would let its pages flutter, and that would foul up its flight path, and if that happens, even God will be too late.

I turn my back, so the swing of my arm won't show above the row of seats, and I make a quick prayer, then I really hurl the tube—way across, to the back of the hall, and when it plops, the dark form whirls around and runs up the far aisle with the rifle aimed to the back—which is when I break for the steps to the stage.

The form is hunting for where I, in the form of the program, am suppose to be hiding, and by now I have crawled up the stairs to the stage and I dive into the wing. The loud sound of my fall makes me curse.

I hear those damn feet padding down their aisle to the other side of the stage. I crouch. I can't see into the theater. Can the form see me?

I rush squints around the greenish softness. Migod, if I only had a gun. My ankle piece—god*dam*mit!—that's in my bedroom drawer.

I see a high vertical bank of unlit light bulbs—covered by plastic discs of red, yellow, blue. And next to the bank, a ladder. . . . Think fast, Pincus, fast. The goddam rifle—

I snap off 2 colored discs and unscrew the bulbs beneath them. The animal in the aisle is grunting closer.

I throw a disc out with all my strength, like it's a Frisbee, and it hums as it sails away and hits the balcony and makes a hell of a clatter. The foot-pads whirl in a circle—then the whole theater cracks lightning and *"Bang!"* the rifle explodes.

At once, I throw a Mazda bulb to my right, and it smashes *"Pop!,"* as the glass shatters.

I now hear the unmistakable *"Clack-clack"* of a pump-action repeater, and another crack and *"Bang!"* echoes all around the auditorium—

"Silkeeee!" comes Kim's scream.

I throw the 2nd bulb, to my left, and it explodes, but the gunner ignores it!

Damn! He must realize he has been suckered—wasted 2 shots—and this is no dummy: He must be trying to figure out where the *pitcher* is, and to hell with where the flying kid-stuff lands.

I skim another disc, and another, and hear them sail and smash. But no gun shots. . . . I desperately scout the light bank and (Oh, God, thank you, thank you!) I see in the back shadows—a switch box. I yank off one of my shoes, then snap down a couple of switches. Like a miracle, all the colored lights blaze on, like a Christmas tree, with me behind the waterfall of red and blue and white and yellow, and I slam my patent-leather shoe right down the whole bank of lights, knocking out bulb after bulb. The panel short-circuits, and sparks fly and smoke erupts—and as the gunner is coming up the far steps I go up that ladder like a hopped-up monkey on 1 of them toys where you squeeze the wooden sides and the monkey jerks up, up, up.

The killer pumps the repeater again. The bullet hits a tin gong. I see the dark form crouch, then stalk.

I grab my ball-point pen out of my inside pocket and toss it below, and the gunner shoots at the sound, and pumps *"Clack-clack!"* and now the shooting form scoots in for the kill he's sure is up there on the ladder.

I desperately yank off 1 of my cuff links, right out of my cuff, and throw it hard down behind the hunched-up hyena. And as, in uncontrolled reflex, he wheels around and away, like I prayed he would, I dive off the ladder, feet down.

My shoe and stockinged foot hit a body in the back, on the spine, and there is a godawful scream and the rifle goes off. I hear a gurgling cry from back where Kim is. The rifle has blown out of the gunner's hold and is sliding across the wooden floor of the stage.

I smash a karate chop on the back of the animal's neck, and again, and another, but that body is super-charged with a fury greater than pain, and it turns under me, rolling me off, and I feel hammers beating into my face and head. I scramble and ram my elbow into the bastard's throat. The Adam's apple splats into sponge.

Suddenly, bedlam: Shouts and turmoil, and shafts of light pour into the whole place from the back and the sides as doors are pulled open everywhere by Security guards and cops and plainclothes heroes who have finally cleared the wax out of their ears and heard the shots and storm in.

I do not smash down on the throat of the killer again: I am paralyzed by the face I behold. Anson Stowbridge.

30
IN THE AISLE

The hubbub is fierce now on the stage. But I am not there.

I am holding Kimberley in my arms, in that accursed aisle, my shirt soaking up blood from the hole in her that Stowbridge's last wild shot had made.

She is ghastly pale and her breathing is shallow. But she half-opens her eyes, and I swear on whatever is holy that she tried to smile as she murmured, "You—took such—good care—of me."

I kissed her, and kissed her, and said things I don't remember.

"How could I—not love you?" she whispers.

And I am conscious that Mike is standing over us. He clears his throat. "A doctor's coming, miss. Hang in there."

I just rock her head, back and forth, like she's a little girl and I'm putting her to sleep.

I feel drops splash on my cheeks. But they are not my tears. They are Mike's.

31
Q. & A.: DOWNTOWN

Lieutenant Perrett put his questions to me Downtown. There were 2 other men from Homicide in the old office, plus a stenotypist.

I told Perrett that Stowbridge must of gone off his rocker when he found out that Melody, his wife, who he was crazy about, was in New York, shacking up with Kenneth Marsh, and they had been making it together 100 times back home, right under his nose.

"From the way the Ballistic boys measured out the angles of the shots," said Perrett, "Stowbridge was behind the big velvet curtains, behind the band, and he fired between the folds when he drilled Melody Navarre in the back of the head."

"He was a helluva marksman." That is "Handsome Jack" Lomax. "I mean, to nail Kenneth Marsh, too. In that madhouse."

"But the shot from the stage—I mean in the auditorium—the shot that hit Miss Kimberley Marsh, that was a wildie, from the repeater, sliding across the wood floor," says Perrett.

"The bullet bounced off the metal of a seat," says the 3rd guy, whose name is Farrow.

Moths are beating dust inside my head, and my stomach is a hollow cave. My legs have as much strenth as a string of fettucini. "Is Marsh hurt bad?" I ask.

Perrett says, "He's dead." He rolls his cigar around his kisser. "But the hospital says *she's* holding her own."

I nod.

"She comes to, Silky, every so often . . . ." says Farrow.

"I know."

Handsome Jack scowls, "How the *hell* did Stowbridge sneak a long rifle past all the goddam Security? Believe me, it was tighter than a pig's ass."

I sigh. "Why don't you ask him?"

"We done that," says Farrow. "But he can't converse, the way you bust his gullet."

"Migod, Pincus, what did you use: a hammer?"

I ask, "Is he booked?"

"For 2 homicides."

"His voice will clear up in court," I say, "when he no doubt pleads he had an unhappy childhood. . . . What type firearm was it?"

"Don't you know?"

"I never got a look at it."

"It was a .22 caliber long-rifle, pump action, mounted with an eight-power scope. It held 10 cartridges. 6 were fired."

"Winchester?"

"Nope. An English job. . . . But how did he get it past all the guards and shooflys and insurance snoopers?"

I ask, "You still don't know?"

"We have some ideas. The usuals."

"Too bad."

"Don't you even want to hear them?" asks Lomax, hurt.

I rub my screaming temples. "I'm on pins and needles. . . ."

"Well, it's possible he snuck the rifle into the premises a day or two ago. Or, an accomplice did." That's Lomax.

"Or another angle," says Farrow, "is Stowbridge drops a line-and-hook out of a window, and his accomplice puts the hook through the trigger-guard of the rifle, which the assailant then hauled up hand over hand. . . ."

"How do those M.O.'s grab you?" asks Perrett.

"If my Aunt Sadie had wheels," I say, "she could of been a bus."

"Ha, ha, ha. Very funny." But the way Handsome Jack says it, he would like to bite off my ear.

"You don't buy any of them, do you?" asks Perrett. He offers me a stogy.

I groan. To me, it's like the 3 Stooges are trying to nail farina on a wall. . . . I can't blot out the memory of her in my arms, pouring blood. Or the way she looked in the hospital . . .

"Silky!" frowns Perrett. "Why don't you answer?"

"I'll answer. A deaf man once heard a mute describe how a blind man saw a pickle turn into a piccolo."

"Lay off, f'Chrissake!" Lomax has his pride up. "You think you're so goddam smart, okay, how do you figure it?"

"Was the rifle all in 1 piece?" I ask. "I mean, could the stock detach, so he might of concealed the 2 parts—like under his coat?"

"No, genius. That's the first angle we checked out! Strike one."

"How long is the weapon?"

"About 40 inches," says Farrow.

"Oh."

"Go on, *shamus*. Any more smart ideas?"

I scrutinize the stogy. I never felt so washed out in my life. "I thought about it—over and over—all night. At the hospital." My heart stops at that word.

"So you came up with a goodie?" That's Lomax.

"Yeah . . . I figure it has to be something like this: That was an all-black band, making the joint jump. Stowbridge came in with them, easy, through the artists' entrance."

"Carrying a 40-inch rifle?!" That's Farrow, goggling.

"In an instrument case . . ."

"I'll be god*dammed!*"

Gawks. Gulps. A growl.

"Maybe in a cello box. Or a bull fiddle."

Perrett says, "You can give us aces and spades. . . . No pun." They all laugh, but weak.

"So now, why was Mr. Stowbridge trying to kill you?" asks Lomax.

"I put him on a stretcher."

"Sure," said Farrow. "We know. But why did you sap him?"

"He came to my office and tried to blow my brains out."

"Sure, sure, but what made him do that?"

I asked for a glass of water, and they gave me a paper cup.

Lomax, grinning: "You weren't laying the chocolate bimbo too, were you?"

The look I gave him must of triggered an angina attack.

"For the record," said Perrett smoothly, "put it in words."

"Don't be *shmucks:* Those are the words . . . I never laid her."

"So what was his motive? To ice you."

I took a long drink, trying to decide what to say and what to hide, and I decide—hell, I don't owe Rodenbaker or Shelby a goddam thing. But my stomach flipped when I thought of Donny Chu. So I told them, "Marsh dropped a lot of dough gambling at the Casino in Port-of-Spain. Then he ran up a bundle of markers—and skipped. No one could find him. So the Chu family asks Donald Chang Chu to put a tail on—Miss Marsh. They figured her brother had to show, sooner or later, in New York. The tail was Stowbridge, flown in, on account of he knew what Marsh looked like. . . . She 'made' him, and was scared stiff, and hired me to tag him. Which I did. He was so flummoxed he lost his marbles and sapped me. . . . So Donny Chu yanked him off the job, plus a ticket back to Trinidad, and Stowbridge was so furious he came to my office that night with a .38 silencer, to get even. . . . I would of had it for good, but my ferocious dog attacked him, and I got an arm around his throat and slugged him with his own piece. I called an ambulance. . . . And before you ask me what I done with the .38—it's in my desk."

"Why didn't you turn it in?"

"You can't remember everything . . ."

The masterminds nod at each other.

I say, "So if this Q. & A. is over—"

"Almost," says Perrett. "How big were Marsh's markers?"

"Half a million."

Someone whistled.

"And did Marsh pay off?" asks Perrett, nice and easy.

"Yeah."

"Where?"

"In the Rodenbaker house."

"How?"

"In big bills."

"That's not what I mean, Pincus. You know damn *well* that's not what I mean! Where did he get that kind of money?"

My skin tightens. "I didn't actualy see the turnover to Marsh." (That was true, as the lettuce never did get into Kenneth's mitt.)

"Did you see the money?" asks Lomax.

"I carried it to Donny Chu. . . . Hell, it was just to pay off Marsh's debt."

Perrett makes a moue. "Where did you take the dough?"

"A movie house in Chinatown. The Yellow Dragon. In the projection room." I look at my watch. "I'd like to get to the hospital."

"We've got a couple of men guarding her door," says Lomax. "They call in . . ."

"Did Rodenbaker put up the ransom for Marsh?" asks Farrow.

"No."

"Did—Miss Marsh?"

"No."

"So back up. Who gave who half a million bucks?"

"Oh, *that.*" I couldn't hold the law off longer—and why the hell should I? Marsh was dead. Melody was dead. "Marsh brought a load of cocaine into N.Y. He sold it to a dealer."

"Do you know who?"

"They called him 'Doc.' " I described him. "And this character hopped into a Mercedes-Benz where, in the back, was . . ." I described the fancy Dan in the Chesterfield. "No, I couldn't see the license."

Perrett is smiling broadly. "The Narcotics files ought to give us a good worksheet. Silky, you done a helluva job!"

"Thanks . . . now can I—"

The phone rang. Lieutenant Perrett lifted the talk part. "Homicide. Perrett." He listened. He gave me a quick look. "Okay." He put the talker down. "Look," he says to me, "I—uh—Mother of God, I *hate* to tell you—"

He didn't have to.

32
KADDISH

I didn't attend the services. They were at St. Bartholomew's. Her brother had been buried the day before.

But I went to the cemetery in Connecticut, near Sharon, where she was born.

Mike drove. I sat in the back with Kathy, who was all in black. She was beading her rosary and whispering Latin words I didn't understand, and every so often she reached over and squeezed my hand.

I don't think 10 words were spoken between us all the way to the burial ground. I was wearing dark glasses.

There must of been 500 people at the grave, and some of the mourners had faces you seen on the Society pages lots of times, and some of their names were like Stuyvesant and Aldrich and Havighurst.

The minister was in purple and white lace. We were too far back to hear what he said, and I didn't want to get closer.

Kathy held 1 of my arms and Mike the other.

We stood under a big tree until it was all over, and we stood there while all the black limousines drove slowly away. I caught a glimpse of Rodenbaker, but he didn't see me. He looked like oatmeal. I didn't see Shelby Maitland, and I was glad of that.

Workmen began shoveling dirt into the open hole . . .

A beat-up Chevy pulled up and out of it got Herschel and Mr. Goldberg.

After a while, pretty long, I went over to her grave, passing many fancy marble monuments with "Marsh . . . Ardway . . .

Livingston . . . Marsh . . ." chiseled in them.

I stood before the fresh mound and I looked down at the flowers and earth under which Kimberley lay. I made myself think she was sleeping. I could see right through the earth and coffin, I thought, because I could see that golden face and honey hair as clear as the first time I saw her, and especially the time I watched her, sleeping next to me, in the bed where we found heaven.

"Uncle Silky," Herschel whispers, "you want I should—?"

"Sure, Hersch. Say *Kaddish.*"

So I put on my hat, and Mike put on his, and dear sweet Kathy covered her hair with a black kerchief.

Herschel took a black *yarmulka* out of 1 pocket and patted it down on his red hair (red, the blood of life; black, death) and out of his other pocket Hersch pulled a worn prayerbook. And before he found the place, Isadore Goldberg began to cry.

"Oh, *hinteleh,*" I said. "Oh, my poor little dog."

The pooch put his head on the grave and then stretched out and whimpered and then he was quiet.

"*Yisgadal v'yiskadash,*" began Herschel.

And Kathy began the Rosary.

THE END

GLOSSARY

(for words I used that are from Yiddish—or the "street-talk" of Manhattan, Broadway, the Bronx, Brooklyn and like that)
by

Sidney ("Silky") Pincus

Alrightnik: A person who has made a lot of dough, so has done "all right"—but the "-nik" is a signal: They are show-offs! Maybe not even college graduates. So you can wish you had their money (after all, you're only human), but you should never admire the way they advertise it.

"Arunter fun bet, hinteleh": "Get off the bed, dear little dog."

bonditt: (Pronounce it "bon-*ditt*") Bandit. But this dandy word is used in a warm way to mean not a real crook, but a delightful type scoundrel, a sharpshooter with a twinkle in his eye, like in "Oh, you devil!" or "He's a clever cookie!" Like Clark Gable or Burt Reynolds.

bonditten: More than 1 of the above. The Marx Bros. were *bonditten.*

boychik: The "Yinglish" for a little boy—but you use it to greet any male you like. Also, a "boychik" is a smart operator plus a bit of a *gonif* (which I will explain in a minute).

boychikel: An even younger guy than above—or 1 who you're fonder of.

bubeleh: (Pronounce it to rhyme with "bookeleh"; don't never, never pronounce it to rhyme with "mood-eleh"—you'll see why in a minute.) *Bubeleh* actually means "Little Grandma," but more often it's used as a very warm way of addressing a kid or a friend, your wife or your husband. Sex has nothing to do with it. Or age. *Bubeleh* is a neat "in" word with the movie and Broadway crowd; also, you hear it tossed around a lot on "talk shows" on TV. Like, "Where have you been, *bubeleh?"* (If you ask me, *bubeleh* could put "darling," "baby" and "honey" out of business.)

bubie: The diminutive and even more affectionate form of *bubeleh;* pronounce it to rhyme with "bookie"—not ever, ever as "b*oo*bie." "Boobies" are breast-works; *bubies* are pals. ("Boobie" is also a dum-dum.)

"Bupkes!": Nuts! Actualy, *bupkes* (or *bubkes)* means "beans," but is used about anything that's not worth a bean—and in this case *I* am blurting it like "Baloney!" or "Peanuts!," to dismiss an idea with heartfelt disgust.

chutzpah: At this date you need *chutzpah* explained?! Man. This word is practicly part of English. It means the absolute top in nerve, gall, "guts" plus brazen brazenness. The mugger who hollers, "Help! Help!" while beating *you* up— that bastard has *chutzpah.*

cockamamy: Life would be pretty blah without this word, which I love; *cockamamy* means absurd, mixed up, ridiculous, fake, foolish, too complex. Sure I know those are a helluva lot of different meanings for 1 word, but, believe me, *cockamamy* is exactly that type word: and a real doll for description.

"Er vet zein besser bahld": "He'll be okay soon."

"Gai in drerd!": "Go to hell!" "Drop dead!" Literaly, this phrase means "Go into the earth," but what type cockamamy curse is that??

Galitzianer: A Jewish person who comes from Galicia, which is a part of Austria but used to be a part of Poland. The geography ain't important: When you call someone a "Galitzianer" you're hinting he's a sharp customer and not up to *your* ancestors. Galitzianers say the same thing about Litvaks (which you'll come to in a minute) or "Poylishers"—who are from Poland. I guess Jews can be just as stuck-up as Cabots or Lodges; and they even have an advantage: longer noses.

"Gevald!": A cry of amazement, a cry for help, a desperate protest; also like "Ye gods!" in Old English. My Uncle Fischel used to say, "We come into this life with an *'Oy!'* and go out of it with a *'Gevald!'* " He was a real philosofer.

gonif: A thief; a crook; but when *gonif* is said fondly, it means a clever or mischievous type character. Jewish immigrants expressed their admiration for American inventiveness by chuckling, "America *gonif!*" My father would laugh "America *gonif!*" maybe 10 times a week.

"Gottenyu!": An exclamation of dismay, like "Oh, dear God!" or "Oh, Lord, help me out of this deal."

gurnisht: I call the phony doctor "Gurnisht" because *gurnisht* means "nothing." He *was* a nothing.

halvah: For *halvah* you need an explanation?! It's found in any big delicatessen, or in Turkish or Armenian groceries. *Halvah* is a very sweet, sticky, flaky mixture of honey and sesame seeds—a dessert (or *nosh*) for children or adults with a sweet tooth, which I am and also have.

holdupnik: Just what it sounds like: A guy who goes around holding up people. I don't mean he holds them vertical; I mean he robs them; a rip-off dude.

Hotzeplotz: A name for "God only knows where!" or "Way to Hell and gone"—like Americans say, "All the way to nowhere." I hear there actualy was a village called Hotzeplotz, but with that kind of name you have to expect funnies. (That's also true of Shnippishok.)

hutzed up or *hitzed up:* Heated up, excited, "hot and bothered."

Kaddish: The prayer for the dead; also a prayer glorifying God's name. (Never joke about this.)

kasha: buckwheat, porridge, groats—or a mix-up, a tough question.

keppeleh: Little head; an affectionate way of saying "head" or "brains."

khallish: (All words beginning with *kh* should be pronounced like you have a fish bone stuck in your mouth and are trying to *khhhhhh* it out.) To *khallish* is to faint.

khaloshes or *khalooshes:* Something disgusting, nausheating, plus revolting.

kibitz: Don't tell me you don't know what a *kibitzer* is?! Well, what a *kibitzer* does is *kibitz*—needle, tease, second-guess, wisecrack, waste time in endless comments.

kishkas: Intestines; also used for a stuffed goodie called "derma."

klutz: A clumsy dope; someone who could use a varnish job of grace or tact, like my nephew Herschel Tabachnik.

k'nock: (Pronounce it "k-nock" and not "knock.") A blow (not a knock on the door).

k'nocker: Altho you could think a *k'nocker* is someone who knocks, this is *not* the meaning of *k'nocker.* A *k'nocker* is a big shot, a success—but 1 who knows it and acts in a boastful, conceited way; a show-off; a fancy Dan. When Mike Clancy calls me a *k'nocker* he is being sarcastic; what he means is, "Don't try and be a hero, pal."

kobtzen: A poor man; but the word is also used to show scorn— for someone you think is stingy, chintzy, or who will never amount to anything.

kochleffel: Literaly, *kochleffel* means a spoon used for cooking, the long wooden spoon used for stirring a pot; but the word is used to describe a hot-shot, a live wire, a busybody, a go-getter, a *buttinski* (a type person who butts in other people's business), a type who stirs up things, even a gossip or tale-spreader or troublemaker. Many a *yenta* (you'll find *yenta* below) is a *kochleffel.*

kotchke: Duck. I mean the duck you eat, not the fast move you make when someone throws a punch at you.

krechtz: This rhymes with "Brekhts"; it means to grunt-groan-wheeze—in pain or in complaint; a gripe, or to gripe. Old folks *krechtz* a lot; so do *shlemiels.*

kreplach: Dumplings that contain meat or cheese, usualy served in soup; Jewish ravioli.

"Kum avek fun ihr": "Come away from her." *"Kum"* is pro-

nounced to rhyme not with "bum" but with "room."

"Kum doo": (Rhyme it with "Room 2.") "Come here."

"Kum mit mir": "Come with me."

Kuni Lemmel: A simple type, a dummy, a guy who you can con out of his jock-strap.

"Laig zich!": "Lay down!" (*Sure* I know you're suppose to say "Lie down" not "Lay down"—but remember, I was giving an order to my dog. Dogs don't know from grammar.)

latkes: Pancakes, usualy potato pancakes (which when they are golden brown and very crisp are something else again).

L'chayim: (For God's sake, do *not* pronounce *"L'chayim"* like in "chain"; the *ch* has to be like the sound you make when you're trying to clear bread crumbs from your throat, or have a fish bone stuck in the roof of your mouth.) *L'chayim* is the most common Jewish toast, made when you raise your glass of wine (or booze); the phrase means "To life!," which is a helluva lot more poetic than "Here's mud in your eye!" (a dopey thing to offer) and a lot more eloquent than "Cheers." (Cheers for *who?* The distiller?)

Litvak: A Jew from Lithuania is what this word means—on the surface; actualy, it's a way of describing someone very, very shrewd, very clever, or a skeptical type. "He's as smart as a Litvak" is praise; but "What can you expect from such a Litvak?" sure ain't.

makkes: Nothing. I mean that's what *makkes* means—nothing, meaning,"I'll (or you'll) get nothing." The word comes from Hebrew, meaning "plagues" or "boils" or "curses." *"Makkes!"* is also an expression of disappointment, like "Damn!" or "Oh, hell!"

maven: An expert. There's a store near where I'm sweating over these very words called "The Bagel Maven." *Maven,* like *kibitz* or *chutzpah,* has really gone over big in English.

"Mazel tov!": Altho this phrase actualy means "Good luck," it is *used* to mean "Congratulations!" or "Thank God!" or even "Hurray, hurray!" Don't never say *"Mazel tov!"* to someone going into a hospital; say it when they come home. This phrase is heard so often at a wedding, party,

b'ris (circumcision), it sounds like someone's shooting B.B.'s at a tin roof.

megillah: A very long report or a long, boring story.

mensh: The best thing you can say about a person is, "Now there is a *mensh!*" *Mensh* means a human being—not an animal—but it is also used to praise the decent, responsible, upright, honorable. "Be a *mensh!*" a parent tells a child. (If both are Jewish.) That's what *I* say to you, too.

meshpoche: (Pronounce it *mesh-PAW-kheh.*) Your whole family, as far as you can stretch it: parents, children, brothers and sisters, grandparents, uncles, aunts, cousins, second cousins, once-removeders, *their* kids and *et cetera,* and it sometimes looks like they will never stop asking you for a favor. But I guess that's what a family is for.

meshuggah: Crazy, nuts, senseless. People who act *meshuggah* go in for *mishegoss* (insanity).

mezuzah: A small, oblong container—about the size of 2 king-size cigarettes—that is attached to the jamb of the front door (in a slanting position) of an Orthodox Jew's house or apartment. A religious or Orthodox Jew will touch his fingers to his lips, then to the *mezuzah,* each time he enters or leaves his abode. Why? Inside the tin oblong is a tiny rolled-up paper (or parchment) on which are inscribed verses from Deuteronomy: "Hear, O Israel, the Lord our God is one," and "Love the Lord your God and serve Him with all your heart and soul. . . ." The *mezuzah* sanctifies the home of a Jew, which is considered a temple. It's a very good idea.

mishegoss: Crazyness, insanity, cuckoo stuff. Persons who are *meshuggah* are not the only producers of *mishegoss*— things that are real far-out, or just don't make *sense.* There's a saying *I* agree with 100 percent: "Everyone has his own *mishegoss.*"

mitzvah: A good deed; a divine commandment; a noble or very worthy act.

Moishe Kapoyr: Literaly, this means "Moses Backwards"; it is the comical name given to anyone who is so ornery or contrary he does things exactly opposite the way other people do—"upside down," I would even say "ass-backwards." The type person who is a *Moishe Kapoyr* is a real pain in the neck—and lower.

Moishe Rebbaynu: Holy Moses! (I mean that's what *Moishe Rebbaynu* means.) Jews say *"Moishe Rebbaynu"* to mean "Moses, Our Great Rabbi/Teacher"—but they also use the name as an exclamation of amazement.

momzer: A bastard; also used in admiration to mean someone very intelligent, ingenious, remarkable. That use of *momzer* has nothing to do with being legit; it probly comes from the old superstition that kids who are born "out of wedlock" are smarter than those born of parents legaly hitched—but I do not go along with this idea, on account of 1) Who the hell, except the mother, really knows if a kid is legit? 2) How come so many geniuses came from nice moral homes? 3) How come bastards are often dum-dums, and also have pimples? 4) I treat a bastard the same as anyone else, on account of some of the worst bastards I ever met can pass the blood test to match the cells of their old man and old lady.

nebbech: This is also spelled and pronounced *"nebbish"*—by people who can't make the *kh* sound the way Jews and Scotchmen do. This darling word has many meanings: l) a weak, ineffective, pitiful person; 2) a Sad Sack; 3) a born loser; 4) a poor guy ("He went to the doctor, *nebbech*"); 5) in sympathy ("She, *nebbech,* can't make a sound"); 6) for "Alas" ("He, *nebbech,* doesn't have a nickel to his name"). My mother used to say, "A *nebbech* will always remain a *nebbech."* And my father would add, *"Nebbech."*

nosh: A snack; or, to eat "a little something"; a "bite" between meals; a sandwich (altho that's really too much for a true *nosh);* a piece fruit, candy, a cookie and like that.

nu: Man, this is an all-purpose word—a question, a comment, a challenge, an answer. *Nu* means anything from "Well . . ." to "What?" to "So?" to "Do me something."

Nu can be sighed (fondly) or sneered (with acid). It's a word for asking, telling, casting doubt, dripping irony. When used by a *maven, nu* is doubled up *("Nu, nu")* or even tripled. *Nu,* do I have to go on?

nudnick: A pest; a bore; a constant annoyer; a nuisance. But all these don't do juicy justice to the word: A *nudnick* must be persistent, even obnoxious, someone who bothers, *mutches,* or *nudzhes* you—but plenty.

"Oy!": I don't know why I have to describe this dandy sound, because it means exactly what it sounds like—except it can sound so many ways that my friend and creator, Mr. Leo Rosten, says in his book *The Joys of Yiddish* (which is actualy a book about English, and you should run right out and buy a copy—retail) that *"Oy!"* is not a word but a whole vocabulary. But I would say that *"Oy!"* is a cry of surprise, or pain *("Oooy! Oy vay!"),* or fear, or sadness, or disappointment, or joy, or relief, or indignation, or irritation, or anxiousness, or sarcasm, or suffering, or despair, or outrage, or horror, or just "I-can't-stand-it-anymore!" If you try, you can produce a pip of an *"Oy!"* to illustrate each situation. If you can't, you need *help,* man.

pisha-payshe: A very simple children's card game, for 2 players.

plotz: To bust open (fancy-pants would say "burst open"); to explode with frustration or anger or indignation.

pupik: (Rhyme it with "look it.") Navel. That's all *pupik* means, but you'd be surprise how much sarcasm this word can be used to express: *"A shaynim donk in dein pupik"* ("A pretty thanks to your navel") actualy means: "Thanks *a lot!"* or "Thanks for nothing." When wishing bad luck on someone, you can say: *"Tsibiliss zollen vaksn in dein pupik!"* ("Onions should grow in your navel"). Other vegetables can be called on according to your state of mind.

Purim: A holiday—the Feast of Lots—which Jews love because its moral is that tyrants or fanatics *can* be beaten, the way the Jews of Persia, who were suppose to be wiped out by Haman, were saved by Queen Esther. The whole story (it's a beaut!) is told in the Book of Esther. On Purim there are feasts, dances, even masquerade parties, gifts of food, and happy feelings all around.

putz: This is a bad word, a 4-letter word, the vulgar or slang name for "penis"; but *shmuck* is more often used as the name of a man's rod, whereas *putz* is a term of contempt for a fool, a jerk, an easy mark, a—well, a *shmuck.*

putzeroo: A *putz* with trimmings; a jerk from Harvard.

rachmones: Sympathy, pity; pronounce this to rhyme with "*loch* (as a Scotsman says it) *mawness*"—and don't *never* rhyme it with "catch pones": A Jew would *plotz* if you did.

Shalom: Peace; used when saying good-bye, like, "Well, Father O'Neill: *Shalom.*" (*Shalom* is Hebrew; *Sholem* is Yiddish.)

shamus: Actualy, the sexton or caretaker of a synagogue; but in English it mostly means a detective, or a private eye. (It *sometimes* means an informer, or an unimportant workman. A real put-down artist will call a guy "a *shamus* in a pickle factory.")

shaygets: A Gentile—boy or man; or a clever kid, a rascal, a handsome, mischievous, charming devil. Mike Clancy, my partner, is a true-blue *shaygets* in all respects.

sheiss!: A strong swearword, meaning "Oh, crap!," and, to be frank about it (you should excuse me), "Oh, shit."

shiksa: A Gentile girl.

shlemiel: It makes me sick to think I have to explain this dandy, often-heard-in-English word—but: A *shlemiel* is a nerd, a pipsqueak, a naïve character, a fool, a joker with simple-type marbles, a loser who don't even complain, a clumsy butterfingers, and like that. I can do better if I compare a *shlemiel* to a *shlimazel*—so keep reading.

shlep: To drag, pull, haul; also, a drag; a clumsy clyde, an untidy, dreary broad. This word gets many a laugh these days on television, like: "But, Lady Fortescue, we shall be happy to deliver this order. Why *shlep?*"

shlepper: A drag, a slow Joe; a wet towel; a hanger-on; a clumsy social type; a sloppy dresser; a cheap peddler; a beggar; even a crook—because he or she *shleps* (hauls or drags out) merchandise.

shlimazel: A permanent bad-luck guy; someone to who nothing ever turns out good. You have to note the difference from a *shlemiel:* "A *shlemiel* knocks things off tables; the *shlimazel* picks them up." A *shlemiel* can be rich, altho funky, but a *shlimazel*—? I doubt it. I doubt a *shlimazel* ever even *inherits* bread. . . . Look at it this way: When a *shlimazel* winds his watch, it stops; when he sells umbrellas, drought sets in; if he sold coffins, people would stop dying. (You can't top that.)

shlock: Cheap, chintzy, crappy articles; fakes. The store that sells such shoddy stuff is called a *shlock*-house. The mail-order "junk ads" that send me up the wall come from *shlock*-houses.

shlump: Bend or slouch, or bend *and* slouch; a person who is that type—so: a drip, a dope, a drab. Also, an icky dresser, not clean, a ratty type.

shmaltz: Cooking fat; melted or rendered fat—usualy from a chicken. But *shmaltz* or *shmaltzy* also mean anything real corny, too gushy; smeared on flattery; overacted; laid on with a shovel; hokey; hoked up.

shmattes: (Pronounced *"shmot-tuss."*) Rags—or dresses; sarcasticly used, it means expensive ladies' clothes; cheap junk. Also, a *shmatte* is someone "you can wipe your feet on": a person of no pride, plus weak character. A broken-down heap (auto) or a porno movie can be called a *shmatte,* which is a very handy word. There's no shortage of *shmattes*—animal, vegetable or mineral—in this half-ass time we live in.

shmeer: Bribe. It actualy means to spread—like butter or oil— so it means to grease, which is why it means to bribe in the 1st place. Also, *shmeer* means "the whole package" or "the whole deal." I don't know why.

shmegegge or *shmeggege:* This is some gorgeous word! But you practicly never hear it outside Brooklyn, the Bronx, or the East Side (Lower *and* Upper, the way things have worked out in real estate) unless it's from a New Yorker who emigrated out to the West Coast. (The Hollywood scene is no place for *shmegegges*, unless they're related to a star or producer.) A *shmegegge* is a no-talent, a cheapo, close to a *shlepper* in character, plus a drip. *Shmegegges* complain and whine a lot. I think a *shmegegge* is a funky combo of a *nudnick* and a *nebbech*—and that's some odd-ball, believe me.

shmendrick: (This is another beaut.) A punk, a kid, a guy who lacks balls; a short *shlemiel*—and skinny. (A *shlemiel* can be a physical brute who is actualy a patsy, but a *shmendrick* can't even *look* big or strong.) Also: A jerk who tries to think big or act big, but always ends up zilch. (A *yenta* was beating up on her "husbar" who crawled under the bed, so she hollered, "Come out!" and he answered, "No! I'll show you who's boss around here!" That's the only guts a *shmendrick* can show.)

shmo: A dum-dum; a fall guy; a clumsy jerk. *Shmo* happens to be the polite way of saying *shmuck* (penis); and even more polite than saying "pee" instead of "piss." *Shmo* is *shmuck* dressed up for company.

shmoes: Plural of *shmo;* and if you look around you'll see there's no shortage of them neither.

shmontzes: Worthless; trivial stuff; cheapos. A way to exclaim *("Shmontzes!")* like "Baloney!" or "Horse feathers!," which I never in my whole life heard anyone say—and have just realized is the cleaned-up version of "Horse shit." (You ask enough, you learn.)

shmooze: You won't find a word like this in any other language! To *shmooze* means to have a warm, friendly, heart-to-heart talk—about anything, plus everything. A *shmooze* is a long chat-up of a special easy type. The telephone is used a lot for *shmoozing,* which means no business, no special subject, just (like we used to say in the Army) "chewing the fat."

shmuck: Okay, okay—if you live on 5th or Park, or are a square who never uses street lingo, you will think this is a real "obscene" word, so you can skip my definition. For those who are still with me, *shmuck* actualy means "penis" (Park Ave.) or "prick" (10th Ave.). But listen: Just as "prick" in English also means a mean guy, a lousy character, a boob, a 2-timer, a jerk, a clown—that's what *shmuck* means. "Don't act like a *shmuck!*" also means don't be cheap, sneaky or crude. (I guess maybe the funniest story I ever heard is the 1 about the Jew, a widower, who went down to Florida and was very lonely: so a *k'nocker* at his hotel sarcasticly advises him that the way to make friends is to buy a camel and ride it up and down the main stem; so— but this is no place for long stories. You want to know how it comes out? You'll *plotz*. Read it, under the *shmuck* entry, in Mr. Rosten's *The Joys of Yiddish*.)

shnapps: Whiskey, brandy, booze.

shnook: (Rhymes with "book.") A real timid type, a sap, a patsy; a form of *shlemiel;* a no-balls character. *Shnooks* are pathetic, I guess, but kind of likable—which no *shmuck* is.

Sholem aleichem: Hello; also "good-bye." Jews say, *"Sholem aleichem"* when meeting or when splitting. The phrase means "Peace unto you." Why do Jews use the same phrase for "Hi!" and "So long"? "In Israel we have so many head-aches and dangers we don't know whether we're coming or going."

"Shoyn genug": "Enough already." (That's how this common expression got into English—via Houston Street and the Bronx.)

shtarker: A strong man (or even broad); a brave type; also a strong-arm. Also, it's used sarcasticly: "Don't be a *shtarker* (hero)" or "Some *shtarker* (big shot). *Feh!*" My partner

Mike and me often rib each other with this colorful put-down.

"Shtay azoy!": "Stay right there"; "Stay that way." (That's my way of getting Mr. Goldberg to—if he was English—"sit.")

shtick or *shtik:* A piece of something. But *shtick* is used mostly for 1) a practiced piece of horsing around or clowning ("That Jerry Lewis with his crazy *shtick*"), or 2) a recognized expression or piece of "business" used by an actor, to steal attention from others; 3) a trick, a con; 4) a clever routine. Like: The "double-take" in movies, or Harpo's chasing quiff, or the fast 3-card drop (a scam that's pulled on suckers all over Manhattan these days by rip-off dudes from East Harlem). Each of the above 4 is a real *shtick.*

shtup: (Rhyme it with "foot.") To push, or a push; but this word is the street-talk for screw, or fornicate. Also, a good lay. So: "You wanna *shtup* her?" or "Wow, does he give her fancy *shtupping!"* or "That doll is some *shtup."*

shul: Synagogue, temple.

shvartzer: A black man or woman. *Shvartz* is black—so there's nothing more prejudiced about a white saying *shvartzer* than about a *shvartzer* saying "Charley" or "the Man."

shvartz yohr: A black year; used to wish a dark future (starting at once) on somebody you're mad on. This is a heated-type curse: *"A shvartz yohr auf aim!"* ("A black year on him!") means "May he have an accursed year!" *"A shvartz yohr auf dir!"* is the same idea "on you."

shvitzbud: Sweat bath; a Turkish bath. Those were great places for relaxing, spilling off fat and hang-ups—and having good *shmoozes* with other *shvitzbudniks.*

tante: Aunt.

tantz: To dance, or a dance.

tararom or *tarrarom:* A hullabaloo, ruckus, big fuss, noisy mess. My partner Mike, being Irish, would say "donnybrook."

tchotchke or *tchochke* or *chotchkeh* or *tsatske* or *tsatskeleh:* Literaly, a toy or plaything, an inexpensive trinket. But

mostly (and best) *tchotchke* refers to a cute plaything—
meaning a lightweight chick, a bouncy number, a sexpot,
a looker—usualy a looker without surplus marbles in her
think depot.

tim-tum: A male/female type; a gay guy. Jews used to use
this word way back in the time of the Bible for beardless
adolescents with high-pitched voices.

toches or *tuchus:* (Pronounce the *ch* as *kh,* rattling your tonsils.)
Ass; butt. I mean the ass you're told to get off of, not the
kind the Hebrews piled things on (or used the jawbones
of).

tsimmes: A side dish made out of carrots, raisins and other
sweet-tasting stuff; but *tsimmes* is used to mean making
a big fuss; or to describe a mixed-up mess; a mish-mosh.

tsiters: Shivers, trembles.

tuchus: See *toches.*

tummel: (Sound the "u" like the "oo" in "took"—not like the
"u" in "tunnel.") A lot of noise, disorder or commotion.
A *tararom* in a less complicated way.

tushy: Look under *toches* (which you must never pronounce
to rhyme with "botches").

utz: To needle or goad somebody. (This word is a sure winner,
a helluva lot better than "getting your goat." Today, who
owns a goat?) Also, a sharp piece of verbal jabbing.

varnishkes: A delicious Russian/Jewish dish of *kasha* (cooked
groats and noodles) and "potato cakes."

vertootst or *fertootst* or *fartootst:* Mixed up, so excited that
you're confused.

"Voos is mit dir?": "What *is* with you?" In school-English you'd
say, "What's wrong with you?"

yenta: (This is practicly English by now—especialy with the
movie, Broadway, Regine or Elaine crowd). A gossipy
woman; a lo-class or vulgar type lady; a tactless repeater
(or spreader) of gossip. The description applies not only
to females: a macho can be a *yenta,* if he is a blabbermouth.

I got a charge out of buttons I saw on some hippies in the Village (Greenwich Village, N.Y.); the buttons read:

Marcel Proust
is a
Yenta

zaftig: Juicy—but especialy: well stacked, with a big bazoom and curves, soft and sending out sex vibes. Every year the TV and flicks give us a new load of *zaftig* no-talents.

"Zaulst brennen, paskudnyak. Boorkess zollen vaksn in dein boech. A shvartz yohr zol dir khappen!": "You should burn, you disgusting creature. May beets grow in your belly! May a black year of misfortunes seize you!" (If you think this curse is too much, remember that I used it on a sonofabitch who'd slugged me, plus had a pistol up my nose and was ready to blow my goddam brains into scrambled eggs. That, believe me, was no time for polite thoughts.)

zayde: Grandfather. A Jew will call any old man *zayde,* to show respect and affection.

zhlub or *shlub:* As clumsy a character as the word sounds; an oaf; a type with no class, grace or manners. A type jerk. A *klutz.*

Shalom, bubeleh

LEO ROSTEN

Evelyn Waugh once said, "Leo Rosten is one of the most brilliant and original writers alive." Mr. Rosten's books cover a truly astonishing range: humor, fiction, religion, language, social science, screenplays, travel, art. But "melodrama was my first love"—and in *Silky!* he has triumphantly returned to it.

Mr. Rosten is the creator of *H*Y*M*A*N K*A*P*L*A*N; Captain Newman, M.D.; The Joys of Yiddish; The Dark Corner,* and twenty-five other works.

He has won many honors for his writing, is a Ph.D. from the University of Chicago, and Honorary Fellow of the London School of Economics.